Taming the Wild Cougar

Heart of the Cougar
Book 3

TERRY SPEAR

PUBLISHED BY:
Terry Spear

Taming the Wild Cougar
Copyright © 2015 by Terry Spear

Discover more about Terry Spear at:
http://www.terryspear.com/

Cover Art by Tell-Tale Designs

ISBN-10: 1633110109
ISBN-13: 978-1633110106

DEDICATION

To my good friend, Dawn Marie Hamilton, who I love seeing at conferences and enjoy getting to hang out with her. Thanks for being such a dear friend!

ACKNOWLEDGMENTS

Thanks so much to my good friend and beta reader, Donna Fournier, who keeps me straight—always. Even though sometimes I'm shaking my head while she's nodding hers.

PROLOGUE

On high alert, Leyton Hill and his teammates, members of the extremely skilled Rangers, a sophisticated raid force in the Army, moved like shadows through the woods, located an encampment of enemy terrorists, and flex cuffed them before they even woke in their beds. He'd had days of firefights at night, one mission after another, when he had a night of reprieve and thought he saw a soldier exchange a confiscated terrorist weapon for money. The guy wasn't a Ranger, just someone with another unit they were working with.

Before Leyton jumped the gun, he did a little checking. The guy's name was Bart Smith, and he was a cougar shifter, just like Leyton, not that anyone else would be aware of their...uniqueness.

For two days now, they'd been in a pacified area, no fighting, no trouble, but they could never let down their guard. The next thing he knew the fighting broke out all over again. He protected his good friend Travis MacKay, fellow Ranger, tackling him and throwing him to the ground, then rolled away to take out as many of the terrorists shooting at them as he could, when he saw Bart Smith aiming a rifle at him. He was *supposed* to be on *Leyton's* side, his blue eyes narrowed as he fired. Chaos reigned everywhere, the fighting forcing everyone to take cover and shoot back. All but Leyton Hill, who lay in a bloodied heap, fighting for his life. He would take down that traitorous bastard, if it was the last thing on earth that he did.

CHAPTER 1

The Colorado summer's day appeared awash in blue—the lakes, the sky, the mountains, even the forest—beautiful, if Leyton Hill hadn't been on a killing mission. His target?

The man who had nearly killed him in Afghanistan, Bart Smith, now known as Butch Sanders, and sniper trained. The bastard had turned a terrorist's rifle on Leyton his last day in Afghanistan, and with all the shooting going on, no one had seen Butch fire the rounds that had nearly killed him.

Now, both, no longer in the military, were running as cougars through the pine forests of Colorado. Butch seemed to know this territory as if he had been born and raised here. Every once in a while, he left tell-tale cougar pugmarks in mud, or a scruff of tan cougar fur snagged on shrubbery, like leaving bread crumbs in the wild that he hadn't meant to. Or had he?

Leyton had never been to Colorado as a cougar, never traveled through White Fork River in the Flat Tops

Wilderness, so he was at a strong disadvantage. Not to mention he'd had to leave his vehicle, clothes, and weapons behind several hours ago in Cheyenne, Wyoming before he crossed the border.

No matter what, Leyton was supposed to check in with his boss concerning news of what he'd learned by next weekend. At this rate, that deadline would be shot to hell. He couldn't do anything about it now. He had to learn where Butch had hidden the gun used to kill Leyton's informant, that he'd planted Leyton's fingerprint on. It wasn't unheard of for some corrupt cops to plant evidence like that. Just use powder to look for prints, then lift the fingerprint with a piece of sticky tape and place it on the incriminating evidence.

Leyton was still torqued off that the guy managed to leave the Army with an honorable discharge and was picked up by a police force!

Butch managed to stay a jump ahead of him, using switchbacks constantly and would wait for Leyton to lose his trail, and then he'd take off again. But Leyton was on his back and the bastard wouldn't get away this time.

They'd passed some isolated cabins in the woods, everything quiet while campers, fishermen, and white water rafters slept until the new day dawned. Leyton would dog him until he caught him, so Butch had to kill him before he could report back in. He hadn't expected Butch to frame him though, so he could misdirect the blame. Because Leyton couldn't go to prison any more than Butch could, Leyton would have to die. Besides, Butch wouldn't want him living to prove he was the real criminal mastermind behind the weapons' black-market sales.

Which was probably why the bastard had led him this way in an attempt to ambush him at some point. Leyton was ready to take the cougar down, cat to cat. He had just reached an isolated redwood cabin when he noticed a raised window, saw a rifle poking out, heard the gunshot fired, and leapt out of the way. *Almost.*

A round struck him in the shoulder, another grazing his ear. Searing pain hit him at once as Leyton ran for cover. Hell and damnation! He'd had hundreds of missions where he had always come out on top. But never in a million years would he have suspected the bastard would be able to arm himself with a sniper rifle and shoot him when they'd been running as cougars in the wilderness.

Despite being hit, he took great satisfaction in the knowledge that Butch had missed anything vital the first two shots he'd fired.

Leyton circled around the cabin, wanting to take him down at all costs. More gunshots rang out. Leyton bolted away from the cabin. Grinding his cougar teeth, he couldn't risk getting hit again.

Cougar shifters healed faster, but he needed to stop the bleeding. Damn it!

Hidden by the pines, he circled wide.

Another five rounds were fired. Hell. He wasn't going to be able to get to Butch this way. And he needed to get something to bind his wound.

Angry with himself for getting shot, but having no other options, Leyton headed way around the cabin, hoping he'd reach civilization before long. The cabins he'd seen dotted about had increased in number, and the few roads had too.

He figured he should be coming to a town before long. Then what? He was bleeding, wearing his cougar coat, and in a real fine mess.

The sun was low in the sky as he moved through the piney woods, wishing he knew the area. He was headed away from the Rockies, which meant he'd probably run into a road that could lead him to a town. He'd loped for about half an hour, resting, and running again when he heard voices carried on the breeze. The air was warm during the day, the sun beginning to sink in the sky, coloring it awash in purples and pinks. The air began to cool.

This was a better time to run, though he couldn't risk delaying until nightfall, not with the way he was injured. Then he saw a lake and a sign saying it was Lake Buchanan, kids playing on the shore, tents and campers on one side, cabin rentals on another. Should he risk sneaking into a cabin? Stealing some clothes?

He moved on, scenting the air, surprised he was smelling so many different cougars in the area. He was moving slower now, his shoulder hurting like a sonofabitch, aching and sharp pains riddling his tired body. But he had to keep pushing on. Had to find a store, maybe where he could get first aid supplies and a few things to wear so he could blend in. Which meant breaking in after businesses were closed.

Home developments appeared, large spacious acre to five-acre lots, treed, no fencing, perfect for him to remain unseen. Again, he smelled the scent of cougars, confusing him. They normally stayed out of housing developments.

The closer he got to town, the darker the sky, but the homes had smaller yards, some fenced-in, and he was having to leap over fences, rather than risk running in front of the houses. Then he smelled food, his stomach rumbling. Chicken wings, barbecue, steaks on a grill, he was starving.

He finally reached a small shopping area—grocery store—open until 11 p.m., a number of eating places, a library, bank, police station, that made his heartbeat quicken, and hot damn! A medical clinic, that looked to be closed. A white Ford Explorer was parked out back, but there were no lights on in the building. Which meant someone had to have just left their vehicle there for the time being.

He shifted at the back door and stared at the damn lock. When he was wearing clothes, he always had lock picks with him. He had no way to pick it. He twisted the handle just in case and couldn't believe his luck when the handle met no resistance. The door opened. Briefly concerned someone had already broken in, he quickly slipped inside, closed the door, and listened to see if anyone was rummaging around. Looking for drugs, probably.

No sounds at all. He moved down the hall, his footfalls silent. When he reached the first room, he peeked in. An exam room. Taking a deep breath to steady his heartbeat, he moved into the room, hoping he could find what he needed, locate a restroom, and turn the light on in there so he could use a mirror to take care of his injury. Even so, there were enough parking lot lights streaming through the blinds of the large window that he could see well enough in the room with his cat's enhanced night vision.

He stalked toward the first cabinet, tripped over something furry, startling him, and he gasped. He smelled a cat—of the housecat variety—at the same time. The furry tiger yowled, making his heart trip, annoying him. Hell, a tiny tiger? No, a cat that looked like a tiger?

The cat began to wind her body around his legs. Animals loved him, but he didn't have time for this.

Before he could move around the cat and reach the cabinet door, he heard footsteps headed quickly in the direction of the room. His heart and breathing nearly stopped. The person who broke in was still here? His first thought was that the person was a drug addict, looking for drugs. But why would he be moving around in the dark?

His adrenaline surging, he readied himself to pounce on the thief and take him out.

***

As soon as Dr. Kate Parker heard her cat yowl in one of the exam rooms, she was jolted from her catnap. She'd laid down after finishing last minute paperwork, shut off the lights, and was taking a nap before she headed out on her trip into the Rocky Mountain wilderness. She sighed, climbed off the couch in her office, and headed for the door.

Once a year, she took a two-week vacation in the Rockies, no matter the weather. Everyone in Yuma Town had given up telling her she shouldn't go alone, worrying about her safety, when she had never had any trouble. Once her boyfriend had split, she had wanted to prove that she could do this with or without a friend staying with her. And for three years, she hadn't had any difficulties.

She'd learned ju jitsu, sparred with the sheriff and his deputies from time to time, and carried a 9 mm. So she was fine.

She sighed again, wishing Queen Sheba would have let

her sleep a little longer. She was a toyger, a domestic tabby bred to resemble a tiger with black and orange stripes and the best little mouser. Humans might have felt a cat would be unsanitary in a medical clinic, but since Kate treated cougar shifters, no problem there.

As soon as she reached the exam room, she flipped on the light switch, expecting to see Sheba, but instead, a naked male body slammed into her, taking her to the floor. She oofed as she landed on her back, the air knocked out of her. She'd only had a split second of seeing him, and gasped—the man standing about six feet one—before he tackled her to the linoleum floor. He was a dead-ringer for Stryker, only his eyes were blue-green, and this man didn't smell anything like the deputy sheriff in town.

He laid on top of her, staring at her for a moment, before she opened her mouth to tell him to get the hell off her. Unfortunately, her gun was not at hand to back up her words.

"Sorry," he said, clamping his hand over her mouth before she could utter a word. "I take it from the white lab coat you're wearing, you work here. I thought you had broken in."

He was a cougar, but no one she'd ever seen before— short, dark brown hair, the start of a scruffy beard, and the most beautiful blue-green eyes she'd ever seen. But right now, she wanted to tranq him and call the sheriff. She tried to shove him off her, but he was too heavy, too muscular. And he knew what she was thinking she swore before she even could react.

His heartbeat was beating as hard as hers. But what concerned her, besides that a naked man had her pinned to the floor of one of her exam rooms and her cat purring next to her face as if she was in on this whole fiasco, Kate smelled the scent of iron—of blood. The cougar was bleeding—all *over* her!

Which must have been the reason for him breaking into her clinic. Not for drugs. They never had any trouble in Yuma Town. Well, rarely. But no one had ever broken into her clinic.

"You're hurt," she mumbled against his hand. "Let me up and I'll help you."

"You'll scream."

"I took the Hippocratic Oath. Let me take care of you."

"Don't cross me."

Her heart beating triple time, she shook her head. She had to gain his confidence. If she could, maybe she could get him to turn himself in. Or...she'd do it for him. If she could reach her desk in her office, she *could* get her gun.

He stood and helped her off the floor. She switched her gaze from his eyes---the way he was watching her, waiting for one false move, ready to pounce again—to his tanned and glorious, muscled body. Except for the blood oozing from his shoulder, and some on his ear, he was seriously perfect. A big cat's version of the statue of David.

"If you keep staring at me like that, I'm apt to bleed to death," he said, his words laced with a hint of humor.

She felt the blood rush to her face, the hazard of being a redhead, when she was never anything but completely professional when on the job. The man had rattled her completely. "Turn around so I can see where the bullet exited, if it did." When he turned, she saw where it had.

"Good. It did. Lie on the exam table, and I'll get the supplies I'll need."

"I'll wait for you to get them. Why don't you give me your cell while we're at it?"

She jerked her cell out of her lab coat pocket and slammed it into his palm. Damn it. She'd hoped she could use it if she had the chance and call 9-1-1. She pulled a patient gown out of a cabinet and handed it to him. "So why were you shot?"

She set the surgical instruments on the tray, but when she reached for a hypodermic needle, he shook his head.

"No shots."

"For pain? Antibiotics?"

His smile was humorless.

"Your loss." So giving him something to make him sleep wasn't going to work either. She directed him to the exam table. "So, how were you shot?"

"Trying to apprehend a killer." He sat on the exam table, bunching the gown over his crotch.

She should have given him a sheet because he really couldn't wear the gown if she was going to work on this shoulder, front to back.

"Why don't you lie down?"

"I'll sit."

She let out her breath in a huff and had to pull a stepping stool over to reach his wound.

She glanced at his chiseled face. "You're one of the good guys?"

"Yeah, but I can't talk about the case."

She snorted, brushing a wayward curl off her cheek,

realizing her bun had come half undone when he had taken her to the floor. If anyone barged in on them right now and saw a naked man on her exam room table and her with her hair in such disarray, they'd surly think she'd just had wild and crazy sex with him in here.

"So where are you from?" she asked, trying not to react to his maleness, when she should have been scared or furious, not, damn it, *interested*. What was wrong with her? No hot guy in her bed for...well, she couldn't remember the last time she'd been with a guy.

"Not from here, wherever here is."

She glanced up at him, having forgotten the question. "Uhm..." Her gaze moved from his abs to his serious face to his wound—which is where it should have been all along. "...Yuma Town, Colorado."

He frowned. "Am I mistaken, or do a lot of cougars live in the area?"

"You're not mistaken. Cougars run the town."

He whistled. "Now that's a new one on me."

Finally concentrating on the business at hand—which she was highly trained for so why he was distracting her so shouldn't have been an issue—she cleaned up the entry wound in front, and then bandaged it. Then she moved around to clean and bandage the exit wound in back.

"Do you live alone?" he asked.

She stilled, her hand still pressing the sterilized cloth against his smooth skin. "No." She finished cleaning up the blood around his wound, disinfected it, then bandaged it. Then she came back to his front and finished washing off the streaks of blood that had run down his torso all the way to the patient gown he had bunched over his crotch, his legs completely bare. She was trying not to notice, but as she washed his chest, the gown began to tent over his erection.

"Two-and-a-half kids, husband, and the dog?" he asked.

"Three kids, the husband, and a cat. You scared Sheba already." No way was she going to let on she lived alone.

"The place was dark when I came in. I didn't see her, but we…"

Sheba jumped up on the exam table and stalked straight to where he was sitting.

"No, down, Sheba," Kate scolded. Her cat *never* did that. Her intruder was a totally bad influence. *Worse*, Sheba ignored her and rubbed up against the stranger's naked waist, and licked his skin, as if she was scent marking him and claiming him for her own.

"We already met. Didn't we, girl?" He smiled down at Sheba and ran his hand over her back, and her little motor began running.

"Sheba," Kate said in her *you'd better obey me or else* tone.

Sheba meowed in her kitty cat way that said, "All right, already. But he's mine."

Sheba hopped down off the table, wound her way around Kate's legs as if to say Kate was hers too, and left the room.

"Cute cat. Anyway, you left the back door to the clinic unlocked, by accident, had to have been. You were tired, fell asleep in your office. No one's calling here looking for you, so undoubtedly, no one's missed you. I suspect there's no one waiting for you at home. You have a cute little accent.

Australian? Not real pronounced, but enough that it shows. Are you from Australia?"

"Born there, but my mother was American and my dad Australian. They met at a writers' conference in New York. They're both nonfiction writers, but there's a problem with being cougar shifters in Australia."

"No cougars exist."

"Right, and years ago when it was rumored American soldiers or a circus had released cougars into the wild—the big cats were blamed for killing two-thousand sheep--no evidence was ever found. But with a twenty-thousand dollar bounty on the cougars dead or alive, my parents felt it just wasn't safe to live there after all that had happened."

"Two-thousand sheep? Sounds like a wild pack of dingoes might have been the culprits."

"Could have been." She threw the bloodied cloths in a wastepaper basket. "You've got to report this to the sheriff."

"I told you I can't."

"Because, don't tell me, you're deep undercover. So what are you going to do now?" She was hoping he'd say he was walking out of here, but with no clothes, and a bandaged shoulder that wouldn't do well with shifting into a cougar? He needed to rest and to heal. And he needed clothes.

"Take me to your office."

"Why?"

"Because I said so." He sounded tired and irritable.

Aggravated with his bossiness, she knew she should be careful and not irritate him further, but she felt just as tired and ill-tempered. She yanked off her lab coat, wanting to wash out the blood before it left stains, but then thought better of it. If this undercover cop, or whatever he was, took her hostage, it would be better if she left lots of clues to indicate that she had trouble after everyone left.

Before she could leave the exam room, he set the bunched up hospital gown on the counter, seized the wastepaper bag containing his bloodied cloths, and said, "Want to put a new bag in there?" He wasn't asking a question, the tone sarcastically demanding. "We wouldn't want the cleaning staff to have to clean up all over again, now would we?"

She wanted to ask if the "we" referred to the frog in his pocket. Only he was stark naked and she took an eyeful of his package—since he'd had the nerve to expose himself instead of setting her phone down to grab the bag. From a medical doctor's standpoint and she-cat's point-of-view, she was damned impressed. He retrieved the gown.

She couldn't believe he'd think of grabbing the trash bag with the bloody cloths. Damn it. She jerked a trash bag out of a drawer and stuck it in the can. She wanted to shove it in and do a really sloppy job of it, indicating someone other than the cleaning crew had done it and something could be wrong. But he was watching her every move.

Transferring the used trash bag to his hand holding the gown over his crotch again, he motioned to the doorway with the phone in his other hand. Letting her breath out, she walked him to her office and flipped on the light switch, wishing she could think of something else she could leave behind as bread crumbs if he took her hostage.

He couldn't leave without some clothes. And she wasn't offering. But then she saw what he was looking for. A photo on her desk of her and Sheba in her arms. Another with Sheba catching her favorite pink ball mid-air.

She knew in an instant, that's why he wanted to come to her office. To see if she had a family portrait. He was good. If he was an undercover cop, he had to be good at his job.

"I'll show you a picture of my husband. Let me have the phone."

He obliged, but stayed right next to her as she pulled up her photo gallery, his hot piney-woods scent drifting to her. Trying to ignore his close proximity, which was damn hard to do as he breathed down her neck, she quickly searched through the pictures until she came to one and clicked on it. She hoped he'd believe that the deputy sheriff who owned the cabins on Lake Buchanan, Chase Buchanan, was her husband.

"Here's Chase. My husband." Best of all, she'd given him a big hug for having taken her to the firing range and teaching her how to fire her 9 mm and his wife had shot the picture of them.

As long as he didn't see the pictures of Chase and his wife, Shannon, and their adorable babies, Kate thought it looked convincing.

"Nice," the man said, studying the photo way too long. "May I?" He waited for her to hand the phone to him, but she tried to turn it off. He took it from her and flipped through the pictures. "And this is his sister and her babies?"

"Uh-yeah."

He flipped through several more photos. "No pictures of her husband. He must be a really close brother."

"He is."

He glanced at the walls in her office. Her medical credentials. More pictures of Sheba. Her Black Belt First Degree certificate in ju jitsu. Great.

Then he focused on her desk, and specifically her large desk pad calendar and studied it. "Vacation from now until Monday, returning two weeks. Rockies." He shifted his gaze to her. "You and who else?"

"My husband, Chase, of course."

"What happened to your three kids?"

She twisted her mouth in annoyance.

He cast her a small smile. "Why don't we go to your house?"

"Sure. You can explain to my husband why you're running around naked, wounded, and forcing me to take you places."

"I could. Let's go."

Quickly, she tried to toss her lab coat onto her chair, just in case anyone might notice the blood and she always hung up her lab coat. But Mr. Undercover Cop looked at it and smiled at her, not in an amused way. More sardonically, like he knew just what she was up to. "Why don't we take it with you so you can wash it out? Blood can leave permanent stains."

He caught her glancing at her desk drawer. "Got something in there you need to take with you on your trip?" He still had her phone in his hand, but dropped the trash bag and bunched gown on top of her desk to free his other hand. He reached past her, brushing against her, and pulled the drawer open.

When he grabbed for the gun in her drawer, she saw her

chance at escape and made a dash for the door.

She should have known he'd drop everything, including her phone. Furious that he might have broken it when it hit the floor, she didn't make it past the door jamb before he skirted the desk in a few long-legged bounds as if he were using his agile speed and turns like a cougar would. He grabbed hold of her with his suddenly very free hands, jerked her tight against his very hard body, and held on tight, his blue-green eyes nearly as dark as midnight, his nostrils flaring.

"Okay, let me make one thing perfectly clear. I'm in a bind as you very well can see. I'm not letting you go until I can safely do so. So don't pull another stupid stunt like this and you'll be fine," he growled, his voice dark and sexy—as much as she hated that it was.

And her darn body was reacting to his—burning up, her nipples peaking against his chest, her pheromones kicking into that feral stage that said he was totally hot, and she was completely interested! Which was the problem with being a cougar shifter. They didn't have control over that aspect of their bodies if someone sexually intrigued them. And she had a mate! Well, not for real. Shannon, Chase's mate, would be surprised to hear it. Chase too. But she was supposed to be pretending she had one! So she shouldn't have had the hots for some strange, naked man, who was pressing his body against hers.

She heard the man's heart beating furiously as much as hers was. But he was also gritting his teeth, and she knew he had to be in horrible pain. She thought to use her ju jitsu on him, but he was holding her as if he knew her every move.

Oh, yeah, her black belt certificate. As soon as she came back from vacation, if she managed to take one without getting herself killed first, she was going to redecorate her office in pictures of the Rockies. No personal information.

"Are you going to go like that?" she asked.

"Have you got some scrubs lying around?"

She smiled. As tall as he was, the pants would be mid shin level, and the shirt? Best of all, he didn't have much of a choice. She and her nurses had extra sets of scrubs stored here, but all were fun from purple dragons on pink fabric to red and pink hearts on a white fabric, nothing that would look quite right on Macho Man.

Before he let her lead him out of the room, he pulled her toward the desk drawer, pulled it open, and found her 9 mm. "Got a bag?"

She motioned to a backpack hanging on her coat rack that was underneath a hoodie.

"Get it." He released her and she stalked over to the coat rack while he gathered up the gun, phone, bag of trash, gown, and bloody lab coat.

She handed him the bag and he deposited the items in there, including the patient gown. "Okay, scrubs?"

She let out her breath, glared at him, then led the way out of her office and into a room set aside for the nurses and doctor—complete with a changing room and kitchen. She pointed to a wall cabinet. "You'll find scrubs in there. No shoes, but you can wear some of those cute disposable shoe covers in there."

"Okay, Doc, sit over there while I get dressed."

She sat down at the table where she and her nurses

would eat a quick lunch. She folded her arms and scowled at him. "Did you break my phone? If you did, you're paying for it."

She said it before she remembered he came here without a stitch of clothes.

CHAPTER 2

The lovely redheaded Dr. Kate Parker was a spitfire, Leyton thought as he made her stay near him and not anywhere near the door so he could keep her in sight while he looked through the scrubs. Hell, he hoped no one saw him wearing any of them. Why couldn't someone be wearing normal blue scrubs, plain, and no decoration?

He pulled out a pair of pants that were neon orange and pink candy canes because they looked longer than the others. He held it in front of him and looked in the mirror. He would look like he was wearing knickers and was in the circus—as a clown.

He shoved his feet into the pants, decided to skip the shirt, and said, "Got your car keys?"

Her green-eyed gaze switched from him to the pocket of the backpack. She let out her breath as if she was totally exasperated with him, or maybe herself. He hadn't even thought of it, but if she had gotten hold of her keys, she could have hit the alarm on it. If she could have gotten away with it, maybe someone would have come to investigate. But she couldn't have sounded the alarm long enough for anyone to have thought it was more than just a mistake.

Leyton pulled out her keys. "I take it these are to the Ford Explorer out back."

She pursed her peach-colored lips in an annoyed way. "No, to my Mercedes Benz, but it's at home. Chase was supposed to pick me up in half an hour."

"Right. Come on." He slung the backpack over his good shoulder and escorted her to the back door. "Have an alarm?"

"Yes." She set it.

Then they walked out and she locked the door. They headed for the car. "Think you can drive it without causing me grief?" He wasn't sure what he was going to do next when he really needed rest, clothes, and food.

"You mean, that I won't drop by the sheriff's office first to tell them I have an armed gunman holding me hostage?"

"Yeah, something like that." He pulled out her phone and turned it on. "Still works. Give me your address."

"Why?"

"Just do it."

She gave him her address. He pulled up Google maps and entered it, then glanced in the car. "You're already packed for your camping trip."

"Yep."

"When were you actually leaving?"

"Why?"

"If it's tonight, you're getting a late start."

"Yeah, well, no thanks to you."

"You're not taking your cat?"

"No. She stays at the clinic when I'm gone so everyone can love on her."

Leyton decided it was safer if he drove. He could see her speeding or driving recklessly just to try and get someone's attention. They climbed into the car and Leyton started to pull out of the parking lot. She might have given him a false address, but he suspected she figured she couldn't pull the wool over his eyes. When he finally reached the location, he saw the sheriff's car parked out front. What the hell? He drove on past, hoping he didn't catch the sheriff's attention if he happened to glance out his window and wonder what Kate was doing in his neighborhood when she was supposed to be on her way to her campsite.

"Wait, that's it," she had the nerve to say, so perfectly innocent-like.

"You're supposed to be married to a deputy sheriff. His car isn't there. So the sheriff's visiting? And no one's home? Hand me your driver's license."

She jerked her wallet out of her purse and shoved it at him.

Leyton checked the address, then fed it into Google. "Your house is next to the damn clinic?" He couldn't believe that she'd pulled this on him. What if he was real trouble? She was just damn lucky he was one of the good guys. Though he had to concede he was impressed in an exasperating way.

She smiled a little, definitely the cat stole the goldfish-out-of-the-bowl look, like she was proud of herself for proving to him she wouldn't be cowed.

"Hell, woman, I feel like shit." He really didn't need the extra aggravation. Not that he blamed her, but he was feeling too damn rotten to deal with this.

When they arrived at the one-story white house, windows up above making it appear as though she had a loft or attic room, he saw the garden at the back of the house, and a path leading to the back parking lot. The house had one light on in the living room, but he suspected no one was there.

Leyton grabbed the controller on her visor and pushed the button. The garage door rolled up, verifying this was her house...this time.

"But I was supposed to be getting on my way. Won't that look suspicious if anyone sees me parking in my garage?"

Ignoring her question, he asked, "Why were you parked at the clinic when you could have just walked over?"

"Some of the ladies treated me to a fun farewell party. I had leftovers to take with me for the camping trip and a couple of ice chests in the back of the car. I didn't want to have to haul the food all the way to the garage."

"Makes sense. But no more tricks," he said, driving into the garage. He didn't want anyone seeing him getting out of her car. It would have been suspicious enough that she'd picked up some unknown man, but when he was wearing a bandage over his shoulder and candy cane scrubs?

He closed the garage door, but when she reached for the door handle, he grabbed her wrist. "Wait." He wasn't taking any chances with her. "Got a house alarm?"

She shook her head. "Yuma Town is usually safe."

"Wait for me." He moved around to the other side of the car and opened her door for her.

She hesitated to get out on her own, looking up at him with an expression that said she was totally pissed that he was controlling her so much. "What? You're going to be a gentleman and get my door for me, but then not help me out?"

He cast her a wry smile.

When he offered his hand, she ignored it and got out of the car. He shut the car door, then they walked to the door of the house, and she opened it. He thought she was going to need a key so he was surprised when she walked right in.

Inside the kitchen, she turned on the light. White tile counters and light colored oak cabinets, white appliances and a big picture window that looked out over the gardens made the kitchen airy and spacious. Red roses lined the white picket fence and solar garden lights made it like a fairy garden as they guided visitors down stone paths and highlighted a fountain and sitting areas.

"Why don't you start the wash, throw in the gown, your lab coat, and the bloody wipes you used on me," he said.

"Why don't you just toss the trash?"

He had to give her credit for not being a pushover. Not that he wouldn't have preferred that in this instance she would do as he asked without giving him grief. But he had to admire her for her backbone and obvious attempts to leave clues as to the trouble she might be in.

She shook her head and led the way to the laundry room where everything was white in there also, except for splashes of pastel colors—pictures of longhorn goats and fluffy white sheep in the mountains—hanging on the walls, colorful bins for sorting the laundry, and a window looking out on the gardens also. She dumped everything in the wash, then started it.

"Where's your bedroom?"

Her back stiffening and her brow furrowing, she turned to glower at him. "Why?"

"Hell, you don't think I can leave town wearing this, do you?" He tugged at the hideous scrubs.

She glanced down at them and smiled. "I might have some sweats you can wear. But they'll be a little short."

"What about Chase?"

She let out her breath on a feigned, exasperated sigh. "He's obviously not home yet."

"His clothes?" Leyton said, not buying into her story one iota.

"We just got married. He hasn't moved his stuff over yet."

Like hell the guy wouldn't have if he was half a man. If Leyton had been married to her, he would have moved in before the big date and been sharing the bed with her long before that. No way could he look at her and not want her—if he was about to marry her.

"Ahh, so that's why there are no pictures of the two of you. Although, I would think you would have a wedding picture at least."

"I'll get you the sweats." She so quickly dismissed the comment, he wasn't expecting her to turn and stalk off down the hallway and into a room.

He couldn't help prodding her about the fake husband.

He wondered why she wouldn't be married already. "The wedding pictures aren't back from the photographer?" he suggested.

"Right. You know it takes time, proofs, small touching up."

"So you were newly married. Like only a few days ago?"

She didn't respond.

"And you're going on a camping trip without him? Sounds like trouble in paradise already."

"He's joining me out there. He had to work a couple of shifts. Why am I explaining myself to you anyway?" she asked, glowering at him.

As soon as they walked into her bedroom, he considered the queen size bed covered in a rose quilt coverlet, lacy bed skirt, and lace and rose shams, he was certain that no man was living here. She began to open a dresser drawer. He was right next to her in an instant, seizing her hand, then pulling the drawer open himself.

"What? You think I have a gun in every drawer in the house?"

"If you lived in Texas, yeah. But since Yuma Town is so safe, no. Well, and it would be too far to get to if someone broke into your house in the middle of the night." Yet, he had reacted to that very real concern, until he'd thought better of it. He frowned at her. "Why did you have a gun in your desk drawer at the clinic?"

"I went practice shooting with Chase in the morning, and didn't have time to run it home before I saw my patient load."

She rummaged through the drawer and he took a

moment to check out the clothes in her closet, keeping an eye on her in the event she moved to another drawer he hadn't checked out yet. "Not even one deputy sheriff's uniform. Nothing?" He'd hoped that if she had been seeing a man, and had no longer been with him as he didn't smell any male scents in her bedroom, the guy might have left some article of clothing behind. Something that would fit him.

"Okay, here they are." She tossed the sweats on the bed.

Pale blue sweats? He put the bag on the floor by the bed and pulled on the sweatshirt, and groaned. Hell, his shoulder was killing him.

She turned a worried look to his shoulder, but when he dropped the scrub pants, her gaze dropped to his erection—that was semi-aroused. Hell, he swore no female doctor who had ever checked him out had ever given him that kind of a rise.

"Have you eaten?" she suddenly asked, pulling her gaze from his growing erection.

"Why? Do you plan to arm yourself with a knife?"

She lost the frown and actually smiled a little.

He didn't like that devious look.

"Not a bad plan. But you look like you need to eat. I haven't eaten since this afternoon either."

"What about Chase?" He knew the guy was married to the woman in the picture and that the babies were his. No way was he the woman's brother as many pictures there were of them together. Not that he had any brothers or sisters that he could relate to, but still, he knew that's what the deal was.

"Hey, listen, I'll give you the benefit of the doubt that you're the good guy and the guy who shot you was the bad guy. So if you need money, I'll give it to you. I'll help you to get some shoes and other clothes. I'll even give you a lift to the next town that has a bus service. Or a rental car place."

He pulled on the sweatpants. They rested way above his ankles.

"I'll take you up on the food." He stopped her before she left the bedroom and checked the rest of the bedroom drawers, looking to see if she had anything bigger to wear. The sweatshirt barely reached his navel, and the sweatpants looked like they'd shrunk in the wash. It was bad enough he had no shoes. Nothing in any of the drawers, though he'd rifled through her silken lace panties and bras wondering just what she was wearing under her Yuma Town T-shirt that said, "Cougars have lots more fun in Yuma Town, Colorado."

Then he checked the drawers in the bathroom.

"What are you looking for?" she asked, hands on hips.

"You're not married and you're not living with some guy by the name of Chase or otherwise."

"Why? Are you interested?"

He smiled back at her. "Lady, you couldn't handle me on a good day."

She laughed. "In your dreams."

Yeah, she'd be in his dreams all right. Underneath him, instead of her on top this time, in a nice soft bed, and she would be just as naked as him.

When they reached the kitchen, he checked her fridge and cabinet. "Unless Chase doesn't eat much, your place is stocked for a single person."

"What do you want to eat?" she asked, a frown creasing her brow, ignoring his comment.

"Anything is good. And...thanks."

"You're not really welcome, you know. I would have been on the—"

"Road by now? You were going tonight? Where?"

"To meet up with a bunch of friends at a cabin in the Rockies. I've been going for years."

"So you know the way already."

"Yes. Why?"

"I need to find the cabin where the suspect fired the shots at me. What would be the chance that he would come upon the cabin as a cougar, break in, and have a loaded rifle just waiting there for him to use on me?"

"He had to have known the area," she agreed, pulling a package of chicken thighs from the freezer.

"Exactly. He was ahead of me the whole time and knew exactly where he was going."

"You've got to go to the sheriff then. Dan and his deputies will go after this guy."

"No can do. I have my mission."

"They're all cougars. They know to be discreet. Besides, if we know his name and that he's from around here, some of us are sure to know him."

"Butch Sanders?" That would be the break he needed.

She shook her head.

"It's an alias, but he probably used another in the area."

"Do you have a picture of him?"

He raised a brow.

"You could use my phone to access your email."

"It's not in an email. I'm undercover. Anyone could hack into it."

"What are you going to do next?"

"Eat. Rest up a bit. Then I'll decide." He started doing a Google map search on her phone of the area he'd traveled through.

She defrosted the chicken in the microwave, seasoned it, stuck it in a roasting pan, and into the oven. Then she started boiling a pot of water for the broccoli.

"Where are you staying?" He showed her the Google map.

She eyed him with suspicion. "Why?"

"I wondered if I saw the area where you're staying when I ran all over hell and back trying to catch up to the shooter."

"There," she said, pointing to a spot in the Rockies. "What do you want to drink?"

"Milk, water."

He was thinking she needed to go with him, to tend to his injury, to show him how to get to the shooter's cabin, and then she would be far enough away from her home in town and close enough to her cabin that he wouldn't have to worry about her going to the sheriff. He'd let her go. But he wasn't mentioning it at first, because he was afraid he'd have a fight on his hands.

She served him a glass of water and milk and then placed a glass of water on her placemat. She set the table next as he sat opposite her chair, his back to the wall, his focus on her, keeping the bag with her phone and gun on the tapestry-covered chair next to him.

Once he letdown a little now that he wasn't chasing

Butch or looking for a safe place to tend to his injuries, he felt exhausted, suddenly experiencing the weariness settling into his muscles and even his brain. Sleep deprivation, running for days, and getting shot could do that to a body, when he really needed to keep his wits about him while he kept an eye on the good doc.

While she worked in the kitchen making dinner, he finally glanced around at the rest of the place. Nicely furnished with redwood furniture, curved legs, a grandfather's clock that looked like an expensive heirloom, or a good imitation. Pots of flowers sat in the kitchen windowsill and on the back patio and front porch too. They would need to be watered while she was gone, he figured.

"Is someone coming over to water your plants while you're away?"

"One of my nurses."

He hadn't expected that. He'd have to watch her extra carefully then to ensure Kate didn't try to leave any kind of evidence that said she had been taken hostage against her will and needed to be rescued.

"You know," she said, slicing up potatoes, "if you need a guide to go into the back country, there are several who are cougars living here, who are perfectly qualified—"

"I don't."

She paused in slicing the potatoes.

He wondered when she'd grabbed a knife to slice them. That made him realize he was slipping a bit where watching her was concerned. She could just as easily have made baked potatoes. No knives involved.

She began slicing again, slowly as if she was thinking

over what she was going to do to convince him to give himself up or at the very least, take off and leave her alone. He watched her this time as she carefully and preciously sliced through another potato like a surgeon would. She was wearing jeans, probably because she'd planned to go camping straight from work. They fit her nice and snug and the image of her cute derriere as she moved about caught and held his attention. He'd never considered a doctor would be built as nicely as she was.

Feeling suddenly hot, he gulped down the rest of his milk.

She was petite and he wondered just how successful she'd be at using her black belt skills to free herself from his grasp or take him down. He didn't believe for an instant that she could get the best of him, yet the notion intrigued him that if they were just practicing—for fun as he didn't want to have to fight her for real—just how adept she would be at ju jitsu.

She finished cutting the potatoes and began frying them.

He was famished, the aroma of chicken baking and the potatoes frying, both covered in lemon and pepper and garlic salt seasoning, making his stomach grumble with interest.

The longer he sat drinking milk and water, the sleepier he was getting though. He'd planned to head on out with her after dinner, but he thought better of it. He was certain he'd fall asleep at some point, either at the wheel if he couldn't trust her to drive, or if she was driving, he'd risk her taking him straight to a ranger station. Or maybe not since he was a shifter. She could head right back to the sheriff's office in

Yuma Town and have him arrested. Safer that way for their kind.

He didn't plan to stay with her all that long. Just take her to her cabin and then after that, he'd try to find his way back to the one where Butch had shot him so he could investigate it. If Butch was still there, even better. But Leyton would be armed with Kate's 9 mm this time if he needed it, and he'd return it when he could.

"When will your nurse water the plants?"

"In a couple of days." She turned to look at him, frowning. "Why?"

He shrugged. "I wondered if we should water them again before we leave."

"They're fine," she snapped.

Maybe she really did need more of a nap. "Do you have medical supplies for the trip?"

"For emergencies..." She looked at his shoulder. "Yes, I do."

He took a deep breath and let it out. He really hadn't meant to take anyone hostage. But she was...sort of going his way. She was a doctor. And he couldn't have her telling the sheriff he had broken into her place, so what else could he do?

"I'm sorry. I'll get out of your life as soon as I can, and you can get on with your vacation as soon as possible."

She sighed.

Maybe she had thought he was going to keep her hostage for the duration of her vacation and beyond.

He joined her in the kitchen. Looking worried, she glanced at him.

"Thirsty." He got some more water. Blood loss could do that to a body. "Won't your milk go bad while you're gone?"

"It's that organic kind. It lasts lots longer. Feel free to drink as much as you want."

He looked at the container, then realized that was probably helping to make him even sleepier. Hell, had she planned it that way? No, he was a big cat and naturally he'd asked for milk. She had only given him what he'd ask for. Dummy him.

As soon as she began to serve up the broccoli, chicken, and potatoes, he refilled his glass with water once more and returned to his seat. He was so hungry, he could have eaten a couple of whole, plump, juicy *turkeys*.

She'd barely served up the food before he was greedily eating his up.

"How long has it been since you've eaten," she asked, looking surprised to see him stab another chicken thigh with the serving fork and dropping it on his plate.

"Two days. I was chasing the bastard for four days. I managed to stop for an hour and catch some fish, rest a bit, and take after him again."

"I've got ice cream, if you'd like some for desert."

He nodded.

"Why don't you let the officers of Yuma Town help you locate this man?"

He shook his head.

"So after I clean up the dishes, then what?"

"We're going to lie down for a bit."

Her green eyes widened.

"If I drive, I'm liable to fall asleep at the wheel. If you

drive? No telling where we'd end up if I fell asleep," he explained. "Back here, even," he added. "So we'll lie down for a bit and start the drive before sunrise."

"You're taking me with you."

He was surprised she hadn't already assumed that. "We're going in the same direction. I'll just be with you until you get safely to your destination."

She ground her teeth, then frowned. "Are you going to tie me up?"

He smiled a little, but didn't say what he was thinking. Not that he was into bondage or anything, but... "If I thought you'd behave yourself, I'd just as soon hold you close. But I don't think that I'll wake if you attempted to slip away. So yeah, I believe that's our only option unless you have a better suggestion."

He was devouring his third piece of chicken while she was poking at her first piece. "I don't have any ropes."

"We'll tear up a sheet or something. Maybe those God-awful scrubs."

"Elsie Miller, one of my nurses, loves those scrubs."

"We'd be doing her a favor." He was about to take another bite of his chicken when Kate's phone rang in the bag. Both of them stared at the bag for a couple of seconds, then he hurriedly fished the phone out and looked at the caller's name. "Who's Dan Steinecker?"

"The sheriff of Yuma Town."

"Answer it. Carefully. Put it on speaker."

Her heart pounding, Kate wiped off her fingers and answered it, with the big cat across the table looking as though he was ready to grab her or the phone if she said anything that would get him in hot water. "Hey, Dan."

Had he seen her drive by his place and wondered what was up? Though that had happened about an hour ago. She was certain if it had been about that, he would have investigated already.

"Hi, Kate. Just checking in on you to see if you're okay. One of the boys staying at Hal's ranch, Ricky Jones, said he saw your light was on in your kitchen. I know when you have the automatic timer lights go on, they're set to go off in the living room when you're away. We thought you were headed out straight after work."

"I took a nap at the clinic. Sheba woke me and …"—she looked at Leyton—"…well, I figured I'd go ahead and fix dinner first, and then get some sleep before I hit the road." She kept her voice steady, though her stomach was flip flopping.

"Okay. Good deal. I'm glad you're going to get some rest before you make that long drive. I was just running over to Dottie's place to have something to eat with her and the kids, but was going to swing on by to check on you if you needed me to."

She glanced back at Leyton and he slowly shook his head, telling her to say no to that. She breathed in deeply, trying to fight her exasperation. One chance to clue Dan in and he wasn't taking the bait. Unless he was, but he was careful not to let on.

"I'm fine. Thanks for checking on me. I'll call you when I can."

"Sure thing. Have a nice safe trip out there."

"Thanks, Dan."

Leyton knew Kate had been wracking her brain, trying to come up with a way to alert the sheriff she was in trouble. He immediately had worried that the sheriff had seen them drive by his house earlier, him, a stranger, sitting at the wheel. And if the sheriff had been able to see clearly enough from the house, he would have noticed Leyton wasn't wearing a shirt either. Besides the fact that Leyton was certain driving in that direction wouldn't be her first choice if she was heading out on her vacation, and the sheriff would have figured something was wrong.

They ended the call and she gave Leyton a scathing look as she grabbed a paper napkin and began to clean off the greasy chicken fingerprints he'd left on her phone. "You could have wiped your hands first before…" She paused staring at the phone for a minute, as if realizing Leyton could have left fingerprints for someone to use to learn who he really was.

He smiled. No one was going to check her house for fingerprints, unless she left a clue she was in trouble, and then he suspected they'd just be trying to locate her and not be investigating the house for prints. Not at first.

"Didn't have time. If you hadn't answered, Dan might have headed on over here, suspecting there was trouble." Leyton finished his chicken. It was so good, he swore he could have eaten the whole package and another.

She set her phone on the table, but Leyton motioned for her to hand it to him so he could stick it in the bag again.

"Didn't give him any hints anything was wrong, did you?" Leyton couldn't help being suspicions. Anything she said could have tipped off the sheriff that something was wrong. Leyton wouldn't have a clue if she'd done so either.

"Sure. He'll be over here with half the town ready to take you into custody within twenty minutes."

He smiled. Not that he didn't believe it couldn't happen, but he liked a woman with gumption. "Aren't you hungry?"

She let out her breath and began eating her food.

"You're a great cook, by the way," Leyton said. "I might be starving, but even so I don't normally pig out like this. This is really great."

"Thanks."

After they finished eating and she cleaned up, she moved the clothes to the dryer while he watched her.

He'd make sure she'd put them all away where no one would see them and wonder why she had a hospital gown and Elsie's scrubs at her house after they dried. But he was too exhausted to wait around for that.

It was time to find something to tie her up with. He had offered to use a sheet to do the trick, but so that he wouldn't cut up her nurse's scrubs or something else, she showed him the rope she had coiled on a hook in the garage.

"So you had rope after all."

"Of course. But why would I have told you, considering what you planned to do with it? I just want to save the scrubs that Elsie loves and my good sheets."

"If she's trying to catch a man, that's not the way to go about it." He carefully wrapped a T-shirt around the rope to protect Kate's wrists and then tied them in front of her. Then he took her back to the bedroom and helped her into bed.

"Shows what you know. The guys all think she's cute in them."

He grunted. "I'm trying to be nice and make this as comfortable as much as I can for you. It's not the safest thing for me to do, so I'm trusting that you'll behave."

"Thanks for trusting me," Kate said, knowing what a big mistake that was on his part!

"Don't kid yourself. I don't trust you in the least. I'm just trying to do the right thing by you as much as I can."

She shook her head. "The right thing to do would be to tell the authorities and let them help you with this since you're obviously..." She hesitated.

Incompetent at his job?

"Well, suffice it to say, you're not exactly in the best shape to pursue this shooter, now are you?" she continued.

"I'm fine. Look at it this way. We're going in the same direction. You can use the company. And I can protect you from the bad guys."

"Ha!"

He smiled and pulled her into his arms. "Just lie still, Doc. Pretend this is all just a heavenly, sexy dream and—"

She squirmed.

"Or not. Let me sleep and we'll get along just fine."

Kate had to be daft to believe anything this man said was the truth. She'd wanted to tell Dan that something was wrong, but she had stuck close to the truth to hopefully appease...hell, she didn't even know the man's name. She'd hoped Dan would realize that no way would she stop by the house and grab dinner, then go to sleep. She always took off on these trips right after work. Which was why the ladies had brought over a feast earlier. Maybe he'd talk about it with Dottie and she'd alert him that something was wrong. She was his police dispatcher so she had a sixth sense about emergency situations.

An hour passed and Kate could tell the man wasn't sleeping. He was tired, but still tense. Just as tense as she was, waiting for the moment that she could slip away from him, free herself, and call the troops. They could learn if he was telling the truth about being a good guy or not. And help him if they could, if he was. But she knew that Dan must have been clueless about her situation.

"Sleep," the man said, as if he could read her mind.

"If we're going to be together for a while, what do I call you?"

"Leyton."

"Your real name?"

"Sleep."

She tried to relax, but his hot and *hard* body was pressed against her back, which also indicated to her that he was *not* sleeping. His warmth warmed her, his heated breath tickling her hair. She hadn't been with a man in forever, but she'd never really been with a man like this before. She didn't mean the bit about being tied up, but the part about sleeping with a man, his breath in her hair, his arms wrapped around her, holding her close as if he didn't want to lose her.

Which of course was the situation, but in her mind, she wanted to think about how it would be if it was a much more normal situation between a man and a woman sharing a lover's intimacy, certainly not a hostage situation.

She thought she felt his arm relaxing about her, but as soon as she tried to move just a hint away from him, he immediately tightened his hold around her. She cursed to herself. After eating, and not having the nap like she'd planned earlier, if she tried to stay awake until he fell thoroughly asleep? She wouldn't last.

CHAPTER 3

Leyton woke to a woman snuggled against this chest, her leg pressed against his groin, her head resting under his chin. His shoulder ached where he'd been wounded, but thankfully he'd been able to get some sleep last night. He closed his eyes, remembering just where he was and why he was holding one pistol of a cougar in his arms. It appeared the doc needed to sleep as much as he had. He would have loved to cuddle with her further, close his eyes, and sleep a little longer, but he didn't want to get up too late and chance having anyone in Yuma Town see him with her when they left.

He rubbed her arm and said low so as not to startle her, "Hey, Doc, let's get up and go."

She didn't stir.

He smiled. What he would have given to make love to the woman, if she was so inclined and he wasn't on a mission, desperate to take Butch down and make sure his own name was cleared of any wrongdoing.

"Kate," Leyton said, rubbing her silky arm again. "Time to go so you can enjoy your vacation."

She jerked awake, saw him, but it apparently didn't register who he was. She slugged him in the jaw with her clenched hands before she attempted to dive off the bed.

He caught her foot and dragged her back, pulled her into his arms, and held tight. "Whoa, it's just me."

Realization dawning, she growled at him. "That's *just* as bad as what I was thinking."

He smiled "Come on. Let's get dressed and get ready for your vacation."

"What are you going to do about having no shoes?"

"We'll stop at a store somewhere—in another town--I'll get some clothes, and we'll be all set." He carefully untied her wrists.

She rubbed them to get the circulation back in them. "What if everyone knows me for miles around?" she asked, as he took her into the bathroom. "What are you doing?"

"I have to pee. Just turn your head. Besides, you're a doctor and when you're running in the woods with your kind as a cougar, no one makes a fuss about what comes naturally."

"I suppose that means you're not going to give me any privacy either."

"I'll shut my eyes."

He needed to take a shower, but he didn't want her to slip out when he was in the middle of it. She probably would like to have one too. Why not kill two birds with one stone? She had a window in the bathroom, so he couldn't leave her alone to do anything in there without being there to watch her.

"I need a shower," he warned her.

"You can't get your bandages wet," she said, her doctor skills immediately coming to the forefront.

He hadn't thought of that. "Well, you might want to take one too and we can wrap some plastic around the bandages."

"Don't tell me. We have to take a shower together because you don't trust me not to escape and tell on you."

"That's the gist of it. But we do have other options."

She raised her brows.

"I can tie you up, keep the glass door open, make you stay in the shower with me, but you can shower after me."

"Not before? Seems a gentleman would let the woman go first."

"Rope or no?" he asked, cognizant of the minutes passing by. "Or you can skip one, if you prefer."

"No rope." Reluctantly, Kate taped plastic over his wound on the front and back. Then she stripped out of her jeans and blouse and shoes. Dressed in her black silky underwear, she got into the shower while he washed up. Never in a million years would she have envisioned being in a situation like this.

She grimaced when he was having such a time of it with washing, and she knew his shoulder had to be hurting. Even though she should have been totally annoyed with him, she couldn't help being a doctor too.

"Here," she said, and took the soap sponge from him to wash his back. He turned around and faced the shower spigot while she ran the sponge all over his silky skin. She washed him all the way down to his feet, trying not to take notice too much of his hard muscled body, and then had him turn around so she could wash the rest of him. She told herself it was just like giving a patient a shower who was having difficulty doing the task himself, but hell, as soon as she saw his erection, that changed her mind about the dynamics between them. Still, he couldn't wash himself adequately, and she hoped if she did this for him, he'd give her some privacy.

She quickly and efficiently washed his torso, trying not to linger anywhere that would make it feel intimate to him, and then under his arms, and back to his body. She quickly washed his penis, pretending she didn't notice it jerk in her hands, and then continued to his legs and feet. "There. My turn. Get out and I'll take my shower in privacy."

"Works for me. Thanks, Doc."

Then he brushed past her and shut the glass door. He didn't watch her, but began drying himself quickly, then used some of her scent-free deodorant, pulled on the sweats, and watched out the window as she quickly showered. She was glad she'd get a shower before they left, but hadn't wanted to mention it because she wasn't sure that just this would happen—that he wouldn't trust her and they'd end up in the shower together.

But she wasn't giving up on trying to get away. She hadn't been able to before. The problem was that he'd locked the bathroom door. That would force her to take the time to unlock the door, then pull it open. She was seeing the whole thing in her mind's eye. Her pretending just too dry herself while he continued to allow her some privacy, but she'd leave the shower, twist the doorknob, unlocking it, shove it open, run out, and shift. She'd bolt out of her cat door and head for Dan's. If she was a cat, no way could Leyton catch hold of her in time. She didn't want to hurt him, but she wasn't going to go with him.

She knew he was better off, if he was a good guy, getting Dan and the other men involved, not being the Lone Ranger. Especially in his current condition.

Not wanting to waste any more time in the shower, she thought for a moment of leaving the water on, and then bolting for the door, but he would hear the shower door opening anyway, and be even more suspicious of her movements, turn, and thwart her.

But would he have enough time to stop her?

She had to give it her all and risk it anyway. If she didn't make it, then what? He already didn't trust her.

She pulled the shower door aside, and he turned his head a little. She knew she could only do this one way. She reached for the towel rack as if she were going to pull a towel off it, but then she jumped out of the shower, grabbed the doorknob, and twisted it, unlocking it. Before she could yank the door open, he was moving toward her, and she frantically called on the power to shift.

***

Wild cat, Leyton thought as Kate shifted into her growly, golden cat form, her teeth bared when he had grabbed her from behind. One minute a woman, the next a big cat. He jumped back, avoiding her razor sharp teeth and claws. She hissed at him and he yanked off the sweats before he called

47

on the urge to shift. Two could play at this game, but he was a lot larger than her, and she wasn't winning this competition. Better get this out in the open right this moment, then they were free to continue on their way. She was going with him and that was all there was to it.

As soon as she saw him shift, she backed up against the door. He wondered if she'd ever had a cat fight with another. He'd had plenty over the years, but what he'd learned was the most aggressive won. And he *always* won. Not that he wanted to hurt her or anything, but he had to make the point she was going along with the program or else.

He was again reminded of the time dwindling in the mental image he had of sand in an hourglass timer quickly sifting to the base of the glass jar. He lunged for her and she rose up on her back legs, powerful, snarly, and aggressive.

So much for *him* being more aggressive. He didn't want to hurt her, and he was afraid he would, just because of his size. But the other problem was, his shoulder hurt like a son-of-a-bitch as the bandages dangled from his fur.

Still, he could easily take her down, though maybe not as easily as he was thinking as she got a good grip on his skin on his uninjured shoulder, not puncturing it, but not letting go either. He retaliated by jerking free, lunging, and pinning her to the floor. She tried to get up. She could wriggle and squirm all she wanted, but he wasn't letting her up until she acquiesced. Her heart was beating pell-mell just like his was, her breathing labored, her tongue hanging out of her mouth, panting.

He waited for what seemed like hours when it was more likely only a minute or two. Then she shifted and he quickly moved off her, but waited to ensure she wasn't going to shift before he got dressed. She was still wet, furious, and looked ready to shift and take him on. Instead, she grabbed a towel, wrapped it around herself, and yanked open the bathroom door. Then she stomped into the bedroom and he followed her, keeping an eye on her. She jerked open the drawer containing the silky panties, dried quickly, and yanked a pair of black and white polka dot ones on.

He waited until she'd put on her bra, jeans, T-shirt, socks, and hiking boots before he shifted, just to make sure she wasn't going to shift back again. He made her return to the bathroom, and he pulled on the sweatpants. She had to bandage his wounds again, her fault, not his. Then he pulled the sweatshirt over his head, growling at the pain that coursed through his shoulder. Still not speaking, neither were in the mood, she fixed coffee, then slammed a jar of over-the-counter pain medication on the counter. He took some, then grabbed some bottles of orange juice, while she filled two thermal travel cups for them, adding cream to both, whether he wanted any or not, but being cats, she probably assumed he would.

He made her show him the paperwork for the rental cabin to prove to him that she was giving him the right location for the GPS before they left. He wasn't about to allow her to lead him astray like she tried to do with the trip to "her" house yesterday.

He almost forgot about the wash in the dryer. Not that he'd think anyone would be inspecting her dryer or anything, but…

"Why don't you put the things in the dryer away before

we hit the road?"

Her luscious lips parted for a second. Then she pursed them and stalked into the laundry room. "As if anyone's going to be looking in my laundry room for anything. For heaven's sake."

"Right, but you never know about people. You think someone's just over here to water plants and then…" He gave a little shoulder shrug, then after he watched her put everything away, they headed out to the garage and settled into the car.

He took the wheel at first, backing out of the garage, then shutting the garage door. He watched all around him as he pulled out of her driveway, not seeing anyone lurking about, waiting to turn on the floodlights and holler, "Police! Step out of the vehicle with your hands up!"

He was glad that if she had given the sheriff any clues anything was amiss, he hadn't caught on.

Leyton kept to the speed limit, just in case anyone was about at this early morning hour, waiting to catch the unsuspecting in a speed trap or for a sobriety test.

"Do you always drive this slowly?" she asked, settling against the seat, a pillow tucked under her head against the window, a soft jaguar throw covering her body. She looked like she was about ready to go to sleep.

She should appreciate that he was driving for a good part of the journey then.

"Rough night?" he asked, smiling, even though his shoulder ached all over again. The non-drowsy medicine only managed to blur the rough edges of the pain a bit.

"I'm used to sleeping against an ultra-soft mattress

instead of a rock-hard body."

"They say a firmer mattress is a lot better for your back."

She didn't open her eyes, but smiled a little.

"I expected you to try and get away from me sometime during the night. I wasn't exactly expecting the cat maneuver in the bathroom." He admired her tenacity.

"I did leave you in the middle of the night. Four times. Didn't you notice?"

"You must have been tired."

"Clearly, or we wouldn't be having this discussion. I'd be on my way, alone, and you'd be talking over your business with the sheriff and his deputies, doing a hell of a lot of explaining about what you were doing in my house last night."

"What did you say to Dan to clue him in that you were in trouble?"

She opened her eyes, a glint of panic in them.

He knew she'd tried to give the sheriff some hints. Any sane person in her shoes would have done the same, given the opportunity.

"If I had, he would have had half the town surrounding the house to free me and take you in."

"He didn't get your hint—too subtle," Leyton persisted. "Or maybe his visit with Dottie was uppermost on his mind. A woman can sure rattle a man like that."

She tilted her chin up a bit. "Like with you?"

"It would take a hell of a special woman to distract me from being concerned something might be amiss. So what did you say to try and clue him in?"

"Nothing. Are you always this suspicious?"

"Yes. You're too cagy to have let the opportunity go without trying something."

She sighed. "If you truly aren't undercover, you must have been a cop before as much as you are mistrustful of people." She didn't say anything for a moment, then finally said, "For one, I hoped when I told him Sheba had disturbed my nap, Dan would have realized she would have only done so if she was upset about something. Like someone had broken into the clinic. Second, I never would have gone back to the house to eat dinner and messed up the place after I had cleaned everything and was ready to go. And third, I would immediately have left for the cabin from the clinic, even if Sheba had disturbed my sleep. I told Dan just what happened, minus any mention of you, because what else *could* I say without making you all growly again? But I figured at least one or a combination of the things might have clued him in."

Leyton smiled. "Dan must have the hots for Dottie."

"Well, it doesn't mean he won't talk to Dottie about it, and she'll start thinking about it and know that's odd. Or if Ricky, the nineteen-year-old boy who saw the lights on in the kitchen, told his boss, Deputy Sheriff Hal Haverton, when he returned to the ranch, Hal might get suspicious. So the whole posse could be on your tail in a massive cougar manhunt in a matter of hours."

"I'll be on the lookout for it. You said you were visiting with friends at the cabin. When we arrive there, you'll say I'm your new boyfriend."

"And Chase?"

"He never was your boyfriend, or I should say husband.

Not when he didn't come home last night."

She let out her breath with exasperation.

The first obstacle he figured they'd meet were bathroom breaks, though he was planning for them to go in the woods. And being that it was only a six-hour drive, they shouldn't have to stop that often. That would alleviate problems with worrying if she'd leave messages that she was a hostage. Still, he was reminded that she couldn't very well turn him in to a regular police force.

Food, no problem. They'd just stop at fast food places along the way. Gas, same deal. No bathroom breaks at gas stations, though he did consider if they had a family restroom, he'd just make her go with him in there. He could just see a clerk eyeing them with suspicion, and he'd show off his injury and tell the clerk he needed her to hold it for him.

He smiled at the image that gave him. He still couldn't believe that she'd washed him, and he'd been ready to return the favor. His body reacted again to feeling her hands on his arousal, which proved she could be more professionally minded them him at times. But hell, when she was washing him...

He shook his head to clear the thought.

They'd started so early, they'd driven five hours before they came to a town where he could grab some clothes. She'd actually slept the whole way, and so except for stopping to get gas once and taking the keys with him while he made a quick pit stop in the woods, she hadn't needed anything. But it was ten, and he was getting hungry.

He pulled into the parking lot of a men's clothing store,

relieved he'd finally found one. This was going to be awkward, but it couldn't be helped. He hiked up the sweatshirt sleeves, and said, "Ready to go shopping? Since you're paying, though once I can, I'll reimburse you, I'll make sure I stick to a strict limit."

She uncurled herself from her jaguar throw like a big sleepy cat, yawned, stretched her arms, and smiled. "Should be interesting."

"We passed a lot of small grocery stores, a Dollar General store, and a department store, but I figured smaller was better."

She waited for him to get her door, but this time he offered her his hand, and she took it. "Where in the world are we?"

He pulled her out of the car, locked the door, and motioned to the town. "About an hour from your rental, I suspect."

"Geeze, Leyton, where in the world have we ended up? I've never seen this place before." She shook her head. "Let me see my phone."

He pulled it out of his pocket and handed it to her while he watched her Google their location. "Ahh, Leyton, you've taken us two hours out of our way."

"What? No way." He took the phone from her, and scowled. "Hell. Must have been the GPS."

"Or the driver."

"Or the navigator. If you hadn't slept the whole time, you could have made sure I didn't go the wrong route."

"Blame me for your mistake, why don't you?"

He smiled.

They headed inside. The clerk said, "Welcome to the Rogers Mountaineer Adventures," then noticed the way Leyton was dressed and glanced at Kate to see what state of dress she was in.

Luckily, the store had just opened and no one else was shopping there yet.

"Robbed, clothes stolen," Leyton said. "Nothing like wearing your girlfriend's sweats to feel like a real man." He draped his arm over Kate's shoulder and led her to the jeans stacked on a shelf. She rolled her eyes at him.

"How are you going to manage this?" Kate asked, her voice hushed.

"What, trying on clothes? No need to. The sizes should be close to what I need and certainly better than what I'm wearing now."

He soon had everything he needed while Kate paid for it. Then they headed out to the car.

"How are you going to get dressed?"

He swore she was attempting to hide a smile. "Hell, Kate, give me a break."

"I don't know. You look so hot in your girlfriend's sweats, I'd hate to see you change into the he-man clothes."

"I'll let you have them back as a souvenir of the brief time we spent together," he said, winking at her.

"Get into the passenger seat. Or the back seat. I'll drive and actually get us to our destination. You go ahead and change."

He did then, trusting her to get them to where they were going. He had finished dressing in the brown T-shirt and camo pants, looking down as he was tying his hiking boots, then decided to rest his eyes. He wasn't sure how long he was out when Kate screamed.

Leyton looked up just in time to see them sailing off the narrow road into the spruce trees and heading down into the ravine, snapping trees in their path, bending others. The collision forced the air bags to inflate and deflate, the trek downward rattling every bone in his body. Right before they crashed at the bottom.

CHAPTER 4

"Kate, are you all right?" Leyton asked, gently taking hold of her arm and squeezing lightly. "Kate?"

"What...what the hell happened?" she asked, staring at the forest in front of them, the windshield glass shattered, the air bags silky white cloth draped over the top of the dashboard and her steering wheel. Bits of glass covered everything. Dappled sun filtered through the spruce, reflecting off the tiny pieces of glass, making them shimmer like diamonds. The car was tilted downward as if they were stuck in a roller coaster frozen in time on the way down, but not going any further.

Through the trees, a glimpse of a rocky shoreline and a creek beyond could be seen, but she still couldn't fathom what was going on. The last she remembered, she was driving on the road.

"You took an interesting detour," Leyton said, unbuckling his seatbelt, stretching, checking himself over.

"Are you okay?"

She couldn't move. She...she wasn't injured, she just couldn't think.

"Okay, listen, Kate," he said, sounding worried about her, his hand on her arm, gently holding it as if he was trying to give her comfort. "You left the road. We're at the bottom of a ravine. There's no way to get your vehicle out of here. It's totaled. We need to assess the damage—not to the vehicle. Just to ourselves and figure a way to get out of here. Where were we when you left the road?"

"A black mother bear and her two cubs were on the road," she finally recalled. Sure, experts always said not to swerve to avoid hitting an animal in the road, but a mother bear and her cubs? The thought left her chilled to the core. She hadn't even had time to slow down, apply her brakes, nothing. And if she'd hit the bears, her car still would have been totaled, and she could have ended up down here anyway.

"Okay, good reason to leave the road."

She frowned at him. "Quit trying to cheer me up. Or placate me. Or whatever it is you're trying to do. I just totaled my car, got us stuck down God-knows-where, and—"

Tears filled her eyes. Damn it. She was not an emotional kind of person. She couldn't be when she had to take care of others who were badly injured and...emotional wrecks.

"Okay." He pulled out her cell phone and tried to get reception. "No bars." He let out his breath. "Do you know approximately where we are? Surely someone will come this way, see the broken trees, and realize a car left the road there."

"I took a detour to try and make up all the time you lost." She chewed on her lip. "Damn it."

He sighed. "Both of us are cougars so we have that advantage. As long as we haven't suffered any broken bones and need to have them splinted, or we haven't had any internal injuries, we should be fine. You have food and water with us, well-prepared for your stay. You have a tent for part of your camping experience. A sleeping bag."

She looked at him. "For one," she said. It really was for two because her nurses had gotten it in the hopes she'd be dating a guy who loved to camp like she did. So for now she'd just used it as an oversized bag for herself. But she didn't want him thinking he could sleep with her in it.

"For two. When I stopped for gas while you were sleeping, I was checking over the supplies. Which will work well for the two of us. It'll get cold at night and I imagine we're going to have a long hike out of here. If we have to, we can hunt as cougars for fish in the creek. But we won't abandon our...your gear. We need to get to someplace where we can call for help."

She stared at him in disbelief. "You're going to talk to the police?"

"I'm going to get you help. Either I'm going to help you get to the cabin you were staying at—"

"I'll be a couple of days late and they'll most likely give my cabin away," she said, feeling defeated.

"I'm sorry, Kate. I swear if I can, I'll make it up to you. Do you need help with your seatbelt?"

"How can you be so calm and collected? Jeesh."

He smiled. "You screamed enough at the top of the ridge

for the both of us."

"The cub ran out into the road. Momma bear ran out after him with the other cub following. I nearly had a heart attack." She couldn't shake loose of feeling so out of it. She knew she was in mild shock. She was glad he seemed fine, but it annoyed her too that she couldn't feel the same way. Probably because she'd been driving, it was her car, and the end of her vacation.

She realized then she was shaking. The adrenaline rush, shock.

"Tell me your name and your address," Leyton suddenly said.

"What?"

"Just tell me."

"Give me a break."

"Damn it, you're going into shock. And you're the doctor. Not that most of our kind aren't first-aid trained, and in the job I'm in, I've taken additional training, but I know shock in a victim when I see it."

"Kate. Ellen. Parker. M.D."

"Address?"

"Oh, for heaven's sake. I got my name right, didn't I?"

"Address?"

"Three-eleven Wildwood Lane, Yuma Town."

He waited for the rest.

"Colorado! I know where I live."

"Good. I'm going to help you out of your seatbelt." He unbuckled the belt and pulled it gently off her, though he groaned when he did it.

She felt bad that he was still in pain, and she was certain

the accident hadn't helped matters at all. "I'll share my sleeping bag with you."

"Thanks, Kate. I swear I will make this up to you."

She leaned back against the seat, her body still shaking. He took the jaguar blanket and wrapped it around her.

"I'm going to get out and look around a bit."

"If you see the mother bear and her cubs, return here pronto, okay?" She could imagine him getting himself killed.

"Yeah, will do." He pulled a piece of hair away from her eye and kissed her forehead. "I'll be right back. Just wanted to check and see if we might be able to climb out of here. If we can get to the road, we might be able to hail someone."

She hadn't seen anyone coming or going on the road the entire time she'd been driving on it, which didn't really bode well for the situation they were in now. "Okay."

She closed her eyes.

"Stay awake, Kate. I'll be gone only for a little while."

After he climbed out of the tilted car, he shut the door and glanced back at her through the shattered windshield.

She frowned at him. "Go."

She realized that this was the first opportunity she'd had to escape him. *Right*. Not that she couldn't make it up the steep incline as a cougar, but then what? She would be shot when she went into town to ask for help. Which reminded her of how Leyton had been shot and sought to get bandages from her clinic. He'd been naked just like she'd be if she had to visit a town as a human after shifting.

She steeled her back, groaned a little in pain, feeling the muscle strain, or whiplash as it was known, in her back and shoulders from being thrown forward so violently, and then back. She tried to open her car door, but hers was stuck, jammed because of a bent frame or maybe a stump or something that prevented it from opening. She just sat there, wanting in the worst way to get out of the car and check out their surroundings too.

Even turning her head made her back and shoulders ache. God, what a nightmare. She could sure use some of the backache medicine she had in her bag, if she could reach it. But climbing over the console seemed an insurmountable task.

She heard movement in the brush behind the car and hoped Leyton had some good news. Like there was a staircase a short distance away and they could climb it up to the road.

She tried to turn to see his expression, but the pain shrieked through her back. There wasn't a thing she could do about it either, except put ice on it and take the backache medicine. She waited until he got to the window and turned her head carefully. Peering at her through her door window was one of the black fuzzy bear cubs, his long wicked nails propped on her door.

Her heart practically seized. Momma bear would be here any second. And the windshield was smashed to smithereens.

CHAPTER 5

Leyton didn't want to be gone long, anxious about Kate's condition. He was really concerned about her, worried she might have suffered some internal injury, knew it was bad news, and that's why she hadn't tried to leave the car. He was afraid she hadn't wanted to worry him. He'd made a pass a mile down the creek, the terrain up the hill too steep to climb. As cougars, they could make it. But as humans without climbing gear, it was going to be difficult to make it up there unless they risked their necks. It was about a half a mile up the steep terrain to the road, he guessed, so not a short trek either.

He headed back to the car, figuring his next job was getting Kate out of it, and checking her over. He needed to give her something to drink, pain medication, if she needed it, and then he'd head back the other way, walk about a mile and see if he could discover anything that way. He wanted to see if he could find a way out of here while it was still light out, just in case there was an easy way to make it up to the road.

His stomach rumbled, reminding him they'd missed breakfast and it was about lunchtime. So he'd fix them something to eat too, set up a camp, and figure out the direction they needed to go. He wondered just how far they had to go on this road. Would it follow the creek? They could get water and purify it to save on their supplies and follow the creek to wherever the campsite was. They'd have to backpack it out. He wasn't sure he could carry a backpack with his shoulder injured so. It would heal faster than a human's, but it was still going to take a week or so. He would have to make a Native American styled travois to carry their gear and pull behind him across the rocky beach. Even if Kate wasn't injured, she wouldn't be able to carry all that weight. He imagined when she got to her destination, she would have just set up at a campsite, her car right there, a tent pad ready for her. And then her cabin, same thing, parking spot right there and she wouldn't have far to lug all her stuff.

Unable to quit worrying about Kate, and finding nothing to help them this way, he headed back. He made it around the bend of the cliff and came to a dead stop, barely breathing. A mother bear was sniffing all around the car, her two black cubs peering in the driver's side window.

His heart racing, he couldn't see Kate in the driver's seat. He wanted to get the mother bear's attention, to scare her and her cubs off, but being a protective mother, if he scared her into thinking he meant her young ones danger, he could be in real trouble. And Kate might not even be in the car. Maybe she had slipped into the back seat to get out of the bears' reach because the windshield was gone.

He couldn't control the anxiety rushing through his bloodstream as he worried about what to do next. Hell, he wished he'd had a noisemaker with him. Even the gun. He could have fired it in the air to scare them off.

Suddenly, the car's alarm went off, startling the bears. And Leyton.

Kate. Thank God, she was all right, and had enough presence of mind to think of using the car alarm.

The cubs ran off and Momma bear chased after them—but in Leyton's direction. *Shit!* He dove for cover behind a boulder, hoping the bears didn't see him. If they did, he hoped the mother bear and her cubs would continue to run and not stop to check him out. Except the direction they were going was also the way he and Kate needed to go, he thought. Unless the road that led to her campsite didn't follow the creek.

As soon as the bears ran on past him, he waited a few heartbeats. The car alarm was still going off, but when the bears disappeared around the bend, the alarm suddenly quit. He jumped up from where he'd been hiding and raced to the car, hoping Kate was all right.

She was huddled among all the camping gear, but tried to open the door when she saw him. He got it first, and as soon as he pulled it open, she practically threw herself at him. He caught her, both hugging and holding each other tight.

"Oh, Leyton, I saw you coming and was afraid the mother bear would see you and attack. I finally realized I had the perfect bear horn, the car alarm, and used it."

"Great thinking."

"Yeah, but then they ran straight for you."

"I managed to get behind a boulder before they ran on past. They weren't going to stop to look for me with the car making such a racket." He held her tight in his arms, her arms wrapped just as tightly about his waist. They were in a real mess, but at least she seemed to have recovered enough and he was grateful for that. He was also glad things seemed to have changed between them enough, that she realized he wasn't holding her hostage any longer. "Are you okay?" he asked, his voice still dark with concern. He still didn't know if she had any injuries.

"Back and shoulders are killing me—muscle strain, whiplash. What about you?"

"My shoulder is killing me. We're a pair, aren't we?"

"Yeah. Not a great way to start a vacation. I think I might need to do something differently next year. I've got a bunch of ice packs in one of the coolers. I need to put one on my back. And I need to dig out the pain medication. Do you think the bears will return?"

"Probably not."

"I'm sure they smelled the food. It's in bear-proof containers, but they can still smell it. If the air bags hadn't knocked out the windshield, we could have used the car as more of a safe spot. Did you learn anything?"

"No way to easily scale the ridge unless we are wearing our cougar coats. Without climbing gear, it looks pretty dangerous and it will take a long time to navigate if we attempt it. Does that road continue to follow the creek? We could walk beside the creek until we reached your campsite, and get hold of someone to pick up the rest of your things."

"No, the road veers miles away from the creek. The cabin is on a lake. I was staying there for five days, which is the maximum time allowed, then tenting at another campsite, and then staying at another for four more days before I left. But we can't carry much with us. You, because of your shoulder and—"

"You can't carry anything with your back injured."

"What are we going to do?" She pulled away from him. "I've got to look for the medicine."

"I'll make a travois like some of the Native American tribes used to make and carry their belongings."

"They'd have a horse to pull it." She found the bottle and brought it out, then pulled out a couple bottles of water. She gave him one and offered him a couple of pills and took a couple of them herself.

"Or a dog." He swallowed the pills and chased it down with some of the water.

"A cougar." She took the pills and packed away the bottle. Then she fished out an ice pack.

"Yeah, I would be more sure-footed while dragging it."

"But doesn't it have to have a shoulder harness?"

"Yeah, it would. So I'd have to do it as a human and just drag it by hand." He took the ice pack from her, grabbed one of the T-shirts he'd just bought, and wrapped it around it. Then he said, "Turn around." He pulled her loose hair away from her back, and began to apply the ice pack to her shoulders, fifteen minutes, moving it to the next area, until he'd reached her other shoulder. Afterward, he put the ice pack back in the cooler and moved things around to make a bed out of the back seat. "Why don't you crawl in and rest. I'll whip up some roast beef sandwiches."

"I'll help."

"No matter what, it's going to be a long haul. I figure after we have lunch, I'll build a travois. We'll repack our gear for the essentials we'll need, the bear bags so we can put our food up in a tree at night, and take any noisemakers you have with us. Too bad we can't take the car alarm with us. Clothes, food, the tent, sleeping bag and whatever else will make us comfortable and that's necessary."

"We don't have a horse to pull this. Despite your strength, you can't carry a car full of equipment."

"We'll do what we have to do. We'll stay here the night, safe in the car, and then tomorrow morning, we'll eat a hearty breakfast, and we'll head out."

"You know, they say it's best to stay with the car in an emergency like this." She began pulling out the bread and mayonnaise, package of sliced roast beef, and a knife. "Maybe we shouldn't go anywhere. We've got enough food to last us here for quite a while, and the creek for fish and plenty of water if we run out."

He let out his breath on a heavy sigh and started making the sandwiches. He was a survivalist and his motto was to move, find a way out of their predicament, not just wait for a rescue. But Kate did have a point. A valid point. Park rangers would say for them to stay with the car. They often would find the vehicle before they found the people, if they wandered off. Because of the wreckage they'd made, a path of destruction all the way down the hill, someone would surely realize someone had ended up down here, given time.

But when he looked back up the mountain, smaller spruce trees had survived the onslaught of the car's path, and instead of breaking, just bent under the weight of the vehicle, righting themselves as soon as the car had passed over them. So there wouldn't be a completely clear path all the way down from the road. If anyone could see the trees that had snapped in two, he could tell the trunks had broken recently.

There were other considerations too though. For one, they were both injured, so no matter what they did, they were going to be in a lot of pain. Even Kate's whiplash could take a couple of days of rest before she felt better. For another, the car would provide them some protection from bears or cougars—the non-shifting kind—if any came upon them. But mainly, if they got really lucky, someone might drive along the road, see the newly-torn up trees, pull over, and peer down to make sure no one was injured. Though Leyton couldn't see the road from down here. Anyone peering down the mountain may not see the car either. Still, the driver might get word to a park ranger or the police that the trail they left could mean an injured party at the base of the mountain and law enforcement officials would most likely investigate. Send a helicopter over even.

And here they would have tried packing it out and risked running into other trouble.

Kate wouldn't be missed for a couple of weeks, unless Dan worried when she didn't call to say she made it safely to the campsite. Leyton figured he wouldn't be missed until the evidence was found that incriminated him for killing his informant. Even though Leyton was supposed to call in soon, when they were hot on a suspect's tail in cougar form or at other times where keeping contact at a minimum could mean the difference between a life or death situation, his boss would just assume he couldn't get in touch.

Leyton couldn't help but be annoyed that he had probably lost any chance to catch up to Butch though at this point. The bastard would be off marketing more weapons on the black market with no one to stop him.

"Leyton," Kate said, touching his hand, sounding worried that something was wrong.

He looked up from making the sandwiches. "I was just thinking over what you said. You're right. Let's stay here for a couple of days. See if anyone comes to rescue us. That will give me a couple of more days to recuperate from the bullet wound, and you time for your back to feel a little better. We can set up camp, you can sleep in the car, and I'll sleep in the tent at night. I can even catch us some fish tonight and cook it over an open fire if you'd like. Maybe someone will see the smoke near the creek and come investigate."

She sighed with a bit of relief. "Okay. But let's eat the food we have. The ice in the coolers won't last forever. We might as well eat up the food in there first."

He agreed and gave her a plate with one of the sandwiches.

She took the plate. "But about the sleeping arrangements..."

He'd raised his sandwich to take a bite, but paused.

"The sleeping bed is big enough for two, and we can't split it."

"I can sleep as a cougar."

Leaning against the car, she shook her head and

groaned. And he knew she had to really watch how much she turned her head.

"I'd have to keep bandaging your wound over again, and I don't want to waste all the bandages..." She paused, her cheeks reddening a bit, and he liked the blush on her. "I mean, I don't want to use them all up in case we have any other emergencies. I don't want to borrow trouble, but it is good to be prepared out here."

"You're right." He couldn't believe her change of heart about him. Was she truly trusting that he was one of the good guys now? Or just felt they had to get along if they were to survive out here. Not that they couldn't turn into cougars and get along fine. But walking out of here as two naked humans wouldn't be smart either. And in a situation like this, it behooved them to work together.

"If the car is too confining, we can sleep in the tent. We can set it up with the car behind us for some protection," she said, then took a bite of her sandwich.

"If we have trouble with bears, we can shift and climb a tree. Even though some bears can climb them too, they'll never be able to reach us if we climb high enough."

"Deal."

He finished his sandwich, still concerned about her. "You seemed really shook up earlier. I was worried about you. Are you sure you're all right, Kate?" She'd seemed so despondent at first when they had come to a dead stop against a couple of trees, he wondered if there had been more to her just being in shock.

She finished her sandwich and said softly, "They died."

He frowned. She couldn't mean someone up on the

road. She would have said something about it before this.

"My aunt and uncle." She took a deep breath. "That's why I became a doctor, you see." She was still speaking softly. With the rush of the creek nearby, he wouldn't have heard her if he hadn't had a cat's enhanced hearing.

"In an accident?" he ventured when she didn't say anything further about it.

She nodded.

"You were driving?" Maybe he should have asked about her driving record *before* he had let her drive them anywhere.

She frowned at him, her green eyes full of tears.

Ah hell.

"I was ten."

"Oh."

She looked back at the ground. "My aunt was already dead, though I thought she had been sleeping, but her head was gashed badly, and bleeding, then it wasn't. My uncle was badly injured, bleeding on his head too. Neither had been wearing seatbelts, old car, no airbags. I was wearing a seatbelt in the back, so except for the belt bruising me, I was fine. I wanted to stop my uncle's bleeding, the pain he was suffering from—he kept groaning and asking about my aunt. I lied to him."

"Hell, Kate. You were only a kid." He pulled her into his arms and held her gently, aware her back could be hurting, and he didn't want to add to the pain.

She nodded against his chest. "I tried to stop the bleeding, kept telling him that he was going to make it. But I was crying and could barely see for the tears. The ambulance arrived but it was too late. After that, I knew I never wanted to be in a situation like that again. Where I couldn't help someone who was injured. If only I could have done something. I started studying all the kids' books on anatomy or first aid. Took junior first aid classes when I was a little older. I vowed I'd be a doctor someday. My parents thought it was one of those phases kids go through. But I kept at it. I even started reading about a cougar's anatomy, and how to take care of big cats. I wanted to volunteer to work at a big cat reserve, but they wouldn't let me. Not until I was eighteen. And then I was right on their doorstep, application in hand.

"Even though I mostly take care of patients in their human form, sometimes because of the injury, they'll be so out of it, they'll shift, and I'll be working on a big cat in his or her place, much to my surprise."

"I'm sure Yuma Town and the shifters there are glad for it."

She smiled up at him a little. "I've found a home there."

"You said your parents are writers. Are they still living?"

"Sure. They're off on jaunts around the world, writing about...the world. Right now, they're up in Alaska on an aurora borealis and polar bear sightseeing tour. They stop in between trips sometimes and stay with me. They have a house in the mountains in Montana, but they don't stay there much."

"Do you feel you made the right choice as far as your profession goes?"

"Yes. All the time." She chuckled and pulled away from him. "I had young men in the clinic a little while back. One had been bitten in a vicious attack, the perpetrator dead, but then the young man bit his brother so that he would be like him. I had to scold them for chasing the nurses in their cougar forms, getting the hang of being newly turned cougars. Best of all, I love delivering babies to expectant parents."

Now *that* was one thing he wasn't really that interested in. Not in his profession. Rescuing kids? Yeah. But having some of his own? No.

"What about you?"

"Except for when I get shot, yeah, it's a good job."

"What made you choose that field of work? Anything special happen that made you believe it was your calling?"

"Nothing noble like yours. I'd just come back from a tour in Afghanistan. My commitment was up. I wasn't sure what I would do with my life when I left the service. Then a man in a suit approached me in a bar, said he wanted to talk to me in private about a job opportunity, and said they were trying to start up a new special undercover operation to take down career criminal cougars. I was already trained as a Ranger, tons of weapons training, physically fit, military disciplined, clean record. And I had just separated from the service."

"So you jumped at the chance to take down the bad guys?"

"Hell, no."

She smiled at that.

"I said I just got out of a high-risk lifestyle, and I wanted something more laid back, my off-duty hours meant grabbing a beer at the local bar, playing pool, and running in the woods as a cougar."

"So what did you end up doing?"

"I hadn't applied for a job yet when I stopped at a burger joint to grab a cheeseburger and three would-be bandits tried to hold up the place. Something just snapped inside. They weren't cougars, but I guess I was thinking, what if they were? I had the training to take these guys down—and if they were cougars, I had the advantage if the criminals took off in cougar form. So I decided that if the organization was going to get off to a good start, they needed me."

She chuckled. "Nothing arrogant about you."

"No. I'm completely down-to-earth, realistic. I broke a chair over one bandit's head, judo sliced another in the throat before he had time to react, and kicked the other guy in the nuts, sending him to his knees. I got a commendation from the mayor even, though I would have done what I did for the sheer gratification of protecting the folks in the fast food restaurant. When people learned I was a decorated Ranger and just home from Afghanistan with no job, I had offers pouring in to hire the vet—as a security officer at most places. But the man who had approached me in the bar, approached me again. I liked that he was persistent, if nothing else. Seems he was a good judge of character.

"All he said was, 'I'll buy you a beer. Nice work.' He didn't say anything more, didn't offer me the job again, just waited to see what I'd say.

"I drank the beer, slowly, just waiting for him to make the offer again. Hell, everyone else had. I wanted to know just how much they really wanted me."

Smiling, she repeated, "So arrogant."

Leyton smiled at her. "The guy drank his beer, studying me in the smoky glass at the back of the bottles of booze and said, 'Ready to come work for us?' as if I wasn't planning on doing anything else but that."

"And you said yes. You had to have."

Leyton laughed. "Yeah. I knew that as long as the organization remained honest and above board, they needed me."

"And you needed them."

He just smiled. "I knew that's what I wanted to do. Will I always want to do it? Maybe. Maybe not. I'm keeping my options open. I've heard of this quaint little town called Yuma in Colorado that I might want to check out further."

"What would the organization do without you?" she asked, quite seriously.

"Hell, I might convince the office you have a need for me right there in a cougar-run town. We don't have any field offices in Colorado. I could open one up right there. Sounds perfect to me."

"Ha! If Dan and the rest of the cougar population learned that you'd taken me hostage, they'd string you up."

"They should've been watching over you better." Leyton pulled her back into his arms and tilted his head down to kiss her, waiting a heartbeat before she showed she was just as interested in kissing him back. Their lips pressed together, gently, as if getting the feel of each other, the softness of her mouth against his, her warm breath mixing with his. He felt her relaxing in his arms, her tongue licking the seam of his mouth in a playful way. He growled a little, his body already aroused with the intimacy. He couldn't deny how much he admired Kate for who she was and how she handled things, how she hadn't tried to kill him for taking her hostage. She could have tried, but seemed to have been waffling between trying to decide if he was the good guy or bad. He suspected some of her reluctance to fight him much was due to his already being injured. But especially because in her heart, she had known all along he wasn't the bad guy.

They touched tongues and then he plunged into her mouth with his tongue, wanting to show her how much he really liked her, how much she turned him on and fired up his blood, his senses on overload as her pheromones spiked and sent his soaring.

"Hmm," she said, pulling away to catch her breath.

He wanted to continue, loving the way her eyes were smoky green now with desire, not wanting this to stop between them.

"Is this a way of convincing me to lie to Dan and the others about you taking me hostage?" She arched a pretty red brow, her mouth curved in a hint of a smile.

"Is it working?" he murmured against her hair, the silkiness soft against his face.

"Hmm," she said back, but he wasn't sure if that was a yes, or just being noncommittal.

He wasn't worried. If he stopped back in Yuma Town to see her, he wasn't letting the sheriff or anyone else prohibit him.

She lifted her chin up to kiss him again, and he was thinking it might be safer if she slept in the car tonight while he slept alone in the tent, as a cat.

CHAPTER 6

After kissing Leyton, and deciding that was enough, probably *way more* than enough, Kate had regained her senses and pulled away from the hot cat so they could get some work done. She organized their gear that afternoon for when they would try to hike out of here, if they thought no one was going to find them. She had it in mind that she wanted to tough it out here for several days, maybe even past the date she was supposed to return, and hope that Dan, or his deputies, Stryker, Chase, or Hal would check on her and see what they could find. But they wouldn't know she came this way. It was way out of the way from where she would have driven. They knew she always took the shortest route there.

Then she had a sliver of a hope. Leyton had used her card at gas stations and at the mountaineer shop...she paused to think about that. If they checked out her purchases, they'd wonder why she had bought men's gear.

Then they'd probably assume she was in trouble.

She sighed. She hadn't planned to mention it. Any of it. That Leyton had taken her hostage. That she had taken care of his bullet wound. That she'd washed him in the shower. Her whole body warmed as she thought about the way he had been aroused in the shower and now him kissing her here. They needed to sleep together in the sleeping bag to stay warm since she had only the one. But if it led to more kissing...

Then again, being practical, she recalled she was hurting and Leyton was too. So that wouldn't come to pass.

She glanced over at him as he worked to make a fire ring. She was surprised to see he'd made it so big. When he caught her watching, he said, "A bigger fire in case we can catch someone's eye from the sky. They might think a fire has been started in the woods, check it out, and discover we're in dire straits."

She smiled a little about the dire straits comment. Sure, they were both injured and her car was totaled, but they could last out here a couple of weeks, without even using their cougar abilities, if they needed to as much food as they had. And they had purification tablets they could use to purify the water. Or drink it straight from the tap—the creek that was—if they needed to as cougars.

Done with organizing their gear for a different setup— i.e. she wasn't going to be setting up in a cabin—she planned to help him gather wood for the fire. It would get dark and cold soon, so it was best to be prepared.

Then she noticed he'd made two other fire rings. She was surprised.

"In the event we have bear trouble. And also to help indicate we've had trouble. If anyone sees three fires going on down here at once, they'll surely realize we are sending up an SOS of sorts."

"Okay, gotcha. You're definitely cut out for this." She was really glad for it. She might be great for her medical knowledge and skills, but she wasn't trained in survival tactics. Though if she had to live as a cougar, she could manage.

"Yeah, it comes in handy on occasion."

When she went to gather wood, he was right next to her. "Let me carry the heavy stuff."

"Don't get all macho on me. We both need to gather wood if we're going to have enough to build three fires that will last any length of time."

"Your back is already killing you. You don't need to make it worse."

"And your shoulder isn't?"

"Now, *that's* me being macho. We'll need plenty of kindling. You work on that, and I'll get the bigger wood that I can find."

"If anyone finds us, we're going to have to come up with a story."

"You want me to say I was driving?"

She frowned, partly in annoyance with him, and partly because he was right, her back was killing her. She desperately needed to rest it. "No. The word will get back to Yuma Town that I totaled my car, and a strange man was with me at the time."

"Strange huh?" He gave her a smirk while he piled a

couple of rotting logs in one of the fire rings.

"You know what I mean." She piled the tinder next to the first ring, then went to fetch some more.

"Well, you could tell them the truth."

"That you broke into my clinic and—"

"I didn't break in. The place was unlocked as if it was open for business. And, the doctor was in. She fixed me right up. Being a kind and concerned cougar of a friendly place like Yuma Town, she even fed me dinner."

"And tied me up and made me sleep with you."

He thought about that for a moment and she looked over from gathering more kindling to see him lifting a heavy log.

"That's too heavy for you."

He plunked it down in the second fire ring. "We need some timber that will last longer."

"All of this is so dry, I imagine it'll burn pretty fast once it gets started. So about you tying me up? Do you have a ready explanation for that?"

"You insisted," he said, and headed back for another log.

"I...I...how do you figure that?"

"I'll have to think on that one."

"I bet you will."

"So then you insisted that I come with you on the camping trip. Hey, your friends should be missing you."

"My friends?" she had no idea what he was talking about.

He dropped a log into the third fire ring and went for more. "Yeah. The people you were going to be camping with. Won't they be worried if they don't see you? Then send word to Yuma Town?"

Oh. She'd forgotten that she'd told him that tale. But she really thought he hadn't believed her. She knew he hadn't about her being married to Chase or having a bunch of kids.

"You really believed that?"

She hauled more kindling to the first ring. She was dying, her back absolutely killing her, but she knew Leyton's shoulder had to be hurting just as bad, yet he was making a real effort to try and catch someone's attention to come to their aid. She wasn't going to be the weak party member here.

He paused cutting up a tree branch with her camping ax, looked over at her, and said, "Why, Dr. Kate Parker, did you lie to me?"

She laughed.

He smiled darkly. "Okay, so in that case, you insisted that I go with you to help drive and give you a break because I needed to be in the area to go after the fugitive."

"And then you drove off the cliff and..."

He smiled. "I thought you said you weren't going to blame that on me."

"No, just the part of why I took the supposed shortcut this way."

Leyton watched her for a moment, and then said, "We have enough."

"Not nearly enough." She had gotten a stack of kindling for each fire ring, but the kindling wouldn't last long. Then it dawned on her. He was hurting too bad. "Oh, sure. Maybe we should put up the tent now and get everything set up the way we want it before it gets dark." That would be enough work for the day anyway. She so wanted to lie down.

"That's a deal."

She couldn't help making sorry sounds of pain, just under her breath, trying not to show how much she was hurting, but damn it, she hurt! He was doing the same, so she knew it wasn't any picnic for him. Before long, the tent was up on the most level spot they could find. They blew up the double-size air mattress, left over from when she was coming here with her now ex-boyfriend.

Once they had one of the lanterns inside, Leyton got a pack of ice. "Before we make dinner, why don't you lie down on your stomach on the mattress, and I'll put some ice on your back."

"Thanks, Leyton." She truly appreciated that he was thoughtful enough to do that.

Once she laid down, she had the greatest urge to close her eyes and go to sleep. But then she'd be awake in the middle of the night. After he finished applying the ice pack, he began to massage her back and shoulder strain.

She hurt, but it helped to relax her, felt like her whole body was going into meltdown mode, and she couldn't keep her eyes open any longer. When she woke, she was curled up against Leyton and he was still sound asleep. Poor man. He had to be hurting like crazy, and she couldn't even massage his shoulder to make it feel better.

Planning to leave the tent, she tried not to wake him. She carefully left the mattress and headed outside to make supper so that when he woke, she could just feed him. She felt so much better, but she knew as soon as she started working again, she'd start feeling bad. She folded shredded cheese and hot dogs in foil and began heating them. Then she brought out the buns and condiments and a big bag of potato chips. She figured this was a good time to have a couple of miniature bottles of wine that might help them to sleep better tonight. Though she sure had conked out for at least an hour or so.

She heard movement on the mattress, a groan, which she knew was because Leyton had carried too many large logs and chopped too much wood for the fires. He pulled the flap aside, smiled at her, exited the tent, and stretched a little, careful with his injured shoulder. "How long have you been up?"

"Just long enough to start supper. Figured if I didn't start it soon, we would be making supper and eating in the dark."

"Watch the sunset, listen to the water rushing by in the creek, sounds rather idyllic. Besides," he said joining her, "we can still see."

"True." She handed him a bottle of wine, figuring he would think they were silly, but for one person, they were almost too much for her, and she didn't need to carry around the big bottles to drink all by herself. "Hope you don't mind having wine."

"I love everything of yours."

She laughed. "I have to admit that though we got a really rocky start, you've kind of grown on me."

"I have to say that even though I'm usually completely gung-ho about a mission and despite our current situation, I can't really complain."

"Is this something you would normally do?" She served

up the hot dogs and chips.

"On a combat mission, yeah, only not half as fancy. No wine. No women. No soft mattress. No campfire. And no relaxing. Otherwise, if I'm chasing down a criminal like Butch, same thing. No tent. No food. Water. Nothing."

"So this is like five-star accommodations for you."

"More than that. Who can say they get to have their own doctor for a camping partner."

"Or Ranger who's trained in all sorts of emergencies." She started to eat her hot dog. "I'd say we make a pretty good team."

"Yeah. Speaking of possible emergencies, did you get some noisemakers for the tent tonight?"

"So much for the thought of it being totally idyllic in paradise," she said, having forgotten already about the bears.

***

After finishing their hot dogs, chips, and wine, they topped the dinner off with s'mores as they continued to sit around the campfire, listening to the crickets chirping and an owl hooting away some distance in the woods. The creek gurgled a few feet away and Kate breathed in the scent of the fresh water. This wasn't what Kate had in mind for her camping experience, but she had to admit, considering her car was totaled and she and Leyton were both in pain, they had survived, and it wasn't half bad. They had plenty of food for two weeks, well, maybe less, because she had planned her meals out for one person. But they could catch fish to supplement meals too, and extend them until they got rescued, or found a way to walk out of here safely.

"I imagine you never thought you'd be doing this when you have a mission to accomplish," Kate said as Leyton made another s'more for her.

"No." He smiled at her. "Can't say that I mind too terribly much. Sometimes it's good to stop and smell the s'mores."

She chuckled.

Then he looked serious again. "I've been giving this situation a lot of thought. See what you think. We'll stay put tomorrow, but I'm going to take the backpack with me up the mountain to learn if there's any sign of traffic. I didn't want to say, but I haven't heard one vehicle pass up on the road. Maybe we can't hear anyone this far down in the ravine and with the creek flowing nearby, but I suspect if someone had driven by, we would have heard it. The only way this will work is if I manage to make it up the mountain in my cougar form, though trying to explain it to anyone would take some doing if I do chance to meet someone. I'll need you to secure the backpack to my back so I can carry my clothes and the phone, in case I can get reception up on the road. Once I make it to the road, I'll shift and dress so that if anyone sees me, I can tell them we had an accident. But in the meantime, I'll see if I can get any bars on the phone."

"Okay. What if they catch you dressing?"

"I'll stay in the woods if I can. It might be too much of a drop-off at the edge of the road, so I'll have to see. I'll look to see if anyone can observe the car from up there, and I'll make a marker to indicate we're down there."

"You're a genius."

"Learned a lot of survival tactics in Ranger school."

"Leyton, I know you said you can't say why you can't go to the authorities and ask them for help..."

He pulled her into his arms. "Right. Because I can't. If I could, I would. How are you feeling? Any better after we napped?"

"The jagged edge of the pain has worn off a bit, but I know that it will come back with a vengeance once we're gathering wood again."

"You need to rest."

"Yeah, like you do. How are you feeling?"

"Sore. Like I overdid it."

"I knew you did."

"I was hoping I could alert someone and get you out of here." He cuddled her tighter.

She loved the feel of him wrapped around her before the campfire. She hadn't had anyone like this ever, she realized. Even her ex-boyfriend wouldn't have done this. Sure, he was always for hopping in bed with her, but just holding her tenderly in front of the campfire? No.

"What about the man you're tracking?" she asked, wondering if he'd be close by and dangerous.

Leyton had her lean forward and lightly stroked her back and her shoulders, easing some of the tightness in her strained muscles again. "Extremely unlikely that he'd just happen across us out here in the wilderness."

"Do you think he left the cabin as a man and not a cougar?"

"He might have. I'd hoped I might find some clues at the cabin, but as cagey as he is, probably not."

"What are our chances that someone will happen upon

us?"

"Tonight? It would be unlikely. Sometime during the day, depends on road traffic and if someone does drive that way, if the occupants are observant of what's around them and not just concentrating on the road straight ahead. Could take a couple of days. Maybe a few hours. Your guess is as good as mine."

The sun had set and their fire was dwindling, the night air growing colder, despite sitting on the log wrapped in Leyton's arms. She enjoyed this, seeing the stars in the night sky, the crescent moon, the black water in the creek rolling on by, the flames sparking and crackling.

Leyton seemed to be enjoying this just as much as she was, not wanting to disturb the status quo. He finally gave her a light squeeze. "Time for us to turn in, if you're ready."

"Yeah, I am." She was cold, but she felt a little better, pain-wise. Maybe because of the wine.

They went their separate ways to have pit stops before they returned, each carrying a lantern, and he let her go into the tent first and then followed.

He zipped up the tent, then turned as she began untying her boots. He sat on the mattress next to her and began to do the same with his. "I like your sleeping bag."

"Special order for Christmas from my nurses. They knew how much I loved to camp so they bought the cougar cat paw print sleeping bag just for me."

"And one other."

"Yeah, well that was in case I had a...partner to sleep with."

"Guess they must have had a sixth sense."

She pulled off her socks and then she started to strip out of her clothes. He did too, only she planned to put on her warm P.J.s and heavy socks. She didn't remember seeing him pick up anything for nighttime wear. Not that he'd planned to spend time like this with her either.

"You didn't get anything to wear for at night, did you?" she asked.

"I can wear briefs. I didn't plan on sleeping with you in a tent for however long we'll be doing this."

"As long as you'll be warm enough."

"Hell, sleeping with you makes me damn hot." He gave her a smile.

"Ow, damn it. I can't reach back to unfasten my bra."

"Here, let me help you."

She turned her back to him, hoping he didn't think she was leading him on, just because they'd kissed and seemed to be getting a lot more familiar than they should be. Not when he had taken her hostage. But it was either allow him to help her or sleep in it.

He unfastened the bra and slid the straps down her arms.

"Thanks."

"Need help with anything else?" he asked, stripping off his sweatshirt.

"No. Thanks." She very carefully pulled on one sleeve of her pullover pajama top, but every movement hurt.

"Here, let me." Even though he was trying to be gentle, it didn't matter how careful he was, she was straining her back muscles to get the shirt on. Even though she thought she could do it, he helped her on with her P.J. bottoms and then her heavy socks.

"I'd help you but you're not wearing anything."

He smiled. "I'm wearing more than I usually do."

"Thank you for that."

He chuckled. Then he pulled the sleeping bag open for her to climb in, and joined her. He hadn't even let her settle in before he was pulling her into his arms as if she needed his warmth and he needed hers, when she was sure they'd be all right for a time, anyway. Though the colder the night grew, she was certain she'd be seeking his warmth like a cougar would her mate.

CHAPTER 7

The sleeping bag's polyester taffeta lining was so soft next to Leyton's bare skin and so was Kate, wrapped in his arms. It was no wonder he dreamed about the tantalizing she-cat as soon as he dropped off to sleep.

Gunfire rang out and Leyton dove for cover—a second too late—ostracizing himself for getting hit again in the shoulder, the pain aching with a dull throb. But the next instant, he was naked and taking down one hot doctor, smelling her sweet scent, cushioned by her soft curves, unable to do anything but enjoy the moment, despite the fix he was in.

And then before he knew it, he was falling again, only this time in a car, flying over a cliff without wings, smashing into every tree in its path. He heard a bear snorting, moving around the car.

In pain, Leyton pulled Kate into the back seat with him, away from the threat of the bear. And then he snuggled with

*her, no more troubles, just her sweet scent, her soft body, and
the sound of the rain lulling him back into a deep sleep.*

***

*Kate only saw the man who looked like the deputy
sheriff, but wasn't him, right before he slammed his hard,
naked, injured body into hers and took her to the floor. She
was trying to recall her ju jitsu. She didn't think she'd learned
any skill to move a heavy, prone, naked man off her. At least
if she had, in that moment, she'd forgotten all.*

*The next thing she knew, she was headed for a cub and
then saw a mother and another cub. She had no choice but to
swerve and miss them. No choice but to tear off a cliff and
land down in the ravine.*

The undercover agent was holding her tight, keeping the
chill out, and she breathed in his woodsy scent as she vaguely
listened to the rain coming down. But then she heard a bear
snort and snuff and her eyes popped open.

She fumbled for the car keys in the dark, and finding
them, she started punching it until she hit the car alarm. The
lights flashed, the car alarm making an awful racket, perfect
for scaring away bears, and Leyton scrambled for the gun.

"What's wrong?" he asked, gun in hand.

"Bear."

"Hell, I only thought I dreamed there was a bear about."

"I was too. But if we both were dreaming about it,
maybe it wasn't a dream."

He peered out through the tent opening, but if a bear
had been about with all the noise the car was making, it
probably had taken off in a hurry.

Leyton set the gun down by the mattress and pulled

Kate gently into his arms. She finally stopped pressing the car alarm and set it next to her side of the mattress, just in case.

"I hope you're having good dreams," she said, dreamily against his chest now that the threat of the bear was past.

"Yeah, I was dreaming about you. What about you?"

"Of you, tackling me at the clinic."

He chuckled. "Me too. I thought you knew ju jitsu."

"I think as soon as a naked male cougar was pressed against me, all my training went out the window."

"I'll have to teach you how to handle someone like that should you find yourself in the same bind."

"Wouldn't that be self-defeating?"

"You mean, if I tried to take you down like that again and you managed to free yourself? More fun for me."

She laughed, then she frowned. "Leyton, it's pouring rain out. What if the creek rises? Is the tent far enough from it?"

"If we don't have a ton of rain. I imagine this whole shore could be flooded, but probably not overnight."

"Okay. Just so you're sure."

"I'm not sure. But we set the tent up as far away as we could from the creek and as close as we could comfortably get to the car."

"Okay." She closed her eyes and hoped Leyton was right.

But he was wrong.

***

The winds had really picked up and the rain hadn't let up when Leyton felt like he'd capsized in a boat and was washed away with a bunch of bedding.

"Leyton!" Kate hollered in his ear as a torrent of water carried the tent and them with it some ways in the dark before it hit a wall of trees. The tent had collapsed and they were wrapped up in it like a heavy wet cocoon.

"Can you locate the opening?" he asked, quickly finding the gun and a backpack, and shoving lanterns and everything else he could salvage into it.

"Here. We're on top of it."

"Okay, just grab your car keys, and anything else you need. I'll flip the tent over so we can scramble out." He was trying to rush her, but not alarm her as panicky as she already sounded.

"It won't budge," she said, trying to lift it with the pressure of the water pouring over the waterproof tent and pinning it against the trees.

"I'll take the bag, and, Kate, when you leave the tent, I want you to move to your right. That's where the car is, up to our right. Grab a tree and hug it."

"But how far back is the car?"

"Twenty or thirty feet. Keep uphill of the car. But wait for me and I'll help you get there." He was afraid she would be swept away with her slighter build and lack of upper arm strength. Not that anyone couldn't be. In the face of a torrent of water like that, it was dangerous for anyone. "Just grab a tree and hold on. We'll make our way to the car. It's wedged between trees. Unless the trees go, it's not moving anywhere. But hold on to the trees. Get above the water line."

"What about you?"

"I'll be right behind you." He couldn't have gotten this

far and lose her in a flood.

He helped lift the tent so she could get out, but as soon as she did, the creek dislodged the tent from where it was locked against the trees and he was carried away. He heard Kate screaming, "Leyton! Oh, God, Leyton."

He couldn't respond as the tent tumbled and he had to find the opening again and risk jumping into the broiling water, hoping it didn't slam him into a tree and break every bone in his body. He was sore enough already.

"Leyton!" Kate's voice was far away now, and he finally managed to open the tent enough as it rolled and the opening was easier to get to.

With a lunge, he was caught up in the water, free of the tent, and scrambling to grab a tree branch and pull himself out of the main flow of water. He wanted to tell Kate he was coming for her. To hold on, but he was trying so hard to keep his head above water, he couldn't manage to get a word out. The bag on his back was being pulled with the flow; his whole body was. He finally managed to dig his boots into the ground and heave himself upward, grabbing for another tree, and pulling himself up again. Each time he managed to climb a little higher as the water threatened to drag him from his tentative perch, he felt the strength of the flow of the water ebbing. Another few feet and he was above the water line and he yelled, "I'm coming, Kate. Hold on!"

The wind swept spruce branches in his direction, the needled branches slapping him, working against him. The rain was hitting his face so hard, he could barely look to see where he was going, but he kept high above the water and kept heading against the strong winds until he spied Kate ahead, but below him.

"Coming, Kate!"

She was still holding onto the tree for dear life in the swift flow of water. He tossed the bag higher above him onto the wet ground, and then headed down into the water to reach her, careful not to be swept away himself. Then he joined her and hugged her and the tree, kissing her cheek, feeling her icy body shaking. Hell, he'd been so intent on reaching her, he hadn't even noticed how cold they both were.

"We're going to move up to the next tree. The water isn't flowing as strongly up there, and we'll keep moving until we are well out of it. The car is above all of this. Don't let go of me, and I'll get us to the next tree. Just don't let go."

She shook her head, then nodded.

"Here we go."

She wrapped her arms around him, and he grabbed for the next tree within reach, not letting go of the last until he had good footing. When he could move her all the way up it, he started for the next tree, each time the pull of the water lessening.

"We're almost there, Kate. And then we'll get warm and dry in the car. Just stay with me." He felt her grip was not as strong as it should be. He was afraid she was hypothermic. And he was afraid she could be in bad shape.

"Kate, tell me your address."

She let out a little laugh. Was she hysterical?

"Kate..." He was almost to the bag. "Wait, let me get the bag." They were well above the water line now. Once he'd grabbed the bag and had his arm wrapped securely around her, they moved against the wind and rain until they reached the car.

He leaned her against the car, then struggled to get the door open against the wind. After tossing the bag inside, he helped her in and climbed in himself, the door slamming shut with the force of the wind. They were soaking wet, muddy, cold, and aching. She still had ice chests and other stuff back there, so he pushed everything to the very back of the car, folded down the seat so they could have a little more room, and removed their sopping wet clothes. Though all Leyton had been wearing were his briefs. He helped her out of her pajamas and they tossed the wet clothes on top of one of the coolers. If the rain stopped tomorrow, which it should, they could hang everything out to dry in the sun tomorrow.

"Tell me your name and address," he said, jerking some paper towels off one of the rolls that was easier to get to than trying to locate a towel and began to dry her, rubbing her delicate skin vigorously to warm her, and then wrapping her in one of the quilts.

She shook her head slightly. "I'm okay, Leyton."

"Like hell you are. State your name and address."

She did, smiling a little, her teeth chattering. "I'm a little hypothermic. Okay? So are you, I imagine."

He turned on one of the camp lanterns to give them some more light. But the cold wind and rain was blowing in through the windshield.

"Be right back." He grabbed a tarp and climbed over the console. "Glad you had plenty of stuff in the car that stayed dry." He began to use the visors to hold up the tarp and secured it well enough against the wind and rain.

She'd been drenched on another camping trip with no reserve bedding tucked away safely in the car. She'd learned from the experience and always carried a couple of old quilts, an emergency reflective blanket with her, and another tarp. She began spreading out the blankets and making a bed for them.

She was chilled to the bone and she knew once Leyton joined her under the quilts, they would both warm up and be fine.

"Thanks for coming for me. When I saw the tent carried away in the creek water…" She swallowed hard, not wanting to think of how she nearly died when that had happened.

"All I could think of was getting back to you. I was afraid with the strength of the water, you wouldn't be able to make it up to the car without being carried away in the creek's overflow. I didn't even think about the way the cold had to be affecting either of us. And I hadn't expected the tent to take off again." He climbed back over the seat to join her.

In her wildest dreams, she would never have imagined any of this to have happened. Or that she'd want to hold his hot body for warmth on a chilly night when just last night, he'd had her tied up in her own bed with him.

She tore off several of the paper towels and helped dry him this time, doing the same with him. Rubbing his body, getting his blood flowing, then pulling him to join her under the quilts.

Once they were snuggled in the bed together, he began to rub her back to help ease the tension again, and then he kissed her and held her tight.

"What's your name and address," she asked.

Leyton chuckled low and wrapped his arms tighter around her. "I'm undercover," he whispered against her wet hair.

"You sure are," she breathed out, feeling his chilly body warming, his arousal stirring.

Naked bodies definitely generated more heat together. Doctor recommended. She sighed, and finally exhausted, fell asleep.

***

The next morning, Kate woke before Leyton, to her surprise. She slipped out of his arms, dressed, and carefully climbed out of the car, trying not to wake him. She couldn't believe she didn't disturb him as she made her way outside into the dim light of twilight where the upper edge of the sun had not yet begun to show itself. Thankfully the rains had stopped and the creek that had spilled over its banks in the middle of the night, but was still a long distance from the car, had receded.

Leyton had to be dead tired to sleep through her moving around him in the tight quarters. But she reminded herself that she had slept most of the drive yesterday, catching up on missed sleep from working on patients in the middle of the night three nights in a row before she went on vacation, then working long hours in the clinic. Even though cougar shifters healed quickly, they didn't heal up immediately, and she'd seen broken bones, cuts, sunburns, poison ivy rashes, car, motorcycle, boating, and camping accident victims, and any number of summer-related injuries that had kept her busy.

But she had to see what had happened to the tent and

sleeping bag, hoping that they hadn't been ruined.

Then she saw the tent on its top, sagging against the brush and trees. She hurried to get them before she tried to start a fire. *If* she could start a fire with everything being so wet. She struggled to turn her tent over so she could pull out her sleeping bag, but it was so wet, she couldn't move any of it. The muscle strain in her back prevented her from doing anything with it without Leyton's help.

She'd wait for him to get up and they could have breakfast, then move it. Then they'd spread it all out to dry in the sun. Between that and the breeze, they should dry out quickly.

She took the paper towels they had used to dry themselves that were already dry and built up the fire, then made coffee. She was going to fix breakfast, when she heard Leyton moving around. He finally emerged from the car fully dressed.

"Good morning," he said, stretching, wearing another pair of camo pants, black T-shirt, and his boots. "Hell of a night." He smirked a little and she got the impression the way they had ended up naked together had made the night's *adventure* well worth it.

She noticed he was still careful with his shoulder, not that she was surprised. His injuries would take some time to heal.

He glanced in the direction of the tent and she could see he was getting ready to tackle it.

"Don't bother with the tent until I can help. The sleeping bag and everything is so wet, it's hard to move. Come, have some coffee. Breakfast will be done soon. Glad you slept a little longer than me. You must have needed the sleep. Feel any better?"

"Yeah. You?"

"I do."

He rubbed his whiskery chin. "I'm going to start looking like a grizzly bear before long. Be right back." He headed back down the beach and into the woods.

"I've got a razor, if you want to use it," she called out to him.

"Nah, easier not to mess with it when we're out in the wilderness like this," he said from the woods.

He was back before she knew it, but when he saw she hadn't finished fixing breakfast yet, he headed into the woods. "Getting firewood for our signal fires," he tossed over his shoulder.

"It's probably all wet. Don't you want some coffee first?"

"In a minute."

She swore he had excess energy to burn this morning, and he was itching to use it up. She got the impression he was always on the move, and sitting idle for him wasn't really his style.

She was that way too, until she was on vacation. Not that this was what she had in mind when she went on the trip.

He began filling up the second of the fire rings. Then headed out for more timber.

Kate wrapped potatoes with sausage and shredded cheese in foil and began heating them over the fire.

"Breakfast will be ready in a jif, but if you continue

working that hard, you're going to burn up all the calories I'm going to feed you before you even eat."

He laughed. "Then you'll just have to make triple the portions."

Kate knew he was anxious to trek out of here. Despite the storm and the bear intruding last night, she really believed they'd been better off staying here. Well, and the car had been perfect for both scaring off the bear, and taking refuge during the storm. Though their heightened senses would give them an advantage over humans lost in the wilderness, if they had to leave on foot. They weren't lost. They had the road to hike out on. It just wouldn't be easy to reach the road and civilization. Beyond that, it was about ninety miles to their destination if they hiked on the road, which meant a lot of climbing up and down hills. Now that they were feeling better, maybe they could plan to hike it out. If they could just haul a travois up to the road, they might be able to do it.

Leyton returned, sat down on the log next to her, and filled a mug with coffee. "Sorry, Kate, relaxing is just not my thing."

"It's probably good that it isn't. In your line of work, you need to keep moving. Will your workplace worry about you?"

"No. I'm deep undercover. The guy was a cop on the force so they had to send someone who wasn't involved or couldn't be bribed."

"Instead, he has to take you out," she said softly, passing over the foiled breakfast.

"Try. I'd take him out but... There are other issues involved."

She wished he could be honest with her. But she guessed that was the deal with being undercover too. "Is Leyton your real name?"

"Yeah," he said. "Makes it easier for me to remember."

She smiled, then got serious. "Depending on how much the road climbs up and down the mountains, it would take us to our destination, and we could manage to hike it out of here in two to three days. If we start really early. The problem was my back and your shoulder injuries giving us fits for carrying the backpacks. And we really need to carry water and food with us if we're to make it."

"Not giving up on your initial plan to stay here and wait for a rescue, are you?" he asked, then ate his breakfast. "Damn, this is good."

"Thanks. Well, I still think it's a good plan to stay put. Especially because of our injuries. My back is feeling better. Maybe I should go up to check out the road and see if we can get reception on my phone instead. Or we should go together." Kate finished her sausage and potatoes. It really was delicious. She was glad that she had brought the fixings for it, never believing she would have had a companion to share her food with.

Leyton had worried about her injures but also about the climb. Even though cougars were excellent climbers, he couldn't help worrying about her safety because she was still feeling so much back pain. But what if he left her behind and she had trouble with the bears again that were undoubtedly drawn to the food?

"We could go together if you think you'll be all right." He finished off his coffee and poured himself another mug.

"What about you? Are you sure you can carry the backpack?"

"My shoulder's getting better." Not really. Not after the work he'd done yesterday, and this morning gathering wood only made it ache all over again. But he was determined to try and get a signal on the phone and leave a sign up on the road, indicating they were down below. They really had to do something, even though he knew they'd be fine here for days if they rested up and tried to signal for help with the fires. He knew it was just as good a plan as any other. Yet, mentally, he was having a time agreeing to the plan to stay there. He wanted to get moving. He wanted to get the doc to safety and he needed to catch Butch. Leyton had to before anyone found the evidence pointing to him in the killing of his informant.

"If you think your back can take it, we'll go together. I'll still carry the backpack," he said.

"Okay, good." She quickly cleaned the dishes and he banked the fire.

Then they worked together to remove the sopping wet sleeping bag and laid it on the rocks to dry, doing the same with the tent. The clouds had dissipated and the day would warm up after a while as the sun began to rise. The breeze would help also.

He figured when they returned from the trip up the mountain to the road and back down again, he would gather more wood for the fire rings. He hoped to keep them going today and maybe some aircraft would see the smoke in three different locations near the creek and believe a fire had begun to spread.

Once they were done taking care of the tent, sleeping bag, and everything else that had been left in the tent in their rush to leave it in the middle of the night, they quickly stripped off their clothes and they tucked them in the backpack. Then he shifted so she could fasten the pack to his back. He waited for her to shift, taking in her long-legged beauty, her dusky rose nipples peaking in the chilly morning air, her breasts full, her skin alabaster except for a smattering of red freckles, and the thatch of curls at the apex of her thighs just as red as her lovely tresses. Beautiful. Then she shifted into her golden cougar form, her green eyes catching the soft sunlight, and he couldn't move for a moment, mesmerized.

She licked his cheek as if to break the spell or say thanks for the compliment, and he rubbed against her in a cat's way of ownership, telling her how much he'd love something more with her. She really had bewitched him from the moment he'd tackled her in the clinic and gotten her scent all over him as if she'd claimed him.

For a moment, she just stared at him with a look of surprise. He smiled, showing off his canines in a predatory, hungry way.

She bit at his shoulder as if to say, "Move it, we haven't got all day, and this is not the time for anything else."

But he was seriously rethinking his need to get her to safety, and chill out a bit more with the hot she-cat.

He led the way then into the trees, trying to find the easiest route for them to go.

They were powerful and agile climbers, leaping from one narrow rock ledge to another, climbing higher and higher. He paused to see her jump, loving the beauty in her form, the agile spring, the powerful leap until she'd joined him again. He brushed his whiskers against hers, then continued up, stopping to make sure she made it, then going higher until they finally reached the road and doubled back to where the car had sailed off it.

Too his disappointment, the path the car had left behind wasn't as noticeable as he'd hoped for. Lots of spruce saplings, willowy enough that during the car's reckless path down the mountain, sprang back into place after the vehicle passed over them. So except for a few larger trees that had snapped off during the assault, the smaller saplings now stood in front of them, hiding the newly fallen spruce. A plane might be able to see the destruction, or if someone was hiking on the road, they could see a couple of trees that had broken from this vantage point, if they were observant. A car passing by? Probably not.

He listened, like Kate was doing, trying to observe if cars were headed their way, the rumble beneath their paws, the sound of an engine climbing the mountain. Nothing. Only nature intruded up here. Wondrous. Peaceful. The wilderness, except for the pavement under his paws.

Kate shifted next to him and removed the backpack from his back and he shifted. Then he began to dress, but she didn't.

"I'm going to run as a cat and check out the road up ahead. I can move much more quickly."

"All right. I'm going to move a pile of rocks to indicate we had trouble here, an arrow to point downhill, and create an SOS next to it. I'd block off the road to force someone to stop, but I'd be afraid they wouldn't see if in time and end up having an accident." He quickly pulled out the phone first and shook his head. "No reception. When you return, I'll take the phone up as far on the mountain as I can go to see if I can get some bars. Don't take any chances. If you hear anyone coming…"

"I won't." She shifted and then she sprinted off down the road.

He hated to see her leave his sight, but splitting up and doing some recon was a good idea too. She disappeared around the bend of the road, and he got to work. Unfortunately, the road didn't have any shoulder, and loose, easily lifted rocks weren't all that accessible. This could take a hell of a lot more time and energy than he had accounted for.

***

At breakfast that morning, Hal Haverton noticed Ricky, the boy he'd taken in when he'd been turned into a shifter, was checking out the clock, picking at his sausage and eggs, and not asking for seconds and then thirds like he usually did.

"What's wrong, Ricky?" Hal asked, thinking Ricky needed to shift, and he didn't want to admit he was still having trouble with controlling it, or he wasn't feeling well.

His older brother, Kolby, who Ricky had turned so that he could remain with them, glanced over at Ricky. "He thinks something's wrong with the doc. He's got a mega-sized crush on her after she read us the riot act when we were shifting and chasing the nurses all over the clinic."

"I do not," Ricky vehemently protested.

"So what do you think is wrong?" Hal asked. He really

didn't think anything was, but he certainly didn't want to dismiss Ricky's concerns if he was right.

His lovely mate, Tracey, a wildlife enforcer, was watching Ricky, just as concerned.

"Her kitchen light was on last night. I...I heard the nurses had a going-away party for her, and so I dropped in to say good-bye before she went on vacation and..."

Ted, Hal's horse ranch foreman, frowned at Ricky, but in a way that said he was more amused than anything. "That's what took you so long when you were supposed to be running by the feed store?"

"They offered to feed me. Man, was it great brisket. Not that you and Hal don't make great brisket, well, Boss Lady, too, but..."

"I knew I should have gone to the feed store instead," Kolby grumbled. "No wonder you didn't ask when we were going to eat like you usually do when you got home."

"So what about the kitchen light?" Hal asked, not getting the picture. Ricky usually took forever to get to the point of the matter, so this wasn't unusual for him.

"Don't you see? She was leaving right from the clinic. You know. To get a jump on her vacation. I even helped the ladies pack up the food in her cooler. She was going to finish up a few things and then leave on her camping trip, heading straight to the campsite. She said so."

"The kitchen light, Ricky?" Tracey prompted.

"Oh, yeah, well, I asked her if she needed me to check on her house for her while she was gone. Cuz what if someone broke in or something? She said she always has the light come on and go off later in the living room. It's on a timer, you see. But the light was on in the kitchen."

"She must have forgotten something at home and dropped by to pick it up, or take care of some business she needed to do before she left for so long," Tracey said.

Ricky looked glumly at his food.

"Okay, so you want me to check her house out," Hal said, putting on his deputy sheriff hat, figuratively.

"I told the sheriff."

Hal let out his breath. "Well, what did he say?"

"He called her, and then he said everything was fine. He didn't even call me back to tell me. Here I am, pacing all over the place, and he won't tell me what was said between them."

"That's probably because everything was fine. Like Dan told you."

Ricky didn't look convinced.

"I'll give Dan a call." Hal pulled his phone off his belt and called his boss, who would clear up the matter once and for all. "Hey, Dan, Ricky said—"

"That the light was on in Kate's kitchen, so I called to check up on her. Doc was fine. Sheba startled her awake when she was taking a nap at the clinic before the trip. Kate ended up returning to the house, having supper, and sleeping there before she took off. I take it Ricky's still bothered by it?"

"Yeah. Elsie's got the key to her place and is going to water her plants. Tracey had offered, but Kate said Elsie was right there and would do it after work. Could you run on over to Kate's place and just make sure everything's okay?" Hal asked, watching as Ricky looked eager to hear what was being said.

"I've got two drunks in jail right now. Stryker's out checking on a B & E. If you have the time, do you mind checking on it? Or you can stay here and listen to these two yahoos singing off tune."

Hal chuckled. "I'll check her place out. Thanks, Dan. Talk later."

"I want to go," Ricky said, jumping up from his seat, his brown eyes wide, his brown brows raised in hopefulness.

"You have chores to do," Hal and Ted said.

"And you need to finish your breakfast," Tracey added.

Ricky sank back in his chair and stabbed a sausage. "Okay, but you're going to call me right away as soon as you've investigated her house, right?"

"Yeah. I've got some other errands to run in town. I'll stop by there."

"First thing though. The trail could already be cold," Ricky warned him.

Hal fought smiling because he knew Ricky was really concerned. He must not have managed well enough though, because Tracey squeezed his thigh in warning.

"Yeah, first thing, and I'll give you a call." Hal was sure that Ricky was making a mountain out of thin air, but the kid's heart was in the right place.

As soon as the boys and Ted headed outside, Tracey pulled Hal into her arms and kissed him. "I love you, you know."

"The feeling's mutual, honey." He sighed. "I better do my investigating before Ricky wastes the whole day fretting about this."

"Call me too about it, will you?"

Tracey's expression told him she was now worried too.

CHAPTER 8

Kate realized she wasn't much different from Leyton as she ran along the road as a cougar, feeling the same need to get to where she had intended to go. She wished she could have run along here forever until she reached the exit for the road that would take her to the campsite, and report in.

But when she came around a bend in the road, it abruptly ended in trees and a drop-off, a heavy railing with warning markings stating this was a dead-end, don't proceed.

She stood there just staring at it in shock and disbelief. What the hell had happened to the rest of the road?

She wanted to scream her frustration, curse the world, but instead, her butt sank to the pavement, her tongue hanging out as she panted, unable to fathom how the GPS could have directed her this way.

Get it together, Kate Ellen Parker, she told herself. Leyton was back on the road killing himself to create a way to show help they'd had trouble and unless anyone took this road by accident, no one would ever see it.

Tears in her eyes, she headed on back, disillusioned again just as much as she'd been after the initial crash, furious with the GPS—at least she had that to blame—and herself for trying to make up for lost time.

They'd have to go in the opposite direction and that would mean another ninety or so miles before they reached any sign of civilization. Unless Leyton's signal fires worked, no one would ever know they were here.

When she finally reached the bend where just beyond she would find Leyton and made her way around it, she saw no sign of him.

He'd moved a few rocks to the side of the road, the backpack still sitting there, but... Her heart was already racing and she was trying to think. He wouldn't just vanish into thin—

She looked up and saw him climbing to the top of the mountain, barely visible for the trees. She raced up to join him. He was struggling, the trek hard without climbing gear, and she imagined his shoulder was giving him fits too.

She startled him, but he held on, glancing down at her, sweat beading on his brow. She shifted, not at the best vantage point to do so as a naked human, but she had to warn him of what she had found. If they could get a signal, they might have some hope.

"The road dead ends up ahead about seven miles."

"What?" He looked as shocked as she had felt.

"The GPS misdirected me, but it was my own damn fault. Why don't I shift and you give me the phone. I'll carry it up in my mouth. This is too hard to climb as a human. You're dressed. I can do it."

He still looked so stunned, she reached over and pulled the phone out of his pocket and handed it to him. "Give it to me as soon as I shift." Then she shifted and he handed her the phone.

"Don't swallow it."

She grunted at him and headed up the mountain and within minutes, so much faster than he would have climbed in his human form, she shifted on a more level ledge. Then she tried to find a signal. The low battery signal began to flash and then the cell phone died.

***

Leyton was busily figuring an alternate plan while Kate was climbing up the mountain. How long had she been driving after they'd left civilization? He didn't think the plan to stay here was an option any longer. Though again, he reminded himself that they could live out here for eons fishing out of the stream and drinking the water from it. If they headed out on a road, they would have to carry what water they could, and food too. They'd have to make this climb up here again, taking both backpacks and lots more gear than when he did it with just their clothes, no food or water. As steep as the mountain was, he didn't think they'd make it up it if he was pulling a travois. He was afraid it would weigh him down too much and make him topple over backwards. With no climbing gear, it would be a risky venture even with heavy backpacks, considering their recent injuries.

He waited where he was, holding onto a spruce sapling, hoping for good news about the phone, not expecting any when he didn't hear her shout that she got it!

When she ran down to him with the phone in her mouth, shook her head, and waited for him to retrieve the phone, he took it from her mouth and shoved it in his pocket. She raced back down to the road and he made his way more carefully to join her. She shifted when he made it to the road and said simply, "The battery's dead."

"Hell."

"Yeah, exactly. But right before it went out, it looked like there were no bars anyway."

"Okay. Let's head back down," he said, stripping already. "We'll have to rethink our situation."

***

Hal dropped by the clinic to pick up Kate's keys from her nurse Elsie and headed on over to Kate's house, assuring Elsie nothing was wrong. Just Ricky being worried. If Elsie hadn't had a patient she was seeing to, he was sure she would have given him the third degree, but he had a million errands to run, so he just needed to do this quickly and let Ricky and his mate know everything was fine. He'd tried calling Kate's cell phone first thing before he'd even hit the road, and there had been no answer, but he knew that in the mountains reception could be spotty.

He unlocked her back door and called out, "Kate? Just me, Hal, checking to see if you're okay." Which seemed foolish because he knew she was gone, but he had to alert her anyway just in case she was at home. An unfamiliar male cougar scent instantly got his attention. And then a hint of the smell of blood.

His heartbeat accelerating and his adrenaline soaring,

he pulled his gun out and began checking every room. He found her bed was unmade and the smell of the man clung to the mattress. But he and Kate hadn't had sex.

Hal frowned, not knowing what to think, but he wondered if she had a male friend she'd been keeping secret, or someone who she'd known before she moved to Yuma Town, he met up with her at the clinic, and they became reacquainted again.

But the blood...

He went into the bathroom and smelled the man had been in there too, used a towel also.

Hal headed for the garage and poked his head in. Her car was gone. Just like it should be if she had gone on her trip as she'd planned.

He sniffed the air in there, the same male scent. He had to have gone with her.

Hal whipped his phone off his belt and started checking her kitchen trash. "Hey, Dan, what did Kate say to you last night again, about returning to her house and staying the night, and how did she say it, *exactly*? And do you know *which* camping areas she was staying at?"

***

When Leyton and Kate finally made it to the bottom of the ravine, she hurried to shift and pull off the backpack so he could shift. Then she jerked her clothes out of her bag and began yanking them on.

Leyton shifted, then pulled her into his arms. "It's all right, Kate. I don't know how many times the GPS has led me on a wild cougar chase in the wrong direction, taken me down streets I didn't need to go on, and misdirected me to the wrong town completely one time. It happens."

She wrapped her arms around him. "It's time to do this your way."

"I don't think I can manage a travois up the cliff."

"We'll wait another day to rest since we've shot part of today. We can start out first thing tomorrow morning. Give the fire signal a chance today, and if that doesn't work, we'll hike out of here. That'll give us another day to rest our injuries, if we quit climbing and running all over the place."

"Okay. So we'll have to figure out what we can take up the mountain."

"We can drag a deer into a tree as a cougar. We're strong enough. Maybe we should just try to drag our backpacks up that way."

"We can give it a shot."

"I'm so sorry. If it hadn't been my stupid idea to try to make up for lost time—"

He rubbed her back. "We would have been all right. We would have turned around and lost time that way, but the bears were the ones that caused the accident, not you. We'll be fine." He lifted her chin when she wouldn't meet his gaze, sensing how disheartened and frustrated she was, and leaned down and kissed her, just sweet and unassuming. Not that he didn't want more, but they had their work cut out for them and they really needed to get to it and then rest. She seemed to feel as reluctant about pulling away from him as he did with her. But business first.

They spent the day figuring out what they were going to take with them, building the fires and making an SOS pile of rocks to direct aircraft to the accident site. They'd leave a note saying which direction they'd gone in too, and that they were fine.

Late that afternoon, exhausted, they settled in the tent to nap some before it was a little darker and they could light the fires and cook supper.

He only meant to rub her back muscles to massage the ache out of the muscle strain, her purring making him smile. But when she turned slowly onto her back, she pulled him down for a kiss. Not hard, because he imagined the strain of doing so would have hurt, but coaxing, encouraging, enticing.

He wasn't sure what she had in mind when he leaned in for a kiss, but she tightened her hold on his arms, drawing him in, and he kissed her slow and deep, the melding of their lips making his blood hot with desire. Every time he got close like this, every time they kissed, he wanted more. He cupped a breast, his hand molding to the shirt and bra covering it, massaging, feeling the nipple tighten and protrude through the fabrics, her heartbeat accelerating, her breathing becoming unsteady.

He continued to kiss her, felt her hands sliding underneath his T-shirt, her warm, soft fingertips caressing his back in a gentle caress. He pulled off his shirt and tossed it aside, then carefully pulled off hers. He massaged her breasts through the pale blue bra, loving the feel of her nipples pressing against the lace. He slid his hands behind her back and fumbled with the hooks until it was undone. He ran his hands under the unfastened bra to have maximum contact with her breasts, his hands covered in the lace for a moment as he massaged and caressed, her nipples taut and peaked against his palms.

When she leaned forward a little to unfasten his belt, he quickly removed his boots and socks, and hers, then his pants. He wasn't sure if she just wanted to fool around a bit, or fool around a lot, so he wasn't about to presume anything, but let her go at her own pace.

But the bra had to go. And then he was kissing her mouth-watering breasts, unable to stop himself from licking and tasting and suckling one, while kneading the other. She was so desirable and he couldn't resist her allure.

He breathed in her kitty-cat pheromones coming to bear, tantalizing his own. The musky heat of their bodies mixed. He unfastened her jeans and carefully pulled them off, then tossed them aside.

Better. He rubbed his stiff cock still clothed in his briefs against her panty-covered mound, wanting to be inside her, thrusting, claiming the cat for his own. But for now, he was kissing her again, rubbing against her like a cat would, showing affection and rubbing his scent over like he was taking her scent with him. He was kissing her again, breathing hard, wanting more when she reached down and tugged at his briefs. When she pulled at them, he was sure she wanted to go all the way, but he still wouldn't assume it and let her guide their actions.

He slid his hand down her abdomen, loving the soft feel of her skin and belly. Lower still, until he pulled off her panties, and then ditched his briefs. Darkened with interest, her eyes were drawn to his erection. He moved his hand between her legs, spreading her for him, then dipped a finger in, feeling the wetness, the need, and began to stroke her.

He caressed the swollen flesh, his mouth fusing with

hers again, wanting this, needing this. She purred and moaned, arching, caught up in the sensation as the late afternoon sounds of nature—the water in the creek rushing on by, the birds twittering and singing, the bugs buzzing and chirping—all faded into the background as he was lost in the feel of her and her responses to his touch.

Her breathing grew labored as she concentrated on his ministrations, but as soon as he probed her parted lips with his tongue, she sucked him right in, devouring him, her hands holding his shoulders, her dark eyes closing.

Then she arched under his strokes and cried out, sinking against the sleeping bag. He was so ready for her, his raw need hungering for her.

"I want you," she whispered and pulled him closer. "No worries."

He took that to mean she was protected because he sure didn't have anything with him for protection.

She licked his ear, then nibbled on it.

He pushed her legs further apart with his knee and centered himself before he guided his cock into her, slowly until he was all the way in. Her wet heat surrounded him, warmed him as he began to thrust.

He slid his mouth over her skin, caressing, enjoying the satiny feel as he continued to thrust into her. Despite his injury, he didn't feel the pain, everything centered on the intimate act between them.

He felt the end coming, held onto the last vestiges of his sanity and released with a growl. She smiled a little up at him and pulled him down to embrace him. He basked in the sensual state of bliss as she ran her hand over his skin. Then he pulled the sleeping bag over them and moved over so she could lay against him, getting comfortable, and then he began to gently rub her back again, hoping he hadn't caused her any more pain.

She melted against him, her soft body hot and perfect, and purred.

He hoped she didn't regret this in the morning, the thought briefly worrying him that she had been his hostage and he had influenced the outcome and not in a good way. He should never have done this with her, unless he had been dating her for a while, and then... well, hell.

CHAPTER 9

"Okay, what do we have?" Dan asked his gathered group of deputies, Stryker Hill, his full-time deputy, Chase Buchanan and Hal, his part-time deputies. All of them had been combing through Kate's house, looking for signs anything was amiss, other than the smell of blood in the house and that a man's cougar scent was all over the place.

"Scrub pants from the clinic, no matching shirt." Stryker set it on the dining table with the other evidence they'd gathered. "It's been freshly washed, folded in a drawer, but it isn't Kate's. Elsie wears these."

Hal motioned to Kate's lab coat. "Kate's lab coat with pale blood stains still visible on it in places, also newly washed and hanging in her closet. She always leaves her lab coats at the clinic. They have a wash machine they use to clean sheets and the like at the clinic, no need to bring it here to wash. And gauze pads, washed and tucked in the pocket of her lab coat, when normally if they had been used, they'd be thrown away. Why would they be in her lab coat pocket? No blood is visible to the naked eye, but I imagine if forensics did a test, trace evidence would be found."

"We need to see if we can pick up the DNA from the blood and run it," Dan said. "Anything amiss at the clinic?"

"The cleaning staff said the wastepaper basket had been emptied," Chase said.

Had Kate tried to leave them clues? Damn, now Dan wished he had checked on her in person that night and not relied on a phone call to ensure everything was okay. He'd gone over their conversation a million times in his mind once Hal had called saying he smelled an unknown male cougar's scent and blood in the house. "How would the cleaning staff know that?"

"Kate had replaced the wastepaper bag, and she did it really sloppy like, not neat like she would have if she'd needed to do it. Which she wouldn't have because they'd emptied it after the clinic was closed," Chase said.

"Anything else?" Dan asked, figuring the man had watched her every move, and she hadn't been able to leave any other clues behind.

"We can't get hold of her on her cell," Chase said. "I have Dottie on it, but she's tried for an hour, intermittently calling, and no response."

"Credit card checks?" Dan asked.

"Still running them down." Stryker folded his arms. "She wasn't seeing anyone steadily. I asked all the ladies in case she had talked to one of them about him. Except for the last guy she was dating four years ago, before she came here, she hasn't seen anyone else."

"I want to know his whereabouts, ASAP," Dan said. "Hal, you said you'd check the campsites?"

"The first she was supposed to go to was a tent site. It's first come, first serve. She hasn't checked in."

"Hotels on the trip there?"

"We'll know when the credit card—" Stryker held up a finger and answered his phone. "Okay, thanks." He ended the call. "She used the card at a station to fill up for gas, way the hell off her scheduled route."

"So she never even headed for the campsite," Dan said, sick with worry for her.

"No, and that was early. Worse? She stopped at a mountaineering shop and bought a bunch of men's gear. No hotels, no eating places, and no more gas stops. In her vehicle, they could have driven four hours without stopping for gas again."

"She might have had some cash with her," Chase said.

Dan hoped they hadn't traveled much of a distance from there, and they could find them quickly. Unless they'd headed into the mountains and ditched the car. "Yeah. They could have driven all night at that rate. What about her bank account? Any ATM withdrawals?"

"No," Stryker said.

"Okay, let's go," Dan said. "I'll call the Muellers and they can pick up this evidence and send it to their FBI buddies in forensics to get a faster response as backed up as they are. I'll alert the state police to let them know we have a missing person."

"The guy's a cougar," Hal reminded Dan.

"Yeah, I know. When we catch up to them, we'll handle

it." Dan just hoped the hell Kate was safe and the man hadn't taken her hostage. But he seriously doubted she had gone with him willingly. Not with the way the blood had been washed out of her lab coat and the gauze, and the scrubs that he must have worn had been washed. "He had to have been a cougar when he arrived."

Chase and the others headed outside with him. "How do you figure that?"

"He was wearing the candy cane scrubs," Stryker said. "Elsie loves them, but they're the longest pair in the clinic so the only ones that he might have been able to wear. I suspect he was a cougar, was injured, met up with Kate at the clinic, probably trying to take care of his injuries, and found her napping there."

Dan agreed. "She said her cat woke her."

"Yeah," Hal said. "Sheba's pretty feisty when it comes to intruders. Probably clawed him up good."

"She needs a wolf to protect her, not a pretend tiger," Stryker said.

Everyone raised their brows at him. Wolves had treed Hal and Tracey a while back. Having a wolf "guard-dog" probably wasn't a good idea for cat shifters.

"Everyone, remain vigilant," Dan said and then they climbed into their respective cars and headed out.

***

Kate snuggled with Leyton and couldn't believe that they'd had sex. It felt so right, and yet...so wrong. She knew he'd be off to kill the bad guy. She'd be back to her clinic, and she'd never see him again. No regrets, she told herself. She'd wanted this, and wanted him. Had she fallen into the hostage-falls-for-the-captor syndrome? But she hadn't been a hostage since yesterday when she drove them off the cliff. She could have left whenever she wanted. And she had no plans to report him to the authorities. At every turn, he'd been kind and gentle with her, even when she was his hostage. He'd proved over and over again that he was one of the good guys. He'd just been in a bind, injured, a cougar without resources, and he'd needed her help badly.

"I'll pay you back, Kate," he said, kissing her cheek.

She wanted to slug him.

He must have felt her tense and he tightened his hold on her as if he was afraid she was going to pull away. She wasn't. She was feeling so relaxed, except for when he made his annoying comment, that she planned to nap a little and rest her back longer before they got up and watched the signal fires.

"I mean, as far as the clothes go, and everything."

She tried to pull away from him then. She should have understood his need to make it up to her, that he wasn't planning to mooch off her, but she couldn't help feeling like he wanted to clear his accounts with her and clear out for good, when, well, damn it, she wished it could be different. Despite the mess they'd been in, she would never forget stargazing, cuddling with him at the campfire, sleeping in his arms in the sleeping bag, or in the car, or making love.

"I can't promise—"

"Oh shut up and go to sleep," she said crossly.

He inhaled deeply and let his breath out, but he pulled her in close again, and snuggled with her until they both fell asleep.

It was dusk when Leyton woke, having loved making love to Kate, but sorry he had annoyed her with his comment about paying her back. No way was he not reimbursing her for all the clothes she'd bought him. But he guessed the timing for mentioning it had been off. He wasn't sure why it had set her off exactly.

He sighed and slipped off the mattress and grabbed some clothes and headed outside to dress so as not to disturb her. Then he started the signal fires. He'd planned to make them some stew, then they'd retire to bed and get a good night's sleep. Tomorrow, they were leaving early. They'd have to hike out of here. No one would have a clue that they had taken *this* road into the wilderness. No one would ever locate them.

His shoulder was sore, and would likely be that way for a couple of more weeks. He was used to toughing it out. He just hoped Kate could manage. He'd thought if they ran out of water, they could leave the road and search for a water source. But that could take them miles out of their way.

He sat at the fire, a cold wind blowing, and he smelled rain coming again, damn it. Lightning forked, spearing into the creek a half mile away. And then the rains came down.

Sheet lightning flashed across the darkening sky. Leyton dove into the tent, grabbed the sleeping bag and Kate's hand, and dashed for the car. They'd be safer in there than sitting out in the open in the tent both because of the threat of lightning, and if they had torrential rains again that swept the tent away. But they wouldn't have time to dry out the bag if it was soaked again. And he wanted to take it with them on their hike.

They managed to get into the car before the deluge really broke loose. Other than fat wet drops all over their clothes, he'd managed to tuck the sleeping bag close to his body, and it was mostly dry. He slammed the door behind him. Glad she'd made a bed in the car and they'd left it as it was, he pulled off his shirt and pants and helped her out of hers, then laid them over the backs of the front seats to dry completely. The tarp had slipped and the rain was blowing in through the broken out windshield again. He climbed over the console into the front seat, then tucked the tarp over the visors and pushed them up to create a makeshift waterproof curtain again, tying it a little differently this time in hopes it would stay put during the brunt of the storm. The rainwater was running down the backside of the tarp onto the floorboard, but at least it was not going anywhere other than there and it was keeping most of the wind out too.

He'd almost miss this time with Kate, just the two of them, isolated from the rest of the world, just two cougars in the wilderness, yet not all that far away from civilization. And for the time he had left with her, he wanted to enjoy it, no regrets.

He rejoined her in the backseat where she'd grabbed one of the old quilts and wrapped it around the two of them. They cuddled together in silence as the storm raged around them.

"I guess," she said, resignedly, "that's the end of the signal fires. And no hot meal."

"Yeah, but how about we have some ham and cheese sandwiches instead?"

She smiled up at him. And he kissed the raindrops on the

bridge of her nose.

After making the sandwiches, they settled back to eat them. "I was going to make the stew, but we can take that with us and heat it up on the way."

Kate sighed. "I don't think I'll ever be able to top this camping trip on my list of wild adventures. What about you?"

"I've had some wild ones, I have to admit. But that's because of the job I'm in, and my wartime experiences before that. But I have to say that this will be my most memorable trip in a good way. Do you think you'll do anything differently on your next vacation?"

"I don't think anything will measure up to this one again. But knowing me, I'll probably just make the same reservations next year, only this time hope to reach my destination."

They finished their sandwiches and not having the ability to cook s'mores over the fire, they just ate a chocolate bar each.

"So where do you go from here?" she asked.

"Not sure. I've got to find Butch. But I'm afraid the trail will have gone cold. I don't have any funds to get me by, so I'm probably going to have to resort to running as a cougar, searching for him, and then if I can't find him, return to where I left my car and my gear. I'll drive back here and search again. He knew the area and he knew that cabin. I'm certain he's got to be from around here. Which could mean he has family in the area. I have to take him down."

"He needs to be. He shot you and you're one of the good guys."

"He's an arms dealer."

"Oh. Then that's another good reason. I'll have to give you money to rent a car. I can call Dan to see if he can have someone pick me up at the first town we come to."

"All right. That works for me."

That night, they didn't have a choice but to sleep in the car again, the wind howling about them, the lightning slamming into the forest and creek, cracks of thunder deafening to their sensitive ears. That made him worry some about hiking out of here should they get caught in another storm, this time without a car to huddle together in, nice and warm and comfy. But he didn't believe anyone would ever find them and he had to get Doc to safety.

CHAPTER 10

The next morning, the rains had thankfully stopped and Leyton moved to the front seat of the car and tried to start the engine.

"Now, why hadn't I thought of that?" Kate asked, thinking he was crazy as she pushed open the door so she could leave the car and relieve herself in the woods.

He smiled at her. "Smart aleck. We have a dead phone. I just thought about it this morning, and I wondered if I could charge it up, and when we got closer to civilization, we could call for help. But the engine won't turn over."

"Must have failed after I used it the last time to scare away the bear. But we can grab the charger. I have one for an electric outlet too for when we reach a town."

"How far away was the last sign of civilization?" Leyton asked.

"Ninety miles."

"Hell, I slept that long?" He thought he had only dozed

for a half hour, if that.

"You did."

"That means we have a three-day hike unless we can hitch a ride."

"Ha! I'm not risking my life to hitchhike."

"Nobody would dare pick me up," he said, looking more and more like a grizzly bear. "But they'd pick you up in heartbeat."

"Yeah, and leave you behind."

"Agreed. No hitchhiking."

He took off into the woods to take care of business, then rejoined her. She was making a breakfast of cereal and fruit, slices of cheese, and ham to give them some nourishment before they took off. "I hate leaving all this behind. Which is part of the reason I didn't want to leave here until we were rescued."

"You can have whoever comes for you retrieve your stuff. Just tell them they need climbing ropes to do it."

They finished packing up their gear, and he helped her on with her backpack, having taken half her load so it wasn't too much. They had raingear in case it began to rain, and as much food and water as they could carry that wouldn't spoil, three days change of clothes, the gun, dead phone, chargers, one of the tarps to make a lean-to for a shelter for the two nights, an emergency blanket, and the highly compressible sleeping bag in its own individual drawstring stuff sack, then wrapped securely in the tarp to keep it dry in case the rain came down again.

She helped him on with his pack, and he groaned a little as the strap dug into his injured shoulder.

"Leyton—"

"I'm fine. "

"You pass out on me on the way up the mountain, and I'm going to have to just leave you behind."

He leaned down and kissed her mouth. "You do that. And if you see anyone, send them back to pick up my half dead body, will you?"

She snorted, then kissed him back. "Come on. Let's get moving before I decide to start ditching everything in my bag."

"Too heavy?"

"No. Same thing goes for me. If I pass out—"

"I'm coming back for you and we'll just live here on the mountain, setting signal fires until we're old and gray."

She laughed. And then they made the arduous climb up the mountain. It was really slow going this time in her human form, gripping trees and rocks with her fingers, trying to watch that she had solid footing with every step she took. The problem was that she just didn't have the upper body strength that Leyton had. So even if she hadn't had a backpack to carry, she was having a time of it. She had to keep pausing, keep catching her breath, and she saw him watching her when she knew, despite the heavier weight he was carrying, he could have been up the mountain in half the time.

"Go," she said, trying to catch her breath. "I'll... be up there...in a moment."

She knew he didn't want to leave her behind. That he worried she'd fall. But if she did, he couldn't have caught her anyway.

"Be back in a minute," he said, and with that, he began to climb much faster with his longer legs and upper body strength.

She knew he meant to help carry her load, and she didn't want him to have to come all the way back down to carry her bag too. He'd be worn out before they even walked a mile.

She continued her slow progress, unable to hurry any faster than she was, her back killing her again. Her foot slipped suddenly on some loose rocks, and she slid a few feet, her heart jumping into her throat, her knees bruised against the rocks. She caught hold before she slid any further and clung on for dear life. Fear made every bit of moisture in her mouth and throat evaporate.

You can do this, Kat, she told herself. Her whole body was shaking from the rush of adrenaline that had flooded her cells the moment she lost her grip on the rocks, but she managed to get a toehold again and started to work her way up. She hated that she'd lost any progress she'd made in the last ten minutes. But she reminded herself she was lucky she hadn't slid all the way back down the mountain and broken something—like her neck.

She was a long way from the top still when she saw him coming back down for her. She wasn't going to tell him not to, not when he had it in mind to do it. And he was already halfway down the mountain.

She continued to climb, carefully, her shoulders aching, her back hurting, her arms and legs shaking.

"I've got you, Kate," Leyton assured her, suddenly beside her. "You're in a good spot. Just turn toward me a bit and I'm going to slide the pack off one arm and then the other. Just hold on tight."

She did, feeling as though either of them could make one false move, and they'd both go flying to the bottom of the cliff. But she did exactly as he told her, and he pulled the backpack off her slowly, one arm, and then the other, and hung it over his good shoulder.

"Okay, can you make it now?" His eyes were dark with concern, his look grim. Had he seen her fall?

"Yes." She better damn well make it after he had to carry all their gear. But she felt so light now and began to climb faster. It was still difficult, but she realized just how much a little extra weight made a big difference. Her foot slipped again on more loose rocks, only this time she was careful to have a better handhold on the rock above her and she held on until she could get the nerve to try again.

Except for climbing cliffs as a cougar, which was a lot different than doing so as a human, she had never done this before. She wasn't exactly equipped with the right gear for it and with her injures, that wasn't helping either.

He stayed next to her the whole way up, when she wished he wouldn't so he could rest after all the effort he'd made, yet she appreciated him for working so hard and being so concerned about her. When they reached the road at the top of the cliff, he threw the pack onto the asphalt, and finished the climb. He turned quickly and pulled her up into his arms and sat down hard against the other pack.

She moved around so she wasn't lying on top of him, but sitting between his legs, using him as a back cushion while he used the other pack for his, trying to catch their breaths.

"What do you think about changing the plans again?" she asked.

"How's that?" he asked.

"Well, since you're in such great shape, you could go back down there and grab the tent, bring it up here and set it up, and we can take a nap. And get started again tomorrow."

He laughed. "If I have to climb down there again, and carry up the tent, we'd definitely have to start over again tomorrow."

She sighed. "Okay, I caught my breath. Let's go." She didn't want to move. Not really. She told herself walking wouldn't be so bad. But she had driven here and she knew how hilly the road was. It wasn't going to be an easy walk back to civilization.

"We'll get as far as we can, Kate. No need to kill ourselves trying to get there."

"Okay, sounds good to me."

He stood and helped her up. And then she helped him on with his backpack first and then he helped her on with hers.

They headed on the first leg of the journey, the road nice and level, but around the bend, it went downhill for a long ways. Driving it was no problem. Walking was going to be some exercise—especially climbing the next hill. At least it was cool that morning, though the sun had begun to rise and with all the exercise, she was already hot.

For a while, he talked about what he'd like to do when they got back to civilization. "A hot shower and a steak dinner. What about you?"

"A nice long soak in a tub and barbecued ribs."

"It'll take about six hours for someone to come get you from Yuma Town. How about we grab a motel room, get cleaned up, and have dinner out when we get in?"

"Maybe I'll have a steak too, mushrooms, wine, baked potato with all the toppings: melted butter and chives and sour cream." She could already taste it. "And ice cream afterward with hot fudge topping, whipped cream, and a cherry on top."

"Plain ice cream or something special?"

"Hmm, chocolate fudge swirl."

"Let's get a double order. Eat out or room service?"

"Watch a movie on T.V. while we're eating dinner?"

"Sounds like one hell of a plan."

She realized by talking about what they would do when they got into town, whether they really did do it or not, she hadn't paid any attention to hiking down the hill, but when they came to the hike up, she had to conserve her breath. Once they were on top and on level ground again—though she'd slowed way down, and he'd offered to take her pack, to which she had politely declined—they had a nice level stretch.

"So what movie do you want to watch?" she asked, a little short of breath.

"Thriller? Comedy? T.V. show? Movie?"

"Space movie. I like Sci-Fi. What about you?"

"Sure. Some of my favorite stories are in that genre. *Star Trek, Star Wars, Firefly, Galaxy Quest,* even *Oblivion* and tons more."

"Maybe I could have a lobster tail with my steak. Side of melted butter to dip it in. Jumbo shrimp appetizer with cocktail sauce."

Leyton laughed. "You're making me hungry."

For several miles, they walked in silence. Leyton figured if they walked thirty miles a day, they'd reach a town about dusk on the third day. But he didn't think they'd get that far today. Not as slow as Kate was walking because of how hilly the terrain was, her injured back, and carrying the heavy pack. At this rate, they were likely going to need four days.

He nearly had heart failure when he left his backpack up on the road, turned to climb back down, to see where Kate was when he witnessed her slip and fall. He'd hurried down as fast as he was safely able, knowing there was no way she was going to make it to the road carrying her pack, despite how bound and determined she was to do it. He hadn't been able to feel any relief that she would make it until he'd pulled her safely to the pavement.

"How far to the turn off where you reached this road?" he asked, figuring the next road would be a main one, and probably less hilly than this. Maybe if it wasn't too far, they could make up the lean-to, someone would drive by and see them and report them to the police. Then an officer in a cruiser would check them out and give them a ride into town.

"I'm not sure. Thirty miles, maybe?"

He didn't think they'd make it that far today and he didn't want to push it if it meant injuring themselves further. "Okay, we'll just walk until we get tired, eat, drink, have a pit stop, and continue on our way. We'll see how far we can get to."

"If you're thinking we might get to a main road after this?" She let out her breath. "We won't. It was a narrow, winding trail too. I should have known it was the wrong way to go. I think I drove on it for about fifteen miles."

"And...before that?"

"The main road. No businesses or homes. But it did have a shoulder we can walk on and it was much more level. A few more cars passed me there. None on the other two roads."

"We're doing great," he said. Because they were. Any progress at all meant they were making...progress. And that's all they could do for now.

They stopped several times and he thought he must have been feeling in as bad a shape as Kate, as far as carrying the packs went. If he knew for certain they'd get picked up somewhere along the way early enough that they wouldn't need a lean-to and everything else they were packing, he'd just dump it and carry water and a little food. But he couldn't risk it if they had to go it alone. They needed shelter from the wind and cold and rain. They needed to stay warm.

The sun was sinking and he was about to suggest that they stop at the bottom of the hill. Right now they were on a nice level spot on top of a hill. "Do you want to go to the bottom of the hill and set up there? Or here?" He was certain neither of them could climb the next hill tonight.

"It would be less breezy down below," she said practically. "And if we get hit with another summer storm, we'll be safer down there than up on top of the hill."

"My thoughts exactly."

They headed downhill, which really was harder on their legs than climbing uphill. When they reached the bottom, he dumped his backpack and took hold of hers and set it down on the ground.

Kate didn't know how to make a lean-to, so she began to gather rocks to create a fire ring on the asphalt. If anyone ever came by here someday, they'd probably think the people who did this were nuts.

She began gathering kindling, while Leyton built the lean-to shelter, creating a backbone to the structure by tying a heavy branch between two others. Then he secured a tarp over it and covered it with branches and leaves for more insulation. He laid the emergency survival blanket on the ground to keep them from lying on the damp, cold ground, and spread the sleeping bag out under the lean to. He grabbed more timber for the fire and before the sun sank completely in the sky, they were seated on the sleeping bag, grilling hot dogs over the fire. They figured they'd have to eat those tonight. Everything else was non-perishable and could be eaten at any time.

"I've never made a lean-to before. I've never had a need, but it's great. I figured we'd be wrapped up in the tarp, trying to keep warm and dry."

"Lots of training. Lots of different environments, usually with a lot less equipment for comfort than this."

"This is great, but only because you're here, sharing it with me." She hadn't meant to get sentimental, good way to throw a bucket of ice water on a nice time, but she meant it. She would have hated being out here like this by herself. But with him, it was romantic.

"I have to agree," he said, surprising her. "Hell, Doc, if I ever get myself into another bind like this, and I'm on my own, you better believe I'll be wishing I was here again, spending the time with you."

They ate their hot dogs, made s'mores, and finished them off. Then they both took pain reliever and washed it down with water before they settled down for the night. They removed their shoes and the rest of their clothes, then crawled into the bag together. In trying to keep a weight limit on what she'd take with her on this trek, cognizant of how long they'd have to walk and such, she had forgotten her P.J.s.

She didn't think they'd make love again, especially like this in a lean-to, practically out there for the world to see as if the world even knew they were out here. She really thought it was a one-time deal when they'd made love earlier. But before she really planned anything, she was kissing him. She moved on top of him, running her hands over his chest, her mons pressed against his groin, and she was already wet for him.

His heart was racing as fast as hers, his hands sliding up and down her naked thighs, his breathing short as she ground against his rock-hard cock. She loved how aroused he'd become with touching him.

Never in a million years had she dreamed she'd be hotly seducing a male cat beneath a hastily-made lean-to out in the middle of nowhere with a man she barely knew. But maybe that's what excited her now, bringing out her wild side, encouraging her feral need to have him. Yet in the back of her mind, she knew it was more than that. Not just a situation where no one could judge what the good doctor was doing. That she'd be with a man she'd never see again, so a couple of feral lovefests would be it and over. Maybe that was making her feel so free with him.

She didn't think so. She felt the real animal attraction between them. Some primitive craving that went beyond their human dictates. She would enjoy every moment of this before it was gone for good.

She was kissing him now, passionately, and felt his cock stirring beneath her assault. His large, warm hands slid over her ass. He made her spread her legs further, to sit more upright, and then he began to stroke her clit. His lust-filled gaze locked onto hers, his other hand holding her in place as she wanted to buck, or arch her back, or melt into him, the sensations so heady all at once, she felt him driving her insane. In a completely, wonderfully hot way.

The cool breeze swept over her as it curled around the lean-to, the bark of a coyote off in the distance, followed by the hooting of an owl. As a cat, the sounds didn't fade completely in the distance, not as wary as they were. Being out in the wilderness, it was important to remain vigilant concerning any troubles they might encounter—bears, chiefly among them. Even so, Leyton stole her attention away, made her body climb in an effort to reach the pinnacle of exquisite pleasure. She realized she was gripping the sleeping bag in her clenched hands when Leyton pushed two fingers into her tight, wet sheath, and set her hurtling over the edge. She cried out, uncaring of who or what might

hear her and was ready to collapse on the male cat who
rocked her world.

Leyton quickly followed Kate's climax by pushing into
her, then moving her until she was beneath him so she'd
stay warmer as the air chilled even more. He was burning
up as he plunged into her faster, harder, rocking into her as
she rocked against him.

He realized what great shape she was in, how taut her
muscles were as they clamped down on his cock. He
captured her mouth and kissed her again, their tongues
twisting around each other in an already familiar dance.

He liked the familiarity he felt with Kate, knowing what
stirred her faster to climax, what actions drew her out. How
she purred when he stroked her, her favorite position to
cuddle against him.

She locked her ankles behind his back, giving him even
deeper access. He thrust hard, his pulse beating out of
bounds, the cold breeze wrapping around his moist skin,
doing nothing to douse the fire burning inside him.

He claimed her lips again, licking and teasing, just
before he released his seed inside her, bathing her on a sex-
roughened growl. Sheer mindless pleasure consumed him
before he hugged her tight to his body, then rolled off her
to pull her into his arms and cover them completely with
the sleeping bag.

He had never been with a woman he'd felt like this
with before, who after sex, he wanted to hold her close and
continue to share the intimacy with as if they had chosen
each other for their mates. It should have bothered him
that he was feeling this way about her. Given he'd never

experienced such passion or need before, he wondered if he should be panicking a bit with the notion that he might want something more from Kate, who had a bit of a rebellious streak, like he had, and who, on the spur of the moment had completely opened herself up to him again.

He had expected that they'd just cuddle and conk out after the grueling day they'd had. He hadn't expected Kate to ravish him like this, which, hell, had energized him just as quickly. The winds had picked up and the breeze was cold, but she was one hot cat as she'd rubbed against his arousal, encouraging him to make love to her. As much as she'd been drooping at the end, he really hadn't expected her to have wanted this. But he was glad for it, when before, he'd so regretted everything that had happened on the trip, taking her hostage and then ending up at the bottom of the ravine, her injuries, and that she had missed out on her vacation. He wondered if she was feeling the need to have a last go of it with him before they went their separate ways.

Yet sharing meals with her and sitting at the campfire, talking and sleeping together, had made such an impact on him. She was the kind of woman he could settle down with, if he were ready.

CHAPTER 11

Dan and his men converged on the mountaineering store after checking out the gas station and the rest of the businesses in town on the off-chance that they had stopped in at a motel, or eaten at one of the restaurants and paid cash. At the store, the woman gave them a description—man wearing women's pale blue sweats, a couple of sizes too small. He was barefooted and he had joked about wearing his girlfriend's clothes because he had been robbed.

The clerk gave a good description of him, but best of all, they had security footage of him. It wasn't the best in the world, grainy, but it was good enough to show his features, and that Kate didn't appear to be coerced or trying to clue the clerk in that she was being held as a hostage. In fact, when the man said he was wearing his girlfriend's clothes, Kate had rolled her eyes.

"Hell, she doesn't look like a hostage," Hal said, staring at the tape as they ran it again.

Chase folded his arms. "He doesn't look like he's avoiding the security camera either, as much as he'd hidden the fact that he had to be the one making her wash the scrubs, gauze, and her lab coat to hide blood evidence."

Stryker glowered at the man. "He's taken her against her will. She's afraid to let on. I'll kill him."

"Hell," Chase said, "he looks like your doppelganger, Stryker. Sure you don't have a twin you've hidden from us all these years?"

Stryker gave Chase a glower.

Dan said, "He must have figured no one would know he'd taken her and so he wasn't trying to hide from the security camera. No security cameras are located on the street in the town, so we can't see what route they took. But if they'd taken the road to the first campsite she was supposed to be at, she'd be there by now. I called again, and she still hasn't checked in."

"When he took the packages from the clerk, he winced right there," Hal said. "He must have an injured shoulder."

Stryker snorted. "Not injured enough."

"So what do we do now?" Chase asked, looking at a map of the area.

"They might have headed for the next big town where he can use her credit card for a rental," Hal said.

Stryker shook his head. "No, she still hasn't used her credit card again. If they are still driving, they'd have to get gas at some point."

Dan ran his hands through his hair. "Okay, this is what we do. Each of us will take these roads out, check the small towns along the way, see if you spot her vehicle anywhere.

State police are looking too. No one's seen any sign of her vehicle. It's like she's dropped off the edge of the world."

"Which means the vehicle could be hidden in a garage or something," Chase said.

"Yeah. All we can do is search for them. And if we find them—" Dan said.

"I'm going to kill him," Stryker said.

"We're going to take him into custody and find out what all this is about." Dan's voice was authoritative. "He's not guilty until proven so. If you find anything, let me know and I'll pass along the word."

Then the men all disbursed except for Stryker and Dan.

Dan waited for everyone to be well out of earshot, then he said to Stryker, "We all are hot under the collar about this. All of us. We want to turn the world upside down and return her home safely. I'm certain he didn't take Kate with him willingly. She would have let us know if she'd had a change of plans. She's good about keeping us informed in case there's an emergency. But, we still need to know the truth of the matter. From that tape, Kate doesn't look scared or concerned. I don't want us getting trigger happy and then learning he needed her help and she was giving it freely."

Stryker looked mutinous.

"All right?"

"If he's a danger to her..."

"We take him in, Stryker. That's an order."

"All right, and if we learn he took her against her will, then I kill him." Stryker stalked out the door.

Dan headed after his men, hoping to hell that Kate was all right. Dottie had never been able to get hold of her, and he feared for Kate, that if she could, she would have let them know where she was and she was all right. It just didn't feel right. Any of it.

***

Early the next morning, Leyton woke to the sound of grunting on the other side of the lean-to. Hell, they had company. He and Kate were naked, so the easiest thing for them to do was shift into their cougar forms and vacate the lean-to until they could safely return.

Leyton whispered to Kate, "Bear's behind our shelter. Let's shift and take off, then we can come back when it's safe."

She was sitting up in an instant and shifting just as fast. He shifted too, only he grabbed his backpack in his jaws, not wanting to lose their food to the bear. Leyton dragged the bag at a sprint while she ran after him.

The bear didn't go after them, thankfully, because dragging the backpack was a monumental task. Leyton leapt into a nearby spruce tree with the bag gripped tightly between his teeth. She leaped onto the branch next to him and shifted, then took the bag and tied it to the branch. "We need to get the other one."

He shifted. "Too late."

The bear was pawing at the bag, trying to get to the food in it, shaking the bag, attempting to rip it apart.

"Damn it," Kate said, then shifted to stay warm.

Leyton shifted back into his cougar form also and nuzzled her face. They waited for a couple of hours, watching the bear moving around the campsite, sniffing where the other bag had been, pawing at the burned out ashes in the fire ring, probably smelling the juices from the hot dogs as they had roasted over the fire. Then finally not being able to get what he was after, he ambled off.

Still, they waited, then believing he wasn't returning, Leyton shifted, untied his pack from the tree, and dropped it to the ground. He shifted again and jumped down from the tree, grabbed the bag, and dragged it back to camp. He wasn't taking any chances of shifting into his human form and carrying the bag if the bear should suddenly return.

Kate was beside him in an instant and helping him to drag the bag back. Then they hurriedly had a quick breakfast of jerky and water, forget making coffee this morning, packed up their gear, and headed back to the road, and were on their way.

"Are you okay?" he asked Kate, wishing they hadn't had such a rude awakening this morning, and losing a couple of hours before they could get to their gear.

"Yeah. Achy. I don't believe back country backpacking is my thing."

"Not when you've been in a car accident and have whiplash. You're doing great for everything you've been through."

"How far do you think we made it yesterday? I was hoping thirty miles, but I imagine with the climb up the mountain first, it was a lot less."

"About twenty. But we should make that other road you were talking about today."

"I wasn't sure I would be able to move this morning at all, until that bear was in the camp."

He chuckled. "Me either. Then I heard him and all of a

sudden, I forgot about all my aches and pains."

They talked even less today, just trying to make the climb up and down the hills, just keeping their pace and not lagging too much until midday with the sun beating down on them as they walked along the road. At least they were on a road and not traversing uneven terrain. If he'd known the lay of the land better, he might have been tempted to cut corners instead of following the road, but he didn't know the area well enough, and he figured they'd end up putting more miles in than necessary.

They took several water breaks, ate tuna in packages and crackers, then headed out again. That night, they reached the second road, and Leyton saw a couple of signs facing the way they had come. He turned back to look. DEAD END UP AHEAD, but to Kate's credit, trees had grown up around them, and they weren't that easy to see.

The second road was just as treed, just as narrow with no shoulders to walk on and like Kate had said, just as winding and steep.

"We'll set up camp here," he said, before the sun began its full and complete descent.

"We're almost there," Kate said, breathing a sigh of relief as Leyton pulled off her backpack, and she helped him with his.

To his surprise, he saw a wayside table a little ways off in the distance. "On second thought, let's set up there." Leyton wanted to take advantage of the tiny bit of civilization.

She agreed, but groaned when he helped her back on with her pack.

They reached the cement slab and the concrete picnic table. A metal cover stretched over the top to shield visitors from the rain and sun. Tall spruce trees surrounded it, creating a nice little picnic spot, but it appeared that no one used it much. The fact they even had one here had to mean more people traveled this road. Well, naturally, because the other dead ended.

A green metal, bear-proof trash can with a lid was even sitting nearby. They eagerly emptied all their trash. Even though empty water bottles and the packaging for their food was light, it was nice to get rid of it.

They set up the lean-to and had a nice warm campfire next to the cement slab where the concrete table rested. Of course the site wasn't set up for camping and it probably would be illegal, but it was the perfect spot to stay off the road in the event that a car did come upon them, and they wouldn't be run over. Given their circumstances, car wreck, injuries, trying to make it to civilization, he knew if any police found them, their transgressions would be forgiven.

After having the can of stew he planned to make them the other night, they settled down to sleep. Tomorrow, if they weren't picked up sooner, hopefully, they would find civilization.

Again, he wasn't sure that Kate would want him to make love to her, but she seemed to need the intimacy just as he needed it, and that night, they fell asleep with a million stars sparkling overhead and a full moon blazing brightly in the dark sky as they cuddled under the lean-to.

In the middle of the night, he had to get up and relieve himself, blaming it on drinking the water to take more pain relief medicine before they retired for the night. It took him forever to wake enough to realize he was just having a nightmare about searching for a bathroom and all of the restrooms were closed, or toilets that he found, not working. He hated having dreams like that.

He thought about waiting until it was light out, but he just couldn't and get any real rest.

As soon as he left the lean-to, he saw headlights, not just one car, but four, which, considering they'd seen no traffic at all today, meant something was up. They were driving slow, as if searching for something. A sixth sense told him to remain where he was. He'd protect Kate at all costs if they had trouble, but he had the sneaking suspicion somehow word had gotten out that Kate had never arrived at the campsite. That he had bought clothes at the mountaineer shop about thirty miles from here. And that the last time they'd used her credit card was several days ago, and probably the state police were looking for her.

He slipped out of his clothes as quickly as he could and shifted. Then he moved away from where he'd left his clothes, leapt into a tree, and waited.

Sure enough in the moon's glow and with his cat vision, he could see the tell-tale markings of four law enforcement cars, three state troopers, and one deputy sheriff's car of Yuma Town.

The troopers would undoubtedly be human. But the deputy sheriff? A cougar. Still, Leyton couldn't leave until he knew that Kate was taken care of, even if it put him at further risk.

Kate heard the cars rolling down the road and hurried to

get out of the lean-to. She saw the police cars. She waved and appeared so happy. He was glad she was going to be all right. But then she looked around the woods, and he knew she was searching for him. She called out in excitement, "Leyton, it's the police. They've come to rescue us!"

He hated leaving her in this way. He wanted to kiss her and say good bye. He wanted to tell her again he'd come back and repay her for her kindness to him. But when the first car rolled to a stop and the trooper hurried out of the car, Leyton faded into the forest and was gone.

***

The excitement Kate felt thrumming through her veins that she was being rescued was quashed by the realization Leyton must have believed he had to run. She knew her place was back home in Yuma Town with her friends and taking care of those who needed her medical skills, yet her heart reached out to Leyton. He couldn't believe she'd turn him in for taking her hostage, could he?

She felt sick and heartbroken, when she should have only felt relief and joy. Looking like he was ready to kill Leyton, but needing mostly to comfort her, Stryker rushed out of his car to take charge of her. She broke into tears all over his smartly pressed uniform.

"We need to know where he is," Stryker said, his brow furrowed as she continued to sob.

Oh, God, Stryker probably thought she'd been so terrified of the ordeal he was going to kill her abductor.

She tried to control her tears, but it was like a dam had broken, and she couldn't stop them no matter what.

"I found some men's clothes over here," a trooper said

from the woods.

"Shit," Stryker said. He knew that Leyton had shifted and run.

"I offered to take him with me camping, Stryker Hill," she blurted out, not caring that she lied. Leyton was one of the good guys and at every turn, he'd been decent to her, as long as she discounted his tying her up and making her sleep with him the first night.

"He took you hostage," Stryker growled.

"My car went off a cliff," she growled right back. "He helped me to get here. I was driving and I took the wrong road. I swerved to miss a mother bear and her cubs, and we sailed off the cliff. He had nothing to do with it! And he has survival skills and put them to good use to keep us alive all this time."

Stryker glowered at her.

Then she took a deep breath and wiped her tears away. "Where's Dan?"

"I've called it in that we found you and that your abductor has made his escape."

"Is Dan here?"

"Fifteen minutes away."

"I'll ride home with him."

"Kate..."

She pulled free from him and glowered.

"Are you injured in any way, Dr. Parker?" one of the troopers asked, as if Stryker was too personally involved in this and wasn't asking the right questions.

Kate was still glowering at Stryker. "I've had whiplash and my back is killing me."

"I'm sorry, Kate," Stryker said, reaching for her arm.

She sat down on the stone bench and stared gloomily at the ground. She wished she could have said good bye to Leyton, just one last time.

CHAPTER 12

Kate was eating a microwave lasagna after work when she got a call from Dottie Brown, their police dispatcher. Kate hadn't wanted to see anyone socially since she had returned home. Her car insurance had paid for the totaled car and she'd found a replacement. Dan and his deputies, and a few others, had gallantly returned to pick up her stuff from the car and given it to her, packed up in boxes.

She hadn't had the heart to sort through everything and wash or put it away because everything reminded her of Leyton, and she wasn't ready to wash him out of her life just yet.

"Kate? A bunch of us women wanted to get together and have lunch at my place. Or eat out or something. We're sorry you missed your vacation, and, well, we thought since it's been a week since you returned home safe and sound, you might be feeling like getting together with us."

Kate hadn't wanted to. They'd all be talking about their

babies. Although she totally adored all of them, having delivered them herself and felt as though she was part of each and every family, everything reminded her of Leyton now, and what she wished she could have with him.

"Or...we could wait a little longer."

Kate was afraid they'd want to know more about Leyton, get the skinny on what had really happened between them. The guys would have smelled her sleeping bag, and that she and Leyton had sex. It was just a part of who they were, nothing wrong with it. Everyone was walking on eggshells around her, and she didn't want them to.

Yet, she felt touchy and protective of Leyton, and she didn't want anyone prying into that part of her life. She realized then, she'd never had a secret like him. A lover who she cherished and wanted back in her life. He'd made her feel special and needed and loved.

"Okay, well, I guess some other time. But we're not letting you off the hook," Dottie said, comforting, yet stern too.

Kate chuckled, though tears welled up in her eyes. She loved the town and all its members. They were her family too. "Night, Dottie, and thanks."

***

Still running as a cougar, Leyton headed in the direction of the cabin where Butch had shot him, hoping not to repeat that situation, and planning to investigate the place when he got a whiff of Butch in the vicinity. Leyton was maybe five miles from the cabin near cliffs overlooking a river. His heart was pounding with excitement with the knowledge he could catch the criminal and take him down.

When he finally reached the treed cliffs and could peer down below, he saw the bastard fishing in his human form, camo pants and shirt, hiking boots, pole in hand. His hair was blond again, growing out, shaggy around the back of his neck and ears. He was sitting on a camping chair on a small bit of rocky beach, relaxed, enjoying the seclusion. Leyton wanted in the worst way to bound down the cliffs and take him out. But right next to Butch's camo colored camping chair rested a cooler and a rifle.

Leyton didn't believe he was feeling Post Traumatic Stress Disorder (PTSD), but he sure was having a hell of a time convincing himself he had to make his way down the cliffs and take Butch out. His gaze kept shifting to the damn rifle.

If only Butch would catch a nibble so that the fish would fully snag his attention. Right now, he was relaxed, but like any big cat, he would be listening to all the sounds around him, watching for any sign of movement. Leyton had to make sure that when he started the climb down, he was behind Butch at all times, completely out of his peripheral vision. Butch would know that Leyton would continue to come after him, so he'd remain alert. Unless he thought Leyton had left him alone for so long because he had been mortally wounded.

Silently, Leyton began to move to the right a little more, keeping to the cover of the spruces and underbrush, picking the first ledge he'd jump to and several below that when he heard voices behind him.

Two men. Even though the season for hunting cougars

wasn't until November 17th through March 31st of the next year, it didn't mean someone hiking with a rifle, for protection, might use the excuse that the cougar in their sights had tried to attack him.

Leyton turned to listen, his ears moving to pinpoint the exact location of where the men were. They were moving away from his location. Good. He turned back to make his descent when he saw that Butch was gone. His rifle was still resting on the beach next to the cooler, fishing pole lying down, fishing line still in the water.

Leyton's heartbeat ratcheting up several notches, he listened, watching, hoping that the bastard was just taking a leak when he saw the cougar bounding up the cliffs in his direction.

Leyton prepared for the assault. Butch didn't attack him, but raced off along the cliffs. Damn it. The guy knew the woods like he knew his own heartbeat and Leyton could see himself in a similar bind as before. Days of chasing until Butch took him just where he wanted and then he'd ambush Leyton again.

Not this time. Leyton was damned determined to end this now. He took chase, diving around trees, leaping over rocks and shrubs, keeping the cougar in his sight.

Rocks rose in his path, no trees or shrubs, but perfect for a cougar to scale. Butch bolted up them, leaping with his powerful legs, and Leyton hesitated. He knew Butch was baiting him. He thought of going around the rock formation, but how far out of his way would he have to go? And he'd be below Butch, which could spell disaster for him. So he raced up the rocks after Butch, expecting an ambush and getting just that.

Naturally, Butch was above Leyton when he pounced. They snarled and teeth clashed, fish-hook claws grabbing hold as they tore into each other. Butch was relentless, strong, uninjured like Leyton was, though his shoulder was getting better by the day.

But Leyton was just as vicious, just as unyielding, just as tough. And damn determined. Neither managed to take the advantage, no matter how hard they tried. They were too well-matched in strength. The slight lead Butch had over Leyton in the beginning by using a higher vantage point to attack was gone. As angry as Leyton was, he didn't feel any pain in his shoulder right now, though he imagined he might later.

All his focus was on killing Butch, not even just taking him down so he could learn where he had hidden the gun that had Leyton's fingerprints on it. He'd have to find it later. But Butch was just too dangerous to leave alive.

Thankfully, because of his power, even though he couldn't overwhelm Butch, the cougar hadn't managed to injure him other than a few shallow bites. Leyton bit Butch on the neck and drew blood. Confident he could take the bastard out, he thrust his teeth at Butch's neck again. But Butch swung his head around and stopped him.

They were standing on their hind legs, forelegs gripping each other, tooth enamel clashing against each other's teeth when he felt the rocks give near the edge of the cliff. If they hadn't had their claws dug into each other's shoulders, they would have leapt away before they fell. Or they could have recovered on a ledge below. Instead, they fell to the river rushing below them.

As soon as he hit the cold water, he realized he'd lost hold of Butch, the other cat releasing him at some point when they freefell. All cougars could swim, so for a moment, Leyton paddled, his head held high above the flowing river, searching for any sign of Butch. He didn't know if he'd fallen behind him or ahead of him. There was no beach along here, though with their powerful claws, they could pull themselves up on the rocks beside the water and begin the climb up the cliffs. While Leyton was trying to keep his head above water in the rapids, he couldn't see the cougar in either direction.

Leyton caught hold of a boulder and pulled himself out, then sat on top, looking from the new vantage point to see if he could locate him. If Butch had been behind Leyton, he would have seen him carried on past Leyton's vantage point by now. No sign of him. If Butch had been ahead of him, he could easily have been swept around the bend in the river, then continued on downriver, or climbed up on the cliff out of Leyton's view, and taken off.

Unless he'd been behind him and done the same thing. Leyton hated being indecisive. If he went up to the top of the cliffs, he could run downstream and attempt to catch Butch's scent. But what if Butch returned to his fishing site and grabbed his gear? That would be more likely.

Decision made, Leyton climbed to the top of the cliffs and raced back to where Butch had left his fishing gear and rifle. But when he peered down at the spot where the gear was sitting, he found it was still there. Was Butch hiding out of sight against the cliff, waiting for Leyton to investigate?

Leyton risked checking it out and headed down the cliff. When he neared the bottom, he saw no sign of Butch, damn it. But Leyton wasn't going to let the bastard return for his stuff either. Leyton shifted, then tossed the rifle, clothes, and fishing pole into the swiftly flowing water. It would all sink to the bottom. Though he hated littering of any kind, he couldn't allow Butch to have his clothes or rifle back. Butch could walk out of there later as if he'd just been fishing. This way, he had to keep moving as a cougar until he could get hold of another stash of clothes. And the rifle? He imagined Butch had more weapons at his disposal, but just knowing Leyton had ruined one of them, maybe even the one Butch had already used on him, gave Leyton a bit of satisfaction.

Covered in bloody bite marks and claw marks, Leyton shifted. He assumed if he went to the cabin, he might find the same trouble as before. Butch ready with a rifle in hand. But if the cougar had continued to allow the river to carry him further downstream, maybe not.

Still, Leyton figured he'd have a better chance at catching Butch there than if Butch just continued downstream. Unless he'd been badly injured. Maybe he had broken a leg or cracked his skull. Leyton could only hope, envisioning the cat drowning or too injured to climb.

Leyton loped toward the cabin, watching, listening for any sign that Butch was also headed in that direction. When he reached the cabin, he saw no sign of movement, heard no sounds inside. He waited, diligent, just watching, listening, circling, looking for a better vantage point. After about twenty minutes, Leyton left the relative shelter of the forest and raced toward the cabin. If he could get close to the side, anyone inside wouldn't be able to shoot him.

No response, no sounds.

Leyton couldn't peer in the blind-covered windows, so he headed around to the door, shifted, prayed he wasn't making the worst mistake of his life and twisted the handle. The door was unlocked and Leyton shoved it open, leaping out of the path of the entryway at the same time.

No reaction from inside.

With his heart pounding, Leyton shifted again, better able to leap at his attacker as a cougar if Butch was inside, waiting with rifle in hand. Leyton leapt inside, but Butch wasn't here. Leyton slammed the door shut, shifted, and locked it. Then he began to search the one-room cabin for signs of weapons, or any indication as to where Butch might go next.

He smelled Butch's scent here, but left here some hours ago, probably when he went fishing. And two other men's scents were also in the cabin. Cougars too. He hadn't found any other weapons, but lots of clothes.

Finding no evidence to help him, Leyton removed any clothes he could find stashed in a chest and left littered about the place. Then he put all of it in a fire ring outside and set it on fire. Anything he could do to create problems for Butch, he had to do. Then he shifted and climbed into a tree to wait and watch, just in case Butch returned. He would be prepared.

As he watched the flames flick higher at the cool night air, Leyton thought back to when he sat fireside with Kate, holding her in his arms, feeling her warmth, listening to her heartbeat, loving the intimacy. Though he had to remain vigilant here, knowing Butch could return at any time as a cougar, or he might have managed to clothe and arm himself with another rifle, Leyton couldn't help thinking of Kate and wishing he was with her.

As soon as the clothes had burned to ashes, making sure the fire was completely extinguished before he left, and with no sign of Butch about, Leyton decided it was time to return to Travis's house. He would get cleaned up, eat a hearty meal, sleep, grab his car and gun, and return to the area to search for Butch until he located him.

***

Kate had worked busily in the clinic for over two weeks since her return. She hadn't heard from Leyton, and still, she hoped she would. She'd never felt like that with any man in her life before. She couldn't believe how much he had intrigued her and despite all their harrowing experiences, excited her. She finally had agreed to have lunch at Hal's ranch with all of the gals. She couldn't keep putting it off because Dottie wouldn't let her.

Everyone had sitters for the afternoon while the ladies cooked steak shish-kabobs on the grill. Everyone had been talking about food and kids, everything but what she knew they were dying to hear about.

All the ladies were married to deputies, or in Dottie's case, not dating, but close to it with Dan, the sheriff. Plus, she was the police dispatcher, so Kate knew they were waiting to hear what had gone on between her and Leyton. She realized she didn't even know where he was from or his last name. She sighed and sat down with the other ladies on the deck to eat.

"Are you going camping at the same location...," Tracey Haverton said, pausing. She was Hal's wife, and helped run his ranch when she wasn't chasing down wildlife exploiters. Her cheeks reddened a bit, and she said, "I mean, where you normally camp."

Everyone looked from her to Kate, waiting to hear her answer.

"Oh sure. Why wouldn't I? I love it there. I fish, camp, run as a big cat in the middle of the night when other campers are sound asleep. Love the peaceful setting."

Silence.

Kate was sure the men would have told their mates that she had sex in the car and the sleeping bag, so there was really no hiding anything from the ladies anyway. She sighed. "Okay, what do you want to ask?"

Dottie smiled. "We swore we wouldn't ask anything about him when we got together. Maybe a few months from now, but..." She shrugged. "We really promised each other we wouldn't put you on the spot."

"We did," Shannon Buchanan, Chase's wife, said. "We are really trying to let you get through this ordeal without questioning you because we know the guys have been doing so as part of their investigation into what happened."

"I helped him out. Leyton that is. He was wounded and going in my direction. I helped him out as anyone in my shoes would have done."

She would never say he took her hostage. No matter how much everyone asked her.

"But you like the guy, more than just in wanting to help

out a fellow cougar," Shannon said.

"Yeah, we were in a couple of bad binds." Kate explained about the trouble with the bears, and the women were all agog.

"Ohmigod, I would have had a heart attack," Shannon said.

Dottie and Tracey agreed.

But at every turn, Leyton had been there for her, protective and caring.

"Then, the storms hit." Kate told them about the one that had swept their tent away. She noticed the raised brows as soon as she said the word "their." Of course it *hadn't* been Leyton's tent too, but since they had shared it, it seemed natural to tell the story that way. "It was awful. I was so afraid he'd been drowned, and here I am, hanging onto the tree for dear life, knowing if I let go, I wasn't strong enough to move to the next tree on higher ground. And I was rapidly becoming hypothermic as cold as the water was. Then like a god appearing in the slanting rain, he was beside me."

She noticed again the expressions of surprise that she would see her captor like that. But he had been that for her. One minute, she'd been alone in the cold wash of water, struggling to hold on, knowing that this could be the end as her body temperature plummeted. And the next, he was there, encouraging her, protecting her, pulling her to safety when he'd faced the strength of the creek all on his own, moments before this.

"Have you heard from him?" Shannon asked.

Kate hated telling them no, that she was hopeful every

waking day that he would get in touch. That at night, she wished he'd knock on her door, sweep her into his arms, and kiss her like he loved her and never wanted this to end between them.

She shook her head.

"He's undercover," Dottie reminded her, very seriously, as if she believed everything Kate had said about him.

Which Kate appreciated. "I agree. I just hope…" She let out her breath. "I just hope he's all right. That the man he's after hasn't killed him this time."

"He's too resourceful for that," Shannon said.

"He's Ranger trained. A real survivalist," Dottie agreed.

"He'll contact you," Tracey said, surprising everyone, because Kate was sure that's what they were all thinking, but she hadn't believed anyone would actually say it out loud. "I know he will."

"I hope so," Kate admitted.

And then the conversation went on to other things, but all Kate could think about was how much she wished Leyton would get in touch with her to let her know he was well.

She was glad she'd shared some of what had happened with the ladies. She knew Shannon had an ordeal with wilderness survival on her own while her ex-boyfriend's family had tried to hunt her down. And Tracey, in the business she was involved in, could relate because of the dangerous situations she would be in when trying to apprehend wildlife traffickers.

Dottie hadn't been, but being the town's dispatcher, she'd heard enough cases where individuals had been in trouble.

Best of all, her friends were there for her, no matter what the outcome. They wanted the best for her, unlike their mates, or the sheriff, who wanted to take Leyton down if they ever caught sight of him.

***

Leyton was exhausted by the time he reached his friend's safe house. Travis was gone on a mission too, like usual. Something covert, most likely. Leyton wished he could have shared a beer and swapped a couple of war stories when he arrived at his house, but no such luck. Leyton had thought maybe they could get together for Christmas, though who knew what either of them would be involved in at that point in time.

Leyton took a hot shower and didn't want to ever leave it. He'd thought continuously of Dr. Kate Ellen Parker, unable to get her off his mind. The way she had rolled her eyes at him, or ran with him as a cougar, sitting on the tree with him as the bear tried to get into her backpack and being pissed about it, making love to her.

Hell, as soon as he thought of his hands running all over that sweet body of hers, he was already hard. He hated that he hadn't been able to call her, not while running as a cougar. And he wondered if he did call her, she'd just be angry with him for leaving her like he had done. But he knew the law enforcement officers from Yuma Town would interrogate him mercilessly, and he wouldn't be able to tell them who he really was or what he really did. He'd told Kate too much already. It wasn't like him to tell his business to anyone who wasn't in their organization and even then only if they had a need to know.

When he'd left Kate, he'd gone back to doing his job and finally located Butch's cabin, though other men had used it. But Butch had used it repeatedly and so Leyton figured that this was his, or maybe a friend's or even a partner's place, who was involved in the same crimes. But there had been no evidence left behind that indicated where he might have gone next.

Once Leyton didn't have any fresh leads, he figured he'd regroup and drive down to search the area again, only this time as a human. He wanted to send Kate the money for his clothes, but he couldn't do it. He was afraid she'd feel offended, yet he had to make it up to her somehow.

Hell, he had done his job as far as he was able. He had to see her and make it right with her. He figured he'd have some explaining to do with the local police force, but he had decided Kate Parker was too much she-cat to leave alone in Yuma Town for very long before some other male cat began making the moves on her.

He called her clinic, but of course couldn't get through to her directly. April, the receptionist at the front desk, said, "May I ask who's calling?"

"Tell her it's Leyton."

"Leyton…"

She was waiting for a last name.

He hadn't given it to Kate. He wasn't giving it to the receptionist.

"All right. She might be in with a patient and then this will go to voice mail."

"Thanks." He hated voice mail.

And that's all he got. Damn it. Kate didn't have a listed

number either so he could call her at home. Now she'd be doubly upset with him, he figured, because he wouldn't leave a message on her blasted answering machine. But he was an undercover agent. He never left messages.

***

Snuggling with Sheba, Kate loved living in Yuma Town. All the outpouring of love for her when she returned home made her know that she was living right where she needed to be, but she couldn't help feeling a part of her was missing. When she'd returned home, she'd smelled all the law enforcement officers had been there—all over her place. Even checking out her bedroom and bathroom. They would know Leyton had slept with her but hadn't had sex with her. Dan had taken over talking to her about the incident because Stryker was too furious about Leyton abducting her, though she'd told them all along he'd needed help, just like he said he had. She told them she had still planned to go to the campground, and he was going in the same direction as she was to check out the cabin where the shooter had been, which had been within a few miles of her campsite. He needed the transportation, and she was willing to help a fellow cougar and an undercover agent. Which had prompted further questions about why Leyton hadn't gone to them for help. And why she didn't let anyone know what was going on with her, even if she was going to insist on taking him herself.

Which led to her telling them repeatedly he was undercover!

She knew they were thinking, yeah, right—in her bed and in her sleeping bag...with her!

She'd been asked a number of times where the cabin was, but Leyton had never said. Dan and the others didn't believe her. They knew she was covering for him.

She was actually beginning to believe the story she was telling herself, so it didn't matter. She thought she'd never see Leyton again, that this Butch Sanders might have finished Leyton off this time for good, though she told herself it wouldn't happen. That this time Leyton would get him. But what if she had just been a convenient and pleasurable way to warm up a cold night as far as Leyton was concerned? Like he'd been for her, if she hadn't fallen for the rogue.

And then, she got *the* call from Leyton so out of the blue, it had sent her heart racing to the moon and back. Though she'd tried to tell herself not to get all worked up about it. Before she went home for the night, April Hightower, her receptionist, had told her she'd received one from Leyton, curious about who he was since Kate never got calls from unknown men who wanted to speak to her specifically, not about a medical problem. As soon as April told her, Kate tried to show unconcern, though her heart was palpitating with excitement. She waited to get home and once she locked her door behind her, she checked her voice mail. And checked her messages again. And again. As if somehow a message would suddenly just pop up on her cell. She couldn't believe he hadn't left a message on her voice mail!

She growled.

Hating to cause April to speculate any more about the situation than she was probably already doing, Kate called her at home, which she *never* did. Kate had to ask what Leyton had said to her...in his *exact* words. Maybe he had left a clue for her. Was she desperate, or what?

"April, about that message from Leyton. Can you tell me exactly what he said and the way he said it?"

"He just said he wanted to talk to you, and he didn't give a last name. I told him his call would go to voice mail if you were busy and couldn't pick up. He seemed perturbed that I wouldn't just walk back there and make you take the call. Didn't he leave a message?"

"No. If...if he calls again while I'm at work, put him right through to me."

"Even if you're in the middle of surgery or delivering a baby?" April sounded surprised.

"Tell him I'll get right back to him. Don't make him go to voice mail. Get his phone number. Or, well, give him my personal number."

"All right. Will do. Is everything all right, Dr. Parker?"

No, it wasn't. Hope had sprung anew that he wanted to see her again, and she knew she'd lost her mind. "Yes, yes, thanks. I'll see you tomorrow."

Kate set her phone on her dresser, praying Leyton would call her back, ready to kill him if he said again that he was sending her the money for the clothes she'd had to buy him. She hoped he had caught the bad guy and had the free time and the strong need to come and see her.

Yet, she knew he only meant to keep his promise— he'd pay her back for all the trouble he had caused her. But she was glad to hear that he was still alive and kicking.

***

When Leyton got the call from his boss that night, waking him from pleasant dreams of making wild and passionate love to Kate wearing only her stethoscope, he swore under his breath. Chuck Warner never called Leyton when he was currently on a mission. Leyton was supposed to call him and...hell, about three weeks ago. Okay, so he'd been rather out of touch while running as a cougar. And he'd been so exhausted, grimy, and hungry when he'd gotten in, all he'd thought of was showering, grabbing a quick supper, and a long Rip Van Winkle's lengthy nap.

"What the hell's going on?" Chuck asked, getting to the point of the call immediately, his voice gruff and irritated. "I send you out on a mission, you get shot, and hook up with some hot she-cat doctor?"

Hell. Leyton sat up in bed, his mind racing over all that had happened, again. He should have known his boss would have been looking into his disappearance when he didn't call in.

"Just got back. Long story. Lost Butch and went looking for him in my cougar coat again, trying to locate him. Lost him when we both fell off a cliff and ended up losing track of him. Checked out his cabin, burned his clothes, and got rid of his rifle. No luck on catching him after that. I'm at Travis's at the moment."

"I know you're at Travis's. That's why I could get hold of you. What the hell was up with the doctor?"

"I was shot and needed bandages. The clinic was dark and looked like nobody was there. But she was there, napping, and caught me. What else could I do?"

"Tie her up? Leave her there? Let someone know she

needed help, *after* you left the area? You're a damn good undercover agent, Leyton. But this is one for the books."

"If you want my badge, the one I don't have to work this job, you can have it."

"What are you going to do about the gun Butch framed you with?" Chuck asked, ignoring Leyton's comment.

Leyton frowned. "You know about that?"

"You think I was born yesterday? Yeah. I know everything. Only a little later than I should have. Travis got hold of another informant who said Butch has been bragging about it."

"Hell." Then Leyton perked up. "Travis is on my case?"

"What do you think? You disappear off the radar, and we have nothing on you for nearly three damn weeks? I gave Travis another job, but he refused to take it. *Refused!* Hell, you guys are working for me. When will you ever learn that? So why did he refuse? Because he wanted to save your ass. And then what does he find? You've been shacking up with some hot doctor! He was furious with me for assigning the job to you in the first place. He wanted to be in your shoes instead."

Leyton smiled a little.

"So now I haven't had any communication from Travis since last Friday, when he was supposed to check in. Everyone is out on a mission and--"

"Where was he at, according to the last report?" Leyton was grabbing clothes out of his drawers. Even though the place was Travis's, he used this guest bedroom whenever he had to use it as a stopping off point. Travis did the same at his place when he was in his neck of the woods, like other agents would also.

"Around Yuma Town thereabouts. Said he was reconnoitering a gold mine and that was the last I heard from him. He was supposed to check back in at noon, yesterday. After you went missing over this same case, I wanted it investigated right away."

"Why the hell didn't you say so?" Leyton growled, pulling on his clothes in a hurry, the phone on speaker now.

"This is the first damn time I've been able to get hold of you."

"What's the name of the gold mine and what are the coordinates?"

"Pine Ridge Gold Mine." Chuck gave him the coordinates, then warned, "If Travis is injured and ends up at Dr. Kate Parker's house in the middle of the night for some tender loving care, it's not my fault. Good luck, Leyton. And don't get yourself shot again. I can't afford it."

"Wait," Leyton said, holstering his gun and heading out the door. "They've got a hot bed of trouble in Yuma Town. I want to be in charge of a field office down there."

Silence.

"Clear it with the locals for me."

"Hell, Leyton, now you know why I picked you for the team. *You* clear it with the locals. It's your office. Though I hear rumors a couple of the deputies, maybe even the sheriff, want your head on a platter. So good luck with that." Chuck hung up on him.

If Travis was wounded and took Kate hostage, Leyton was killing him, forget saving his ass. As to the field office in Yuma Town? They'd better be ready for him because he wasn't giving the notion up. Next vacation Kate took, he was riding shotgun, and anything else she needed him for. He couldn't quit thinking of her the whole time he'd been running as a cougar while trying to locate Butch. His focus definitely hadn't been totally job-related. He knew then that he might have taken her hostage, but now she held him hostage.

He headed out to the car and called Kate's office. Because of the late hour, all he got was the answering machine telling him the office hours, but if this was an emergency, to please stay on the line.

He hated to have to talk to anyone else about this, just Kate, especially when it wasn't a medical emergency. But it might become one, so he was going to give her a heads up this time.

"What is the medical emergency?" the woman asked.

He thought she might have said something else, but he'd missed it if she had.

"I need to speak with Dr. Parker. Tell her Leyton called."

Silence.

"This is the service that takes any calls for medical emergencies, sir. Is this an emergency?"

"It sure the hell is."

"What is the state of the emergency, sir?"

"It's private. Just tell her I called and I'm coming in."

"Sir, I can't forward a call like this without knowing what the medical emergency is."

"Just. Tell. Her. I'm. Coming," he gritted out.

"Sir, are you in pain? Just calm down. I've heard

everything, so you don't have to be embarrassed to discuss this with me."

"I'm having chest pains. All right? In the vicinity of the heart. Tell her that." He hung up. Damn it. He wanted to talk to Kate, not discuss his personal problems with some stranger on the phone.

But he was desperate to find his buddy, Travis, too, as long as he wasn't at Kate's house.

***

Kate was sound asleep when something woke her. Headlights flashing through her blinds in her bedroom. Then more. And more. What in the world was going on?

Worried there'd been a medical emergency and no one had alerted her about it first, she got out of bed and hurried to dress in scrubs. Then she looked out the back door and saw all the police vehicles in Yuma Town sitting either in the parking lot between the clinic and her home, or parked out front.

Omigod, had her receptionist told Dan that Leyton had tried calling her at the clinic and then he'd gotten all worried and thought Leyton was going to come and spirit her away again?

She'd had her vacation, and she had no plans to take another anytime soon. Then again, something more must have happened. No way would Dan have called the whole force up to "protect" her unless there was some indication Leyton was actually coming to see her. That made her heart skip a little.

She looked at all the forces outside and was angry all over again. Damn it. She'd told them already Leyton was harmless. At least with her. If he got hold of Butch, she doubted he would be. And she wanted to see Leyton. Desperately wanted to see him. If Dan and his deputies were going to make that difficult for him, she would...

Well, she didn't know what she would do except she wasn't going to stand for it!

She slipped on her tennis shoes and headed outside, the glare of lights in her eyes, and she folded her arms and glowered. She couldn't even see anyone, just knew they all were there, no conversation at all. Then Dan moved beyond the lights as if to rescue her and pull her to safety.

She yanked back from him and growled, "What the hell is going on, Dan? Unless any of you have a medical emergency, you'd better just get back in your cars and hightail it out of here."

"Kate—"

"Don't you 'Kate' me. I told you Leyton was one of the good guys. So leave this business alone. If he wants to call and talk to me, then he's welcome to do it. And no one's going to bother him. Do you hear?"

"Kate—"

"I have a long day ahead of me, starting at five. Go on. Go on home to your loved ones, or go deal with a real emergency."

"Kate, damn it, he's coming here. He told your emergency hotline number that he had a medical emergency."

Kate's jaw dropped. She was furious with all the underhanded, aggravating—wait, why hadn't she gotten the call?

"Does he have a medical emergency?" Considering the last time she saw him and that he was after this Butch guy, he could very well be sporting a few new bullet wounds.

"No. He—"

"She's fired. Off my property, now."

"Kate, listen, Becky said the guy was angry, insistent she give you the message. It's for medical emergencies only. You know that. And then when she insisted he give her one, worried he was in a lot of pain or stress and that it was something kind of personal and he didn't want to share it, he said he was having chest pains. Damn liar."

"Chest pains?" Kate frowned, then smiled. "Thanks, Dan." She hugged him and gave him a big kiss on the cheek, then turned to enter her house.

"Kate, he said he's on his way."

She scowled at Dan over her shoulder. "Then unless there's a law against a cougar visiting another in Yuma Town, leave him alone." She went inside and slammed her door and locked it.

Ohmigod, Leyton was having chest pains. For her. And it was personal. Something he hadn't wanted to discuss with anyone else. Just her.

If Dan or anyone else on the force had him arrested, well, they'd just better not.

CHAPTER 13

Leyton had reached the gold mine in question, but there was no sign of Travis or anyone else for that matter. He explored inside, saw the telltale signs of where rounds had hit boulders and pinged off walls, chipping them, but it had happened a while ago, as if someone had been in a shootout. Which was another reason he needed to set up a field office here. Looked like the regular force could use some help. Besides, he would be canvassing the whole state and surrounding states, not just here. He'd have to hire some guys to work for him too. He hadn't really thought of what it would be like to be the boss of a bunch of undercover guys, just as wild and unpredictable as him. He almost felt sorry for his boss. *Almost.*

But he did smell that Travis had been in here recently. But not Butch. Leyton wondered what information Travis had that had led him here.

Leyton went back to his car and grabbed a headlamp,

and just to be on the safe side, he tossed a rope and medical kit into his backpack, and slung it over his shoulders. Then he went deeper inside the cave until he reached a ladder, peered down, couldn't see anything, and climbed down into the pit. He hoped he wouldn't find Travis in trouble down here. He was hoping that Travis was off on a cougar hunt and just couldn't check in like Leyton hadn't been able to do for so long.

When Leyton reached the tunnel, he found no sign of Travis here, but his scent led to a ladder that dropped into another shaft. Leyton peered down into it, but couldn't see a thing. No sign of light if Travis was at the bottom exploring. Leyton climbed down the ladder, smelling Travis's scent all the way into the next tunnel. Still no sign of his friend. The walls were covered in water and algae and Leyton felt uneasy being even this deep underground. He'd had a couple of missions where he'd had to rescue cavers, but it wasn't his favorite job to do.

He walked down the tunnel until he came to another ladder leading down. "Travis?" he called out.

Leyton really didn't want to go any deeper if Travis wasn't there.

"Is that you, Leyton?" a voice from deep within the tunnel called out, faint, hopeful.

"Travis, what the hell are you doing down there?" Leyton hesitated to climb down the ladder. He really didn't want to go down there.

"I'm in...kind of a bind."

"Why the hell didn't you say so?" Leyton was already to hurry down the ladder, but then he paused. "What kind of a bind?"

"You might want to grab some material to make a splint, if you don't have anything readily available. And watch out for the missing rung on the ladder about five steps down."

"Ah, hell, Travis. If you injured yourself on purpose just so you could get my Kate to doctor you up..."

Travis laughed. "Yeah, hell of a way to get her attention, but it seemed to work for you."

"Okay, be right back, buddy. Hang in there."

"*Don't* take your time. Butch's liable to come back down here at any time and finish me off."

"He did this to you?"

"No, but he's got some shit down here. And if he finds me down here sitting pretty with his stash..."

"Hot damn!" Leyton was thrilled that they finally had located one of Butch's weapon caches. Leyton planned to get some other materials to make a more reliable splint now. "Okay, gotcha. Be right back."

At least that was the plan.

***

Dan gathered his men together out front of Kate's home. "You heard the doc. She's fine and she wants to see this Leyton character. There's nothing we can do about it."

Everyone looked as worried about it as he felt, but really it was Kate's life, she was a grown woman, and it appeared she had real feelings for the guy.

"You can't mean it," Stryker said.

"We'll investigate him thoroughly, on the sly and we'll keep an eye out for him. I don't want her getting hurt. But we're not arresting him, picking him up for questioning, or any of that."

Chase frowned. "Unless he breaks the law."

"There is that."

"Speeding violations?" Hal asked.

"Jaywalking?" Chase added.

"Wearing candy cane scrubs and no shirt or shoes—indecent exposure?" Stryker asked.

Everyone smiled.

Dan slapped him on the back. "Let's call it a night and unless this Leyton proves to be real trouble, we'll let him and Kate be."

Hal's phone jingled and he answered it. "Yeah, honey?" he looked at Dan, frowning. "Thanks, we're on it." Hal ended the call and said, "Looks like we have a real police emergency to take care of. There's been a blast at Pine Ridge Gold Mine near my ranch."

"The one Tracey and Ricky had the shoot-out at?" Dan headed for his vehicle.

"Yeah, same one." Hal jerked his door open. "I'm beginning to think that place is really bad news."

Dan got on his cell. "Dottie, got a blast at the Pine Ridge Gold Mine near Hal's ranch. No telling if anyone's been injured, but alert key personnel who can help at the mine if we need them."

"Right on it, Dan, and be careful."

"I will be. Check in with you later." Dan had planned to have a special crew seal off the tunnels for good, but the mine was private property and the owner was on a year-long cruise. Dan couldn't have it done without his permission, but maybe the mine blast this time had sealed it off for good.

***

Laying prone on the rocky floor, his body covered in small rocks and dust, Leyton wasn't sure what hit him in the back of the head, or why he was flat on his back. The way his head was pounding, he felt like a sledgehammer had hit him. Good thing he had a damn hard head.

His shoulder was killing him too, and he looked down at it. Fresh blood soaked his shirt, only it was the other shoulder this time. Damn it to hell.

No light was coming from the shaft above like there had been before. For a moment, he just remained there, trying to get his bearing, trying to figure out what the hell had happened. Luckily, his head lamp was in good working order, and he quickly checked himself over and found the only two injuries he'd sustained were to the back of his head and his shoulder. Well, and he couldn't hear anything except some ringing in his ears.

He saw dust and small rocks falling, but couldn't hear the sound at all, neither of which boded well. Cave-in? Ah hell, now that would be just great.

He didn't even remember being shot. He remembered being struck from behind. Was it Butch?

He smelled two other men there who had been at the cabin where Butch had shot him.

Leyton fished out his phone. No reception. Not that he expected it would have any, but he still was disheartened by the lack of signal. At least the phone was fully charged so if he could get to someplace with a signal, he could call for help. Then he remembered Travis. Damn it, anyway. Travis needed his help pronto.

"Travis, you okay, buddy?"

His friend didn't answer and Leyton quickly tore off his shirt and made a half-ass bandage to stop the bleeding from his shoulder wound. Then he carefully made his way toward the ladder leading down to where Travis was. He gripped the ladder and began the descent, carefully watching for any missing rungs. When he reached the next tunnel, he surveyed the floor, looking for Travis, then saw him sitting against a wall, his head tilted over to the side like he was sleeping or dead.

"Travis!" Leyton hurried over to him and felt his wrist, saw his chest rising and falling, and knew he was still alive. His head was sporting a knot probably as big as Leyton's, only his was on his forehead, not on the back of his head.

"Hey, buddy, time to get out of here."

Travis groaned, his eyes opened, and then widened. "What...the...hell...happened?"

"Mine blast. I think. Not sure. I was knocked out before it transpired, but what happened to you?"

"Hell, he and another couple of men came back. Butch laughed about me being stuck down here and he said he'd help make it my tomb. Then one of the other men struck me in the head. You nailed the bastards before they left the mine, didn't you? Tell me you got the three bastards when you went to get the... Why do I smell your blood?"

"What happened to you?"

"Broken leg. Rung on the ladder broke. My own damn fault. Too impatient. Informant told me to check out this gold mine for Butch. It was the best lead I had."

"Your car's gone."

"Figures. I kept going until I was down here and found a *real* gold mine. After I fell and broke my damn leg." He looked over at another area of the mine, then back to Leyton. "You got them and you got the weapons when they took them out of here, right?"

"About that…"

"Ah, hell, Leyton."

"We'll get out of here. And we'll get them. But I've got to move you up to the next two levels."

"You're going to carry me with my bum leg when you have a round in your shoulder?"

"Got to do something. You know me. I never like to sit still. And a little pain never hurt anyone. I'll splint this the best I can. I'll have to carry you up on my back. But we need to do this now before I can't manage."

"What are you waiting for?"

Leyton tore open Travis's pant leg and saw the bruising, swelling, and it appeared the bone was out of place, but not too terribly bad. It was a simple fracture, not having broken the skin. Leyton began splinting the leg using a couple of pieces of wood he found and hoped they would last and not disintegrate, but as soon as he tore up Travis's shirt and used the strips to tie up the splint, the pieces of wood disintegrated under the pressure. He swore and pulled the backpack's metal frame out—there was always more than one way to make a splint in an emergency—and bound Travis's leg with that.

Before he could toss his supplies back in his bag, Travis said, "Give me the gauze and let me bandage your gunshot would, Leyton, before you bleed all over me. No wonder you had to see the doc the last time to take care of your wound."

Leyton smiled a little and sat down next to Travis, who groaned as much as Leyton did as he applied the gauze and wrapped it around his shoulder.

Then Leyton stood and got ready to stand Travis up first, while Travis held onto Leyton's shoulder to prevent setting any weight on his leg.

As soon as Leyton hoisted him in a fireman carry, he groaned.

"We're a pair," Travis said.

"Yeah, reminds me of a couple of binds we got into before, but we always came out all right, scraped, beat up a bit, but we survived."

"How bad is it?"

"Your leg?"

"No, up top?"

"I don't know. The tunnel I was in was okay." Then Leyton made the climb up the ladder, slowly, watching he didn't miss his footing where the missing rung was, hoping that double the weight wouldn't break any more rungs.

When they made it to the top, he set Travis down easily and took a breather. "I'm going up to the cave tunnel to see how bad it is. See if the dust and rocks have settled."

Travis was breathing through the pain. So was Leyton. Next time he got shot in the damn shoulder, he wanted six weeks to recuperate, even if he only needed a couple of weeks to feel better with his enhanced healing genetics.

He headed up the ladder, made his way through that tunnel, climbed the last ladder and surveyed the cave-in. Massive rocks and smaller ones filled the entrance to the top.

But if he could climb nearer the top and pull away some of the smaller rubble, maybe he could squeeze out and call for help. They had about twenty feet of space to rest in. Or at least, Travis would be resting. Leyton had his work cut out for him. All he had to do was make a small enough hole for him to crawl through, then he could use his cell phone.

Wait! Could he call for help here? He snatched his phone out of his pocket, and turned it on. Hot damn! He had a signal. The clinic wasn't open, naturally, but he got hold of the same woman he talked to before that took calls for medical emergencies after hours only.

"I have two medical emergencies. One bullet to the shoulder, and the other, a simple fracture. And on top of that, the ambulance you send needs to bring a crew to clear a cave-in before we can get much needed medical assistance. Do you get that? This is an emergency medical situation. One gunshot wound and one leg fracture. Get the doc for me ASAP. Or faster," he said quickly, the pain in his shoulder just now hitting him full force.

"Your name?"

"Leyton Hill."

"Ohmigod, are you related to Stryker?"

"Who? I'm an agent with the Cougar Special Forces Division, CSFD, and Field Director of the new office in Yuma Town. And my buddy, Travis MacKay, is the other agent down. He's the one with the broken leg."

"Location?"

"Pine Ridge Gold Mine."

"I'll send help right away."

"And Dr. Parker."

"I don't know that she'll go out to the mine. The EMTs will and she'll be waiting for you at the clinic."

"*And* Dr. Parker."

"Yes, sir, I'll tell her. Wait, she said to give you her number if you called with another 'medical emergency'." She gave him Kate's number.

Halleluiah! Only he wished the woman had done so *way* before he'd talked himself to death, trying to convince her he did have a medical emergency.

Then he called Kate, but the signal dropped as soon as he headed for the ladder. He called down to Travis, "Good news, Travis. Help's on its way. Coming to carry you up in a minute." Then he stalked back to the blocked entrance and called Kate again.

"Hey, Kate."

"Leyton—"

"I've got kind of a medical emergency. Real this time. Not that I didn't mean it about the other."

"What's happened? I'm getting dressed. What's wrong?"

"I'm in a gold mine, cave-in, buddy of mine has a simple leg fracture. I've been shot, other shoulder this time, I imagine the same bastard who shot me the last time. I didn't get to see him. This is really getting old. But I wanted you to know I came back for you. I cleared it with my boss and he okayed me opening a field office here. They need me here in the area."

"You're injured and you're buried in a mine," she reminded him.

"Just temporary."

He thought she was crying. "Kate, don't worry. Just bring a splint for my buddy and some more bandages for me and we'll be good as new."

"I'm on my way over. Which mine?"

"The one off Highway 15, maybe twenty-five miles east of Yuma Town. Pine Ridge."

"Near Hal's ranch. I'm on my way."

"Okay, got to get my buddy. He's in a tunnel two levels below this, but I don't want him going into shock. I'll lose the connection as soon as I move toward the ladder."

"Don't kill yourself before I get there."

He smiled. "I'll try not to. See you in a bit."

Then he ended the connection, worried about Travis, and headed back to the ladder and then went down it. "Hey, Travis, hang in there." He traversed the next tunnel, and went down the other ladder, the pain in his shoulder pounding.

Travis looked pale, but he smiled a little as soon as he saw Leyton.

"Have anything in that bag of yours that will curb the pain a bit?" Travis asked.

"Yeah, hold on." Leyton joined him, dug through his bag, and gave Travis some over-the-counter-pain medication, and a bottle of water, then took some himself. "I don't know how we get ourselves into such binds sometime."

"I do. I was trying to save you."

"I'm glad you found the weapons."

"But we lost them."

"You took a picture of them, didn't you?" Leyton half joked. He knew as good as Travis was, he would have if he could have.

"Hell yeah. Got a shot of Butch and his men too when they thought I was passed out. They were hovering over their weapons. Took a shot and shoved the camera back in my pocket before anyone looked in my direction. One of them must have seen me with my eyes open though because that's when Butch told me he'd bury me down here and then the curly redheaded guy slugged me in the head with the butt of one of the rifles."

Leyton sat down next to Travis.

"Bad up top?" Travis asked, probably wondering why Leyton didn't try to carry him up to the next two levels.

"Nah. I just think I'll sit this one out. Help is coming. Let someone else do their job for a change." Leyton had lost too much blood. He needed a doctor to take care of him this time, well, and hauling a six-foot man up ladders wasn't the same as carrying a backpack. Besides, with the injury to the back of his head, his whole skull felt like a jackhammer was rat-a-tat-tatting on the back of it.

"You okay, Leyton?"

Travis must have realized Leyton would have still made the effort to carry him up the ladder unless he just couldn't. Despite the way his head and shoulder were paining him, he was thinking over the situation here, wondering why they hadn't smelled Butch down here. And then he thought about the photo. He'd been down here. He had to have worn hunter's spray. Maybe afraid that now that a cougar was after him, he could follow his scent and track him down faster.

"Yeah, I'm okay. After we take down this bastard, or,

maybe I should say, after we recuperate from this, then take down the bastard, want to work for me in my new field office?" Leyton asked.

Travis smiled and leaned his head against the rock wall. "Same pay?"

"I'll have to ask the boss."

"You'll be the boss."

"Only of the field office and I'll be out working just like anyone working for me. I might have a little higher pay to put up with dealing with the undercover agents under me."

"And the boss will still be the boss?"

"Yeah, but you won't have to deal with him, just me."

Travis closed his eyes. "After we recuperate and take down the bad guy."

"Yeah, it's a deal."

***

Dan and a crew of men were checking over the rocks blocking the mine, figuring as long as no one was in there, it was a good deal. But when he smelled the recent scents of several men, one being Leyton, the man who had taken Kate hostage no matter what she said had really happened, he wondered what the hell the guy was really up to. He didn't recognize the scents of the other men.

Stryker was fuming. "He's been here, caused a mine explosion, and who knows what else."

"Several men have been here," Chase warned. "Not just him."

Dan's phone rang and he saw it was Kate's after-hours emergency service. "Yeah, Becky?"

"Oh, Sheriff, that Leyton guy? He's Leyton Hill. He didn't

say he wasn't related to Stryker, but he said he and another man are injured in the mine."

Dan looked at the blockage again.

"He's an undercover agent with the Cougar Special Forces Division, CSFD ...and he's setting up a field office in Yuma Town."

"Like hell he is."

"He's been shot and I told Dr. Parker. She's already on her way."

"Hell."

"And the other man's got a simple fracture—his leg."

"What the hell were they doing in there?"

"I don't know. He just said that he had two medical emergencies and he wanted to talk to Dr. Parker. But she told me to give him her number so I did. And then I called you."

"All right, got a call coming in. Thanks!" He took Kate's call next. "Okay, what the hell is going on?"

"I've got the ambulance on its way. Have you cleared the rocks so that you can haul the injured agents out?"

"That's my next call. We'll need some heavy equipment for the job. We didn't think anyone was in there."

"Well there is. And I better see that everyone is moving rocks when I get there or else."

Dan smiled. "We're on it, Kate. I'm ordering men and equipment right now. Talk to you in a bit."

"What the hell was that all about?" Stryker asked.

"We've got two injured men in there. Move what you can. I'm going to make some calls."

CHAPTER 14

When Kate arrived at the scene of the cave-in, it was worse than she had expected. All of the men were lifting rocks out of the way, trying to clear at least a small hole big enough to extract the injured men. She moved in to help, but Dan stopped her. "Doc, damn it, you don't need to cut your hands up on all this rough rock. They'll need you to do surgery on them when we get them out of there. So just let us handle it. Heavy equipment is on its way."

She hated feeling useless. As soon as the EMTs arrived, she knew they knew their job, but she wanted to have her hands on the situation. She couldn't stand this waiting around. Yet, that's just what she had to do and was glad no one called for any other emergency services while she was here. Four hours later, they'd made a hole big enough that Stryker climbed through. Even that was dangerous in the event another slide occurred.

"Leyton!" Stryker called out.

He moved farther away from the cave-in and she heard him call out again, "Leyton! Stryker Hill, Deputy Sheriff of Yuma Town. Where the hell are you?"

Kate began moving toward the hole and Chase seized her arm. "Kate..."

"We have to move them. They're obviously not mobile enough to walk out on their own. And they'll need fluids."

"The EMTs..."

"I'm going with them." Only she went first.

Dan hurried to give her a headlamp. Then she crawled through the narrow opening, though it wasn't as bad for her as it had been for Stryker because he was bigger framed than her. When she reached the other side, she felt a distinctive claustrophobia settling into her bones. But she breathed through it, knowing Leyton and Travis needed her badly.

The EMTs followed, and then several other men to help carry them out.

The air was still dusty from the cave-in, but there was no sign of Stryker. She heard him calling from the tunnel below them. Then deeper when he went down another ladder. And swore.

Despite allowing her to go down there, as if she was going to let Dan stop her, he and the other men preceded her, and then when they reached the tunnel, Stryker hollered, "We're over here."

When they reached them, both men were passed out, pale-skinned, Leyton's arm around Travis as his friend's head was planted against his neck. Despite his own injury, Leyton had provided a shoulder for his friend up until he couldn't any longer. She helped the EMTs start an I.V. on each of them. As sturdy as Leyton was, she had imagined him pacing across the stone floor, anxious to get his friend out, not leaning against the wall, unconscious, still as death.

And worse. She smelled blood at the back of Leyton's head, and he was bleeding profusely there too. She quickly bandaged his head and ordered the men to be removed at once, worried she might still lose the wild cat who had taken her down in one pounce and altered her life forever.

***

When Leyton woke, he expected to be sitting in the damp cave, the underground water running down the rock wall he'd been leaning against, soaking his back, the rough stone digging into his skin, his head and shoulder on fire. He expected to smell the musty air, and feel the cold temperatures, hear the distant yelling of men and banging at rocks, the shovel grinding back and forth, and the sound of Kate's worried voice, calling out to him from far, far away in a distant galaxy.

He was still cold, only the smell of antiseptics clued him in right away as to where he was now. The clinic. He recognized the scent from when he was here before. Instead of an exam room, which, when he thought of tackling one hell of a sexy doctor, still made him smile—he was resting in a clinic bed on rough, thousand times, heavily bleached sheets. The railings were up as if he was a child and someone was afraid he'd fall out of bed. He glanced across the room, thinking he'd have a private one, but instead saw Travis, sipping from a straw, as if a broken leg meant he had to take precautions when drinking...well, whatever he was drinking.

Leyton glanced at the door, listening, trying to hear

Kate's voice. He realized he'd grown addicted to hearing her voice, her breath against his chest as they snuggled to sleep, her heart beating against his.

"You're finally awake," Travis said. "The doc was so worried about you. You lost a lot of blood, she said. More than you did the last time. So no going home with her tonight."

Leyton looked back at him. Travis was smiling.

Leyton felt like shit. "How are you doing?"

"Enjoying being pampered at the moment. Though we've got a guard on the door."

Leyton raised his brows.

"For our protection since Butch wants us dead."

"Or for Kate's protection?"

Travis propped his head against his arms resting on the pillow. "A little of both. There's some guy named Stryker Hill who looks a whole lot like you, dude. If I didn't know better, I'd say you were related. Twins even. Only you're meaner looking."

Leyton smiled.

"He really doesn't like you. Think he had the hots for Doc and then you butted in. Doc was worried about your head too. Said you'd taken quite a beating. She had a bunch of tests run on you, worried you might have had your brains scrambled a bit. I told her they were fine. That you were completely coherent, rescuing me, talking with her, ordering her emergency call person around. That doesn't sound like a man with a head injury to me. She said that head injuries can turn out bad sometimes after the ordeal. Think she'd like to take you home with her and watch over you, just in case. But you had lost so much blood, she left you here for the last two days."

"Last two days?"

"Yeah. We were both in pretty sad shape. She worried about my head too, but not as much as she worried about yours. Mine didn't bleed. You had a real mess on the back of your head. Blood everywhere. So you didn't suffer blood loss just from your shoulder wound."

"The round?"

"Exited. She said she'd never seen a body where bullets went right through every time and didn't ricochet off ribs and such."

"She hasn't seen me when they did."

"True."

"Don't tell her either."

"Don't tell who what?" Kate asked, stepping into the room.

At once, Leyton was ready to get out of the bed. He couldn't help himself. He hadn't seen her in over two weeks and it was like he'd never been apart from her. "I'm ready to leave the hospital," he said, getting ready to help her with the I.V. if she didn't yank it out fast enough.

She put her hand on his good shoulder, or at least better shoulder, and made him lie back down.

Travis was smiling. "I've never seen a woman put you down without you putting up a fight."

"He fights with women often?" Kate asked, a brow arched.

"He's just spouting off. Come on, Kate. You can okay me to leave this place."

"I could, but I won't. You both need medical care, and you need armed protection, for the time-being. Dan, the sheriff, wants to talk to you both. But I told him he couldn't until you're both feeling all right. And I'm the doctor."

"Did she pull the doctor card on you when you were off on your camping trip?" Travis asked.

Leyton just smiled. He wished she'd come over close enough so he could drag her into his arms for a kiss. Maybe if he'd had a private room, she would have. But with Travis in the room, she was keeping her distance.

"Travis, can you vacate the room for a moment?"

Kate gave Leyton the evil eye. "No, he's to stay put. He's got therapy in half an hour."

"Will you come back and see me then?" Leyton asked, feeling as soon as he said it, he sounded like a lovesick puppy dog.

She smiled, and he loved that smile. "I have surgery then. I'll check in on you before I go home tonight." She let out her breath on a heavy sigh. "Glad you both are all right. Check on you later."

Then she left. Without kissing him or anything!

"She's trying to be a professional, dude," Travis said, trying to explain her cool behavior. "What do you expect? She's on the job here, not off camping with you in the wilderness where the two of you could be a couple of fun-loving, wild and sexy cougars."

Leyton gave him a quelling look.

Travis finished his drink and shrugged. "Just saying. Here, she's not the same person as you were involved with before. She has appearances to keep up. Everyone expects her to be a certain way. Kissing a patient isn't part of the job description no matter how you want to look at it."

Then as if he was sympathizing with Leyton, or worried he was thinking the worst, Travis added, "She's not given up on you. She's been in here a dozen times checking on you, worried because you hadn't woken up any of the other times she came to see you. She could have sent one of her nurses, but she didn't."

That cheered Leyton some. But he was still dying to get her alone to himself and show her how much she meant to him. That he was starting a field office here and he was staying for good. It didn't mean they were jumping in the sack as soon as they could or that he was moving in with her. He understood her need to be a professional. Well, kind of. He understood, sure, but he wanted to move right in with her, claim her, prove to her he was the right one for her and then marry her. He didn't want to live down the street from her if he could even find a place that close by.

He saw his phone on the table next to the bed and grabbed it.

"I called the boss and gave him an update on what happened to us. He was pissed we let Butch get the better of us, which means double pissed he got the best of you twice," Travis said.

"Is he sending more men?"

"No. He said we'd better clear this up or he's canceling his offer to allow you to set up a field office here. You really told him there was a hot bed of trouble down here?" Travis laughed.

"I'm setting up the office with or without his approval."

Leyton searched for a real estate agent in the area and found only one listed. "Ms. Tremoine, my name Is Leyton Hill and I'm looking for two things. Office space near the medical clinic and a house available right next door to the doc's house. Money is no obstacle."

"I'll get right on it, though I don't think there's anything right next door to Dr. Parker's home or her clinic, but I'll see what I can find and get back to you."

"Thanks, just make it happen." Leyton gave her his phone number and ended the call, then looked over at his friend whose jaw was hanging.

"Damn, Leyton, way to crowd the woman. What if she really *isn't* interested in you? That the camping experience was a little lighthearted fun and that's all? Now she's back to her real life and—"

"Travis—"

"Just saying, dude."

"There's probably nothing close to either location that's readily available. I figured if I said to make it close, the realtor will try and find the closest to that location she can get."

"I can just see the two of you being next-door neighbors and you borrowing sugar from her." Travis laughed again.

Then a man loomed in the doorway. Dark-haired, about six-one, his green eyes spearing Leyton, not giving Travis the time of day. Damn, if the guy didn't look just like him, only he had green eyes and not blue-green like Leyton's. He was as tall, muscular, but not half as handsome. But Leyton swore he was looking at a brother, if not a twin.

"Leyton Hill, where the hell are you from?" the man asked.

"What's it to you?"

"If you think you're going to continue making the moves on Kate, it means everything."

"Time for your therapy," a pretty nurse said, coming into the room to get Travis.

"Do you want me to stay and protect you from whoever he is?" Travis asked Leyton.

"Stryker Hill, and there's no damn way in hell we're related."

Travis's jaw dropped. "You've got a brother, Leyton?"

"No. People have been known to look similar who aren't related in the least."

"With the same last name," Travis said, skeptically.

"Go on. Get your therapy. We have a job to do and lying around in the hospital isn't helping us to do it," Leyton growled.

"All right. Yell for help if you need it."

Leyton ignored him and turned his glower on Stryker. "Okay, so where the hell are you from?"

Stryker leaned against the wall and folded his arms across his deputy's uniform. "Ely, Minnesota. You?"

"White Bear...Minnesota."

Stryker narrowed his eyes at him. "Who were your parents?"

"Foster. Left home when I was sixteen. Joined the service."

"You would have been too young."

"Lied about my age. Big for my age. Served as a Ranger until my time was up and went home."

"Who were your biological parents?"

"Hell if I know, and I really didn't care. Except that Leyton Hill was my name, and it stuck. Foster parents collected their checks, and when I was old enough, I moved on. You?"

"Fostered until I was sixteen, and then I moved on."

"To Yuma Town."

"Yeah, joined the service with the rest of the sheriff's department before we *were* the sheriff's department—Dan, Chase, Hal. What's this crap about setting up some damn field office?"

"You need my assistance. Seems there's a lot of trouble in the area."

Stryker smiled, albeit a little evilly. "Seems to me that you're some of the trouble, and you needed *our* assistance."

"Slight inconvenience. We would have dug a hole and been out of there in no time."

Stryker snorted. "You're just lucky we didn't leave you in there after what you pulled with Kate."

"Excuse me," Kate said, interrupting the "talk."

Stryker immediately straightened and shoved his hands in his pockets.

"You had to have a lot of blood," Kate said to Leyton.

Leyton thought this should be confidential patient information and was about to tell Stryker so when Kate added, "Stryker gave you blood. But I have to say, I ran a DNA test. Only men have a Y chromosome. A father will pass on the *exact* same Y chromosome to all his sons. Both of you have the exact same Y DNA patterns. Which means at least your biological father was the same. Not only that, you have much more DNA in common, which would indicate that you had the same birth mother as well. That means you are most likely full brothers."

Stryker looked a little pale. Leyton felt a little woozy himself, only he told himself it was from the blood loss.

"So I guess the question is, if you know your accurate birth dates, what are they?"

Stryker looked at Leyton as if he didn't want to be the first to say and waited for Leyton instead.

"June 5th, 1985," Leyton said.

"June 6th, same year," Stryker said, wearing a self-satisfied smug.

Kate smiled, pulled out her phone and checked on something. "I can see it now. Both are a bit of a rebel, but you're both curious and want to learn new things. Family is important, you're playful, charming, sociable, and...you both have a mischievous sense of humor. Independent, but super responsible, good natural instincts. Yep, sounds like the both of you."

"You're reading a horoscope?" Leyton asked, not trusting the doc would believe in that nonsense.

"You're brothers. Congratulations. Be nice to each other. I don't want to hear any fighting between the two of you. Oh, and your strength of character is having the art of diplomacy, charm, and wit. Just remember that." Then Kate stalked out of the room.

Leyton scowled as much at Stryker as he did back. He knew the deputy had the hots for Kate. "Wait, Doc? What does it say about romantic relationships?"

That met with dead silence.

Stryker turned on his heel and stalked after Kate. "Kate,

there's got to be a mistake."

"DNA testing proves there isn't."

"Our birth dates…"

"You are only one day off. One of you has got it wrong. Which means either Leyton's a day older than you, or one of you has to decide to accept that you've got your birth date wrong. Or, you were born a few minutes after midnight, Stryker, and you're the youngest, by nearly a day."

"Hell, Kate," Stryker said from the hallway as he walked with her down the hall toward her office.

Travis returned on crutches.

"I thought you were getting your therapy."

"I am. This is some of it. I'm supposed to walk back that way in a minute. So is Stryker your brother?"

"Seems that way." Leyton grabbed his phone and checked the Zodiac sign for his birth date.

"What are you looking up now?" Travis asked. He glanced at the page on Leyton's phone and smiled. "Romantic relationships. She was right, you know. You're too curious for your own good. Charming? Well, I guess with her you are. Diplomatic?" Travis laughed.

"Idealistic about romance. Rare to make the first move and takes time to settle down with someone long term."

"Well, that's true," Travis said.

"Not this time it isn't." Leyton set his phone on the table and was still smiling when he got a call from the real estate woman. "You got a place for me?"

"A rental with option to buy. It's a vacant building two doors down from the lot where the clinic stands. A cougar made a go of a craft shop, but it didn't go over. So she wants to rent it out with an option to buy—"

"I'll take it."

"Don't you want to see it first?"

"Yeah, all right. I'll meet you over there. Just as soon as I find my clothes."

"You're at the clinic, right?"

"Yeah, but it's time to check out."

"Do you want me to pick you up?"

"I wonder what happened to my car."

"Sheriff probably dropped it off at the clinic."

"Then I'm good. Meet you in ten minutes."

"Will do."

He ended the call.

Travis said, "Got a place for us already?"

"I'm going to check it out."

"Okay. I need to head back to the therapy room." Travis hobbled off.

Leyton still felt tired from the blood loss, but he figured he needed to eat a juicy steak and...that's just what Kate had wanted when they were making that long hike back to civilization. But should he just bring over the works, or wait until he had a place and invite her over so she wouldn't feel...crowded, as Travis said. Then they could put on appearances they were dating, and she could keep up her nice family doctor image without offending anyone.

He was ready to take her back to their campsite by the creek and just enjoy being with her again alone, without anyone judging them or giving her grief. Like Stryker. Of all the damn things. Leyton had a brother!

He still wasn't sure if that was a good thing or not. Not

good, if Stryker thought he had a chance with Kate.

He yanked on his clothes, ignoring how rotten he felt, and once he was finished dressing, though he was shirtless— he guessed someone had thrown away his bloody T-shirt— he headed out of the room. He heard Elsie talking to Travis in another room, telling him to walk with her some now. Hell, Travis should have been running laps by now. Stryker was talking low to Kate in her office.

Leyton reminded himself he needed to get on with business. Buy the office for work and then see if the real estate agent had any residences nearby that he could buy, or lease with the option to buy.

He had considered that Kate might not be ready for settling down with him. Maybe never.

He let out his breath. That just wasn't an option with him. Not the way he felt about her. Even now he had to curb his growly cougar nature when she was holed up in her office with Stryker.

Then he headed past the reception desk and three women sitting in the waiting area. April had the phone to her ear. "Yes, Mrs. Haverton, I can get you in—" But then she looked up and saw Leyton heading out the door. "Wait, Mr. Hill. You haven't been discharged yet!"

"I'll take care of it later. Got to take care of some business." Leyton headed out the door before April called the doctor and she stopped him. He was soon in his car, glad to be out of the clinic, and on his way down the road to the building a couple of doors down. He could have walked, but the way he was feeling, this was probably for the best anyway. On his phone, he checked the property values in the area, taxes, utilities, then parked in the parking lot for customers, once a yard for the quaint, two-story home with a wrap-around porch and fenced-in backyard.

When he saw Ms. Tremoine get out of her car about ten minutes later, all prim and proper in her jacket and skirt, heels, her hair done up in a bun, he smiled. But she looked aghast, her blue eyes wide, her jaw dropping.

"Omigod," she said, staring at his naked torso.

"I work out a lot." He flexed his good arm, though he knew that's not what she was referring to. He was certain she wasn't used to showing property to a shirtless man who was wearing a thick bandage over a gunshot wound. "Let's see the property."

She fumbled to get the key in the lock of the two story-building, that had once been a home with a kitchen in back and an expansive living area that had been used to display the majority of her handmade crafts, he imagined. Same with the stairs. "Bathrooms?"

"Two and a half. And three bedrooms, though she used one for teaching crafts, one for supplies and storage, and the other for her crafts on clearance." She showed him the backyard with patios and walkways, treed and had several pretty flowerbeds. "She displayed garden decorations for sale out here."

"I'll take it."

"Three-hundred and twenty-thousand."

"That's highway robbery."

"You said any price."

"I guess I should have said any *reasonable* price." He looked over the kitchen. "Needs updating."

"If it's not going to be used for anything but an office…"

"Needs updating." He headed up the stairs and looked into each of the bedrooms. One for Travis and one for him, until they could make other arrangements. But for now, they had enough bathrooms, bedrooms, a kitchen and an office. Another room for another agent if they brought on another until he could make his own arrangements. "Bathrooms need updating also." Not that any of them would care, but if they ever needed to resell the place, it could use some renovations.

"One-hundred and seventy-five thousand," he offered, figuring from the other home prices in the area, that was about right. Maybe a little low. But the listing showed it had been for sale for over a year, so she definitely had the price jacked up—just so someone like him would offer less.

"She won't go below two-hundred and ten."

"I'll take it. On the condition we can move right in."

"I'll call her and see if she agrees." Ms. Tresmoine pulled out her phone and called the owner. "Mrs. Tipton? We just had an offer on your craft store."

CHAPTER 15

As soon as April frantically told Kate their patient Leyton Hill had walked out of the clinic without being discharged properly, Kate wasn't surprised. She wasn't going to allow it either. Her clinic, her rules.

"Stryker, go get your brother and return him here at once."

"He's a big boy, Kate. He can check himself out—"

"You're supposed to be guarding him. Those were Dan's orders to you."

"Hell."

"Besides, he's your brother. Show some brotherly love."

Stryker snorted and headed outside, but she swore he was not all that upset about having a brother, more that the brother and she showed a mutual interest in each other.

Kate saw Travis using his crutches to get back to his room. "Leyton escape?"

His hair was nearly black and his eyes nearly as dark as

he made his way down the hall. He was as muscular as Leyton, and he looked like he could take down the bad guys every bit as much as Leyton could.

"Yeah. I should have known. He doesn't like to sit still."

"I probably should warn you he's got a real thing for you," Travis said, hobbling back to the room.

She joined him, wanting to hear just what he knew of Leyton's interest in her.

"He wants to buy a piece of property right on top of your business to set up his field office. And a house right next to yours."

Amused, she smiled a little.

"I told him you might be feeling a little crowded, and he should back off a bit."

She could slug Travis, if he wasn't having a hard enough time getting into bed, and she had to help him. Or maybe that was just his ploy. He would be staying here based on the leg fracture. It was simple enough. It was the crack to the skull and the fact Butch Sanders had tried to kill both him and Leyton, that forced her to keep them here longer than necessary. Well, and Leyton's blood loss too.

"So he's getting a place anyway on top of your clinic if he can find one. And a house." Travis got a call and raised his brows. "Okay, sounds good." He finished the call and smiled. "Well, he did it. Do you know the craft shop two doors down from the clinic? He bought it. And he and I are moving in. Pronto."

"When I say so."

"Okay, you tell him that. As far as I'm concerned, I could use some more bedrest. The bedrooms are upstairs. I can't see climbing up flights of stairs any time soon, or I'm liable to fall and break my neck."

"Like hell I'm returning to bed per the doctor's orders. I'll clear it with Kate," Leyton said in the reception area.

Kate smiled. "Looks like my patient is back."

"If you want him in the bed, he'll probably need a sedative. Knowing him, he'll be buying the furniture, having the place set up, and open for business tomorrow." Travis pulled his blanket over his waist.

"No he won't. Get your rest. You're not going anywhere where you'll have to climb stairs to get to bed." She headed out of the room and nearly collided with Leyton. He grabbed her arm to steady her, the heat instantly flaring between them, and though she only meant to get him back to bed and to demand that he stay there, the way he looked at her like a starving cat, his gaze shifting to her mouth, she couldn't stop the inevitable even if she'd tried.

His mouth was on hers, hungrily kissing her, licking her lips, biting, his tongue diving in, tasting her like she was tasting him, her arms sliding around his neck. He pulled her in tight, unwilling to leave it at a sweet kiss, but something hotter, more passionate, more desperate.

She'd missed him too, and this. The passion igniting between them was as if they had some sexual physical bond that couldn't be severed either by time or distance. When they were close, they couldn't fight it.

Then she remembered where she was, that her shirtless, bandaged patient needed to be in bed, though she was thinking he needed to be in *her* bed with around-the-clock care, and she reluctantly pulled away. Her heart and his were racing, his eyes dark as she imagined hers were. His pale cheeks were flushed with heat, not embarrassment, but hot-blooded heat. She realized then that he was trying to do the right thing, setting up close to her, but not automatically thinking he had the right to just move in with her. She appreciated that. Though she was still wanting the moving in part, when she knew it was better to take this slowly.

She had to remind herself she had been a hostage in the initial part of their relationship, and that she needed to really get to know him on a day-to-day basis.

"Your bed is waiting for you," she said, trying to say the words firmly or she was afraid he'd take it as a suggestion and not an order. But her words came out breathy instead.

He smiled down at her in that cat way that said he knew just how she was feeling, and he knew how to make her feel even better. Or maybe he was thinking that the bed she was referring to as his was hers.

"I hear you've bought the craft shop just down from the clinic and plan to live there." She took his arm and led him back to the room.

"Yeah, I've got to set up shop somewhere and I got a real bargain."

"Travis can't climb stairs for some time," she warned.

"I'm going to get a couch to sit in the office that can make into a bed for the time being. Our office isn't like a real office. We just use it to drop in and get our job assignments, crash if we need to, do research on computers, but it's not like a police station where folks off the street come in to report crimes. We'll be taking our cue from our boss in Minnesota. But we'll have this area to monitor, and the states surrounding it."

She nodded, waiting for him to climb into bed.

He frowned at her. "I have plans, Doc."

"Think about them some more." She pulled the covers aside. "While you're resting. I promise I'll release you both tomorrow. But I don't want you moving furniture and the like. Not either of you since you've both suffered from head injuries. And Travis isn't to move anything."

"I can't. Not with a bum leg," Travis said as if he needed to emphasize that point.

"I'll buy the furnishings and the deliverymen can take care of it." Leyton started stripping off his clothes, then climbed into bed wearing just his briefs.

"Hospital gown?" Kate picked it up off his tray and handed it to him.

"I'll put it on when I have some privacy." He winked at her and she felt her face heat.

She took a deep breath. "I'm clocking out and Stryker is staying here until Chase relieves him."

"We don't need all this high security," Leyton said.

"Yeah you do. If someone were to injure you while you were at the clinic, none of us would forgive ourselves. Besides, I need someone here to make you stay put."

He jerked the covers up to his waist. "I had other plans for tonight."

She smiled. "Night, boys. See you on rounds tomorrow."

Then she left the room and saw Stryker speaking on the phone to Dan. "Yeah, okay. Hell, I had no idea Leyton was my brother. What do you mean Dottie will want to celebrate it? No way."

***

Two hours later, Dan stalked into Leyton and Travis's clinic room and closed the door. "Okay, I'm Dan Steinacker and the sheriff here in Yuma Town, and I want to know exactly what this is all about."

"The boss said we could share what we've been working on undercover with you, so this is what's going on." Leyton told him all about the arms dealer, the way he'd slipped away from him, and how he'd managed to come back for his weapons, but set off the mine blast afterward to get rid of two pesky cougar agents breathing down his neck. He also mentioned the previous history between them—the shoot-out in Afghanistan where the bastard tried to kill him for looking into his background.

Dan swore under his breath. Being a military man, Dan knew the stakes in combat. They sure as hell didn't need the "friendlies" trying to kill them too.

"I want to know about *the doc and you*," Dan said, his arms folded across his chest, his eyes narrowed, his expression condemning.

"Oh, that." Hell, Leyton thought the sheriff would be interested in apprehending the bad guys and not worried about what went on between him and Kate, since obviously she had no trouble with what had gone on. Not with the way she kissed him in the hall earlier. Leyton swore he could still feel her warm lips pressed against his lips. And he definitely could smell her delightful she-cat scent on him too.

"Well?"

"Surely she must have told you what had happened." Leyton thought he and Kate had talked enough about it that he had the story down pat. He just hoped she hadn't gone and given a different version.

Dan still waited, his look growly.

Leyton told him the story, minus tying her up in bed. He still hadn't come up with a plausible reason for that except that he was holding her hostage.

"I don't believe she went with you willingly," Dan said.

"Okay, listen." Leyton plumped up his pillow. "We haven't seen each other in a couple of weeks. She could have told a different version of the story without any threat or coercion from me. She didn't even know that I'd ever return. So unless she gave you a different version..."

"If it wasn't that Stryker saw the two of you kissing in the hallway, I wouldn't have believed it myself."

Leyton tried to hide a smile. She was one hot kisser, and he wanted to get back to that part of their relationship as soon as he could. Though he kept telling himself he needed to do the friends without benefits first. Well, maybe partial benefits. No way could he date her and give up kissing her good night. Hell, he'd only planned to wait here for Dan's arrival so he could tell the sheriff what the deal was concerning Butch Sanders before he left the clinic again. He needed to get his place in order if he was going to be ready to have her over pronto.

Would she care if he had everything fixed up first? He didn't think so. That meant he only had to have the patio set up—barbecue grill, patio furniture. It was kind of romantic out there, even though he loved being in the real wilderness with her. Still, it was kind of like her gardens, yet more treed, lots of birds singing away. He figured she'd like it while he grilled steaks and lobster tail.

"When are you getting married?" Dan asked.

"Don't you think that's something that should be decided privately between Kate and me?" Leyton knew the town was a tightknit community, mostly because they were cougars, but hell, this was not a community affair.

"She's a professional, highly-respected by the community. She takes care of families in her practice and she has a reputation to uphold," Dan warned, as if he was her father and was ready to pull out his shotgun and either chase Leyton off or force him to do right by his daughter, even though Dan appeared to be about the same age as they were.

Leyton suspected Kate would not appreciate the sheriff's interference.

"Okay, not that it's any of your damn business, but if Kate would have me, I'd marry her in a heartbeat." Leyton really didn't want to hurt Kate or her business in any way. "But I want to date her first, before I spring anything of the sort on her. And that's between the two of us."

Dan didn't look like he was satisfied with the answer. Probably didn't believe Leyton really intended to marry Kate, just fool around with her and then decide he wasn't ready to settle down. "What about this damn field office you intend to open up?"

"We'll be working on it tomorrow." Leyton explained what it would entail. His agents would be seeking criminal cougars in the whole state, not just the county, and their jurisdiction would extend to the states bordering Colorado.

Dan narrowed his eyes at Leyton again, and fairly growled. "You get any fugitives in our county, you let me know about it before you go off trying to take them down in my jurisdiction."

"Fair enough."

"Got a picture of the guys you're after?"

Leyton looked at Travis, who said, "Yeah, got a picture of them hovering over the weapons cache in the tunnel." He pulled it up and showed it to Dan.

Dan studied the shot. "Not a very good shot."

Travis snorted. "*You* try taking a shot of a bunch of criminals who would like nothing better than to put a bullet through your head, when your leg is broken, you're in pain, shaking from the adrenaline flooding your bloodstream, and you're trying not to let them see you take the picture in a hurry, then shove the phone away or they'll destroy it and the evidence."

Dan cracked a smile.

Leyton didn't think Dan was a smiley kind of guy, the way he'd stalked in here and looked like he meant business.

"So you think this guy's name is an alias?" Dan finally got back to what Leyton thought he should have been asking about all along.

"Yeah, I know it has to be. He had a different name in the military, Bart Smith, and one as a cop with a human police force, Butch Sanders. I think when I caught up with him, he'd left the force so he could do his business without having to report in to any job. He's changed his hair color, and eye color by wearing contacts a time or two."

"As a cat?" Dan asked, surprised.

"No, he'd have to remove the contacts when he shifted. I think it's more for official photos. He gains weight, loses weight, wears different clothing styles from formal to homeless so he can fit in wherever he needs to."

"I smelled two men there, other than the two of you," Dan said.

"Yeah, Butch's wearing hunter's spray. I figure that it has to do some with me trying to track him down and he knows I'm a cougar. But I also think he's from around the state. He knew that area well where the cabin was."

"But he wasn't covering his scent then, was he?" Dan asked, hopeful.

"No, he wasn't. He didn't know a cougar was tracking him at first."

"What the hell are you doing in the bed still?"

Leyton smiled a little at him. "Doctor's orders."

"You've got a job to do. Get your clothes on. You're coming with me." Dan glanced at Travis. "You're staying here. Then at least I'll only get in trouble for checking one of you out of the clinic against the doctor's orders."

Leyton was out of the bed, well, not really fast as he hurt too much to move really fast. But he was moving and Dan watched for a moment as if making sure he wasn't going to have a dead man on his hands, and one pissed off doctor. Then he nodded to Leyton and left the room.

"What the hell was all that about?" Travis asked.

"What? Going after Butch? I suspect Dan wants to head over to the cabin, only I know where it is and he'll see if he smells the guy's scent and can recognize him."

"No, about Kate."

"What about Kate?" Leyton asked, wishing the hell he could dress faster. He couldn't believe how achy and sore he was, or how hard it was to move. He supposed running around earlier to buy a place had zapped more of his strength than he had imagined. What he needed was a few juicy red steaks with Kate to help build up his blood. He had his trousers on before he realized he didn't have a T-shirt. "Okay, you stay put." Leyton tied on his boots. "And I'll give you a call when we learn something."

"Wait, what about Kate?"

"What about her?"

"The marrying part?"

Leyton smiled, then frowned. "Don't you dare say a thing to her about it. I need to do the dating stuff first. Work up to it nice and slow and..."

"You don't ever work slow."

"This time I will."

"Want to place a bet on it?"

"No," Leyton said.

Travis just smiled. "Because you know you'd lose."

Leyton smiled back. "I don't see how I could lose. Rest up. We have work to do when I get back."

"Take a pillow with you. You look like you still need to rest up. You said it was a six-hour drive back there. You can sleep. Let the sheriff drive."

Now how would that look if the new field director of the office in Yuma Town had to go on his first joint mission, but had to take a pillow and blanket and sleep on the trip there?

He headed out of the room and was surprised to see Stryker, Chase, and Hal there with Dan, waiting on him. Dan handed him a T-shirt. "If you're going to be one of us, you need to be at least half-dressed for the job."

Leyton tried to pull the shirt on without groaning, knowing the men were all judging him. Was he too injured to go with them? Hell no.

Stryker handed him his gun. "Surprised you didn't use it on the bastards." He cocked a brow.

Leyton still couldn't believe he hadn't heard the men sneak up behind him before they bushwhacked him.

"You're taking the whole damn posse? Who's staying behind to watch out for Travis if Butch learns he's at the clinic unprotected?"

"I am." Hal looked cross about it.

Then they headed out, but he was surprised Stryker would go with them. As soon as they exited the back door where several vehicles sat, Kate came out of her house. "Dan said you were going on a hunt. Which I vetoed. But he said you insisted on catching the bad guy. Did you?"

She arched a brow at him as if she didn't believe it for a moment. That she thought he had been coerced into going along with this.

"Hell yeah, I did. I am. I've got to take this guy out once and for all. If Dan and the others can identify him as a local, we've got to do it."

"You can't just tell him where it is?" She gave him a look that said she knew he could, but he stubbornly was going because this was his chance to bring down the bad guy.

He move toward her to give her a hug, but she held up her hands and wouldn't let him get near her. He knew from the irritated expression she was pissed at both of them, Dan for taking him, and Leyton for going.

"All right. Hate tearful good-byes anyway." Leyton

headed for the passenger door of the sheriff's car.

"Back here," Dan said, opening the back door for him. "It's the only way Doc will go along with this, begrudgingly."

Leyton glanced in the back seat and saw her cougar paw print sleeping bag and a pillow. He looked back at her.

She was standing there, head cocked to the side as if saying, "Try me." Her arms were folded across her chest. And she was *not* smiling.

"Either you get in the back, or you can tell me where the cabin is, and we'll take it from here," Dan said, looking just as serious as Doc. "I don't want to get on Doc's bad side if I ever need patching up."

Chase and Stryker were smirking, waiting for Leyton to decide what he was going to do.

"Ah hell, Kate." Annoyed to the max, Leyton climbed into the back seat.

"You have a six-hour drive there. Sleep, Leyton," she said. "If you don't, and you come back in worse shape than you left...well, you don't want to know what I'll do to you."

He smiled a little, thinking just what he'd like for her to do to him. But he climbed into the back seat and sat there.

"Down," she said, pointing at him, like she was commanding a dog to obey her.

He growled and laid down on the back seat and said to Dan, "As soon as we can safely do so, pull over and I'll climb up front with you."

"Like hell you will." Dan closed the rear door, then climbed into the driver's seat. "I promised Kate and I'm not breaking my promise. She's right. You need rest. You have six hours to do it and then you can earn your pay. Tell me the location of the cabin so I don't have to disturb you if you do manage to sleep at all."

Leyton grumbled under his breath, showed him the location on Dan's GPS, then he frowned. "How did she know about us leaving? We only just decided to check out the scents at the cabin."

"While you were dressing, I called her. And she laid down the rules. She didn't want you going, but she knew you'd need a straightjacket to keep you from leaving the clinic. So she figured this was the next best solution. If you weren't going to sleep in the clinic, you could sleep in the car on the drive out there."

"Hell." Leyton pulled the sleeping bag around him and realized Kate hadn't washed it. He could smell her on the sleeping bag and the pillow too. He snuggled against the pillow, pulling the sleeping bag closer, thinking about her in the sleeping bag with him, smiling.

He thought he heard Dan talking to him about learning from Kate that he was a Ranger. Dan wanted to know everything about him. But Leyton soon drifted off and didn't hear anything more but a chuckle from Dan.

CHAPTER 16

Kate paced across her living room floor, understanding that Leyton had to do this. But she knew he really needed to rest more than anything. He wasn't strong enough this time to go chasing after Butch. Dan had assured her Leyton would sleep in the back of his car. She knew he was good at his word. Not only did Dan not want to rile her, in case she had to take care of his injuries at some later date, and she had reminded him of it, just in case, but also, he didn't want Leyton dying on them.

Even so, she didn't trust Leyton to sleep the whole way there. When Dan stopped for gas four hours into the drive, he gave her an update. "He's sound asleep still. I began asking him about his time in the military, but he was already out."

Then she worried that Leyton was still sleeping! She knew he had needed the rest.

"Just like a baby all rolled up in his sleeping bag," Dan

said.

"Yeah, well that's why he should have stayed at the hospital. Is he looking paler than normal? He is breathing, isn't he?"

"Yes, Doctor. He's breathing, and no, his color hasn't changed. We should have brought you with us so you'd quit fretting. But it might not be safe."

"Do you think Butch would return to the cabin? After Leyton would have undoubtedly told you where it was?"

"Maybe not. But we can't trust that he wouldn't. He might very well think he was safe in returning."

"Is Leyton's pulse okay?"

"Yes, he's sleeping, Kate. He's fine. He better be worthy of your affections when he asks you to marry him."

She stopped pacing. "What?"

"Uhm, just that we think a lot of you, Doc, and none of us want to see you get hurt."

"When did the marriage issue come up? You didn't threaten him to marry me, did you?"

Dan sighed. "No. He said he was going to do this right and date you first."

She felt her heart swell with excitement. "I want to talk to him."

"He's sleeping, Kate. He needs to sleep. Doctor's orders. Besides, I don't think he wanted me to spill the beans. Got to go. We'll be there in two hours. You need to get some sleep. You've got a busy day ahead of you. I'll call when we get there and if Sleeping Beauty wakes up by then, he can call you."

"Don't you need to find out from him which cabin it is?"

"He told me before we pulled out."

225

"Then you could have left him behind!"

"No way. He needs to do this and find closure. Any of us would feel the same way. Talk to you later."

"All right. Keep me updated."

"Will do."

Kate couldn't help being both excited that Leyton wanted to actually date her, which she thought was cute of him and that he'd even talked it over with Dan, and worried that Leyton was too injured to be out there with the rest of the men. Sleep? No way would she get any sleep while she waited to hear word of what they learned.

***

Leyton woke as they pulled into the parking area of the cabin where Butch had stayed. "Hell, I slept the whole six hours?"

"Yeah," Dan said. "Thought you wouldn't wake up until we returned you to the hospital. Want to call Kate and let her know you're all right before we check out the place?"

"Yeah." Leyton pulled out his phone, expecting Dan to get out of the car and give them some privacy, but he just sat there, waiting in the car like Chase and Stryker were waiting in theirs. "Hey, Kate—"

"Are you all right?" She sounded half asleep, like he'd made love to her and was not quite awake.

Did he say he was going to spend a whole lot of time dating her? He had to be nuts. No way would he last.

"Yeah, we're here. Just wanted to let you know that we're safe for the moment but..."

She waited.

"Hell, can we have some privacy here?" he asked Dan.

"Forget it." He groaned and exited the car. "Hey, I want to set up our first date."

"After you heal—"

"Tomorrow night. I'll take you out for supper."

"You need to rest."

"Okay, I'll eat at your house. I'd have you over to my place, but it's going to take a little bit to get it fixed up. And damn it, I can't wait that long."

"My place. When you get back."

"Any time, day or not?"

She laughed. "I thought it was for a date. Like supper?"

"Depending on the hour, we could make it breakfast. Or brunch. Or lunch. Let's just wing it."

"I'll be working, most likely. You'll have to wait until I get off from work."

"We'll talk about it when I get back. The guys are getting out of their vehicles. I have to make sure they stay safe."

She chuckled. "They better make sure *you* stay safe. You're the one who's been injured."

"Damn it to hell," Dan said, gun out as Chase and Stryker both pulled their weapons.

"Got to go, honey. Call you later." Leyton pulled his gun too and hurried after Dan and the other men, but no one was at the cabin. "I thought you heard or saw something."

Dan was on his phone and said, "Dottie, I want you to make sure your place is locked up tight. Your ex is back in the area. Smelled him all over the place and his scent at the cabin is recent. I'm sending Hal and the Muellers over. But it'll take them time to reach you."

Leyton *knew* the bastard was from the area. Chase and

Stryker were checking out the cabin. Leyton was examining the area around the cabin in case he had missed anything the last time. But nothing.

Dan was on the phone to Hal and the Muellers next, telling everyone to get to Dottie's place pronto.

After that, he seemed torn about what to do.

"They haven't been here since the last time I was here," Leyton said.

"Okay, we head home, now."

"You want me to drive? Spell you?"

"No. Come on. Let's go."

"You're dating Dottie," Leyton said, climbing into the passenger's seat.

"Who the hell told you that?" Dan asked, tearing off down the road. "I watch out for her."

Leyton smiled a little. "Yeah, well, I never thought I'd be falling for a she-cat either. Sometimes life just happens. I don't know any of Butch's past history. Want to share? I've told you what he's been up to of late."

"He was married to Dottie for three years. They had twins, a boy and a girl, blond-haired, blue-eyed, both taking after their dad, though they have their mother's smile, curiosity, and friendliness. They were a year old when he split. So he's been gone for nearly two and a half years. They'll be four in November. He didn't look anything like that blurry picture Travis took."

"Butch's a master of deception. His hair was dark brown and he wears brown contacts. But when I saw him more recently fishing at the river, he was a blond, his hair shaggier. He's been into arms dealing all this time." Then Leyton had another concern. "He hasn't returned to see Dottie since he left, has he?"

"Just once. She'd divorced him for abandoning her and the kids. He'd tried to convince her to leave Yuma Town and reconsider leaving him, meaning, he wanted to work things out and remarry her. He really wanted her back, but he wouldn't tell her why he left her in the first place. She wasn't buying it. You don't just leave your wife and kids if you truly love them. I figured he got anxious about having to raise a couple of twins, only a year old, panicked and took off. But when he didn't return? That was another story. She had loved him once and it was hard on her to see him with the kids. They were shy to begin with, then had fun playing with him, she'd told me. But it was over between them when he'd left her in a real financial bind without word. Still, she couldn't deny him seeing his own kids as long as she was right there with them."

"Probably his criminal dealings had caught up with him, which was the reason for him running in the first place."

"Yeah, now that we know what he's been involved in, I'd say that is a good bet. When I learned she was about ready to lose her home—she'd kept his abandoning her a secret from everyone, but the banker made me aware of her troubles and the imminent foreclosure on her house—my dispatcher decided it was time for her to retire, and I gave Dottie the job. Everyone stepped in to help watch her kids while she works. We're a community of cougars who will do anything to help one of our own. She's great at her job too. Gave her the confidence she needed to get back into the mainstream."

"So why don't you marry her? You're not married, are you? Or have had a bad experience with a divorce, ex-girlfriend, or something?"

Dan gave him a quelling look.

"You've given me the third degree about Kate and my intentions. So what's the deal?" Leyton wasn't letting go of the issue. Dan obviously had real affection for the woman, much like his own for Kate, and he'd decided when he had met her, and got to know her, he wasn't giving up on the issue of claiming the she-cat.

"Dottie had a lot to work out on her own after her husband left. She was upset because she was about ready to lose the house and had two little ones to provide for. She needed the self-assurance that she could manage fine on her own. She didn't need another man taking over her life at that point. Just for someone to be there as a friend if she needed someone."

"Seems to me there's more going on than you want to let on. Are you afraid of taking on the responsibility of a readymade family?" Leyton thought even if Kate had a whole slew of children, he'd be fine with it—now. Kids hadn't appealed in the beginning, but Kate just gave him a totally different perspective about life in general. Which was another reason he felt he needed her in his life—permanently. She did something to him that no other woman ever had.

"No, the kids are great."

"Then what? Commitment phobia?"

"I have a wife already, damn it!"

Leyton stared at him for a moment, then said, "Oh." He

should have kept his mouth shut after that bit of revelation. But he couldn't help it. Part of it was owing to having the natural curiosity of a cat. But part of it was his law enforcement training. "Dottie knows about it, right?"

When Dan just sat there staring out at the road looking gloomy, Leyton figured the worst. No one in Yuma Town knew Dan had a wife. Sure-fire way to kill a new blossoming relationship. He was sure glad he didn't have any skeletons in his closet like that.

"You've got to tell her, Dan. If this is leading anywhere between the two of you, you've got to tell her." Then Leyton, feeling exhausted all over again, leaned his head back against the seat and fell asleep, thinking of holding Kate's naked body in his arms.

It was two in the morning when they arrived at Dottie's house. Hal greeted them and Leyton offered, "I know you're going to take turns watching over Dottie. And I'd liked to help. Howdy, ma'am," he said. "Sheriff?"

"Hal, take him back to the clinic."

"No, wait, I need to do this."

"You need to rest. And that's an order." Dan's stern look meant he wasn't changing his mind about this.

Neither was Leyton.

CHAPTER 17

As soon as she got a call from Leyton, telling her he was back in the clinic, per her orders, Kate was on her way over there. She couldn't help it. Even though it was three in the morning and she had to go into work at six, she wanted to see him and learn what had happened.

"Thanks, for coming back here," she said, standing beside his bed, the privacy curtain drawn around them, trying to keep her voice low so as not to disturb Travis.

"I didn't have a choice," Leyton said. "Dan ordered Hal to bring me back here and stand guard." Leyton pulled her closer for a kiss, and she obliged, tongues dancing, deepening the contact. He groaned. "I've got to get my place set up pronto."

"I'll let you out of here in the morning."

"Breakfast?"

She shook her head. "You rest until I can release you. Maybe we can get together after I'm through with work."

"Okay." He sounded like he was backing off, afraid she felt he was trying to move too fast with her.

"Dan let everyone know that Dottie's ex, Jeffrey Brown, is back in the area and to call if anyone spots him, but to let the police handle it. He's going under the alias of Butch Sanders, but he might have a new one by now," she said.

"Yeah, he might not intend to go near her place, afraid he might get caught."

Kate shook her head. "I wouldn't count on it. If you didn't know his true identity, he may figure no one else will realize he's the same man."

"True, but he's also been using the cabin for a while, knows the area, and that may be the only reason he's in the area." Leyton held her hand and rubbed it tenderly with his thumb. "I just want you to know that if Dan had permitted it, I would have been taking turns watching over Dottie and her kids."

"Then I'll have to thank Dan for sending you back here. You need to recuperate before you tackle that man any further."

"I just want you to know I'm not giving up on the notion."

"I wouldn't expect you to. I'm sure if they need you, Dan will call." Kate leaned over and kissed Leyton again. "See you on morning rounds."

Before she could leave, he pulled her in for another devastating kiss and left her breathless.

"That's so you don't forget about me."

She licked her lips and smiled. "Doubt that would ever happen." Then before she moved him to her bed, she said goodnight for what was left of it, said goodnight to Hal sitting outside the room, and then headed back home. And wished Leyton really was there when she went inside.

***

The next morning, Kate came by to discharge Leyton and Travis, to his relief. He would have already left the clinic if it wasn't that he wanted his good morning kiss from her.

He'd been dressed and ready to go while Travis was grumbling, "Can't a body get any sleep in a place like this?"

"I was afraid you might have left already, so I came here first," Kate said, greeting them.

"Nah, waiting for my good morning kiss."

Kate smiled at him, then he looked at Travis, who yanked his privacy curtain shut.

Kate chuckled and wrapped her arms around Leyton's neck. "You're almost as addictive as chocolate."

"Almost?" He slid his hands up her waist, wanting to just sweep her away and take her right back home. But he had to set up his place and check with Dan about serving a guard shift at Dottie's today, because tonight, he was keeping his time open for Kate.

She smiled. "I'm releasing you. As soon as Elsie can bring a wheelchair for Travis..."

"I'm on it."

"Hospital procedures would dictate that you have one also."

He snorted. "I've already left the clinic so many times already, I'm just a visitor."

"Just as long as you don't end up back in that bed."

He watched her leave and smiled. Travis used his

crutches to join him. "I don't think I've ever seen you with the hots for a woman like that before."

"Can you blame me?"

"Not in the least."

Leyton dropped Travis at the empty house and dumped their bags. "Dan has put an alert out on your stolen vehicle, if someone didn't tell you already. We'll have to get some of our things from our homes up north. I'll get the furniture arranged so we have some place to sleep tonight."

Travis sat on the floor and propped his leg up on one of Leyton's bags, his back against the wall. "You're wearing me out just thinking about it."

"I'll bring breakfast back in a jiff. You just relax."

"See you in a bit."

Then Leyton was off to the donut shop, picking up cinnamon buns for the hospital staff, though he didn't have a chance to see Kate, and then headed back to his place. He carried in the cinnamon buns and a coffee maker.

"That was quick," Travis said.

"Yeah, just wanted to grab a quick breakfast, some coffee, and then I'm out of here."

Leyton spent the day shopping, asking Hal if he could deliver some pieces in his truck rather than wait for a delivery date later. Stryker helped too, and before long, well, most of the day was gone when they had some semblance of a furnished house—wraparound sofa, two beds, a couple of desks, a kitchen table and chairs. They'd have to get the rest later.

"Hey, Stryker, I was wondering if I could pull guard duty soon at Dottie's house to relieve the rest of you. I take it he hasn't come by, or I would have heard something."

"Yeah, no word on anything. Dottie wants to have a barbecue tomorrow. Maybe you can do it after that. After all the work you've done today on your place and the injury you sustained, you've probably had enough of a workout." Stryker sounded like he thought Leyton couldn't handle facing another confrontation with Butch and protect Dottie.

Leyton was disappointed and damn if Butch did show up, he wanted to be there to take the bastard down once and for all. But then he thought about the kids. Hell, no way could he kill their daddy in front of them, unless he was hurting her or the kids.

"Tomorrow then."

Hal jerked his thumb at Travis. "We're taking him to dinner. You were out getting the T.V. off the truck at the time. Want to come with us?"

"No, but thanks for asking. And thanks for taking Travis out."

"Are you sure?" Stryker asked.

"Yeah. I've got a date."

Stryker nodded, looking like he was kind of accepting the inevitable.

As soon as the guys left, Leyton got busy again. Forget making beds or doing anything else. He had to go to the grocery store again and pick up special fixings for dinner to share with Kate—so he could fulfil his promise to her to make it up about the camping trip. At least, this was one of many occasions he had planned.

***

Kate curled up with Sheba on the couch, trying to

concentrate on a Sci-Fi adventure story in space on T.V., but all she could think of was Leyton, and his kiss, and that he wanted to stay here near her. That he wasn't leaving. He was setting down permanent roots. She'd been so upset when she'd heard from him in the gold mine, recognized his calm voice that said no matter how drastic the situation was, he wasn't going to give up, or act like he was in dire straits.

She stroked the top of Sheba's head and listened to her contented purring, wishing she could have taken Leyton home with her, but this was for the best. They'd taken off running as far as the relationship went, needing each other when they had the car wreck, but now it was time to take this more slowly. Really get to know each other. What if the two of them weren't suited to each other in the long run?

In the short run, she wanted him here with her now. But they both had jobs to do. They'd take it slow and easy.

She needed to think about having something for supper, but she just wasn't hungry. She couldn't believe it when Leyton and his friend had been injured in the gold mine. And how serious his wound was this time because of all the blood loss. And what was he doing? Heading out of the clinic to buy a place so he could stay near her, not making assumptions that he could just move in either.

She smiled. She couldn't help appreciate him for who he was. Hal had called her earlier in the day to update her on Dottie's situation, all quiet on that front, and just mentioned he and Stryker were helping to move furniture in to the new field office. He told her that he really believed Leyton was overdoing it and if he wasn't careful, he'd be back at the clinic.

That had worried her, but when she had called Leyton to check on him, he didn't pick up.

She heard something on her back patio and Sheba instantly jumped off her lap and ran for the door. Then she meowed, wanting out.

"You don't go outside," Kate said, heading into her bedroom to get her gun. She hadn't really thought she'd ever need it, but that had all changed when Leyton had barged his way into her life.

A knocking at the back door startled her. No one would have come knocking at her back door after work, unless he or she had called ahead first.

She grabbed her gun and opened the blinds on the door and saw Leyton, with packages in hand, smiling. But subdued, and she was afraid he was hurting. She wondered how bad off he was, this time.

"I thought you might be busy tonight, trying to set up your place to impress me," she said, ushering him in, then locked the door.

He carried the groceries into the kitchen. "We talked about having steak and the works when we got back from our wild hike in the wilderness. I was going to buy you dinner out. But we were going to have room service and chill out until someone came and picked you up."

"*You* were going to buy me dinner when we were up north?" she asked, dying to see what he had bought and if he was not going to listen to the doctor about taking it easy, so be it. "As I recall you didn't have any money."

"Yeah, slight technicality. I wanted to do this right. You know, wait until I had a place and had you over for a date."

He looked up at her. "But hell, Kate, I couldn't wait. I'd be killing myself trying to get ready for you and it would probably take more than a few days to furnish the place and get everything ready for you."

"So you picked up steaks and...omigod..." She came around the counter to see the steamed lobster. "You drove to the city to get these?"

"Had to. They didn't have any at the local grocers and I told you I wanted to make it up to you."

She began helping him prepare the rest of the food. "Sit down and I'll fix it."

"But I meant to do the cooking."

She took his good arm and forced him to sit on a dining room chair. "Sit. I'll fix this or I'm calling the sheriff's office and having you confined to the hospital bed again..."

He rose from the chair pulled her into his arms and kissed her. "I've been thinking about what you said in the hall of the clinic about me being in your bed." And then he kissed her again. "Let's eat. I should have held off on getting fresh lobster this time around, but..."

"I love that you did." She pulled away and prepared the feast, but instead of fixing it for the dining room table, she took a tray and set it up for them on tray tables so they could have dinner and a movie like they planned, except not in bed. She knew that's where they'd be headed next. And for the moment, she wanted to just share a meal and a movie...first. "Travis said he warned you to take it slow with me."

"Yeah, well, Travis shouldn't have said anything about it. Besides, I don't want you to believe everything my horoscope says."

"What's that?"

He smiled as they got comfortable on the couch.

She held up her phone. "I can check it out myself."

"That it's rare for me to make the first move."

She was happily eating her lobster, then dipped another piece of lobster tail in his butter because she'd run out of in her dish, and laughed.

"And, that it takes me a long time to figure on settling down."

"Now *that,* I can believe."

They finished their meals and then took their dishes into the kitchen.

"I don't want to take that long." Leyton pulled her into his arms and began to kiss her. He broke free for a moment, their hearts beating faster, their breathing labored. "I mean it. I'll take however long you need to say yes, but I'm not giving you up for anything. All I thought of while I was chasing down Butch was you. Everything about you. Our fireside chats and holding you close, dealing with the weather and the bears. Settling down for long summer naps. Hiking out of there. I couldn't put you out of my mind even if I'd wanted to and I sure as hell didn't want to. When I arrived back at Travis's place, got cleaned up, and ate, it was so late and I realized I didn't have any way to call you, I figured I'd try to get hold of you first thing in the morning. Then the boss called and said Travis could be in trouble.

"When I learned he'd been down in your neck of the woods, I knew then it was providence. I headed down to rescue him, and when your clinic was open, I tried calling you, desperate to let you know how much you mean to me. And how much I want you in my life. Believe me, when I'm tracking down a suspect, I am totally focused on the mission. Nothing else. So for me to keep thinking about you when I was trying to track down clues of where he went? Well, I knew there was more than just hot chemistry between us."

She smiled up at him. "I didn't think you'd come back. Everyone knew I was not myself when I returned. They tried to make me feel better, and I'd heard whisperings that folks figured I had fallen for the hot cougar who had taken me hostage."

"You told them that?"

She snorted. "No. But it doesn't take a brain surgeon to figure that out." She tightened her hold on him. "I couldn't stop thinking of you either. I swear I've been in a fog the last two weeks, worrying if you were okay, thinking you might not be because I never heard from you. Hoping you were running as a cougar like before and still trying to catch up to Butch, hoping you would take him down and not be injured again. Then you didn't leave a message on my answering machine!"

"I'm undercover. I never leave messages."

She shook her head. "If I say yes, will you promise me that if you get injured, you'll listen to doctor's orders?"

He just smiled and kissed her again. "I take that as a hot damn yes!"

"I didn't think you'd ever ask."

"You've made me the happiest cougar alive," he said, sweeping her up in his arms and heading to the bedroom.

She loved that he was, that for the first time in their relationship, they would have the comfort of her soft mattress while making love. Although, she reminded herself of the last time she was in bed with him there and just how "hard" her mattress had become.

"I love you," she said, kissing his cheek.

"I love you, Kate, with all my heart."

He set her down on the floor next to the bed, and jerked the comforter aside, then began stripping her clothes off her as if she might change her mind about this. No way would she. She was struggling with his belt buckle in earnest, and he finally yanked it free, sat on the bed, and began removing one of his boots. She helped with the other, now wearing only her purple panties and bra. But he was way too dressed.

As soon as his feet were bare, she tackled him, sliding her body up his, licking his throat, her hands drawing his arms above his head, pinning him. His eyes were already dark with lust, his mouth curving up just a bit.

She rubbed her body against him, arousing him, his cock already rock hard beneath his jeans. Her blood was hot with the smell of his arousal, the scent of his pheromones doing a hot blooded tango with hers as she leaned in for a kiss.

He kissed her mouth, licked it, and drew her down for more. She slid her hands down his arms, releasing them, and he quickly took charge of the situation. He moved her onto her back, straddling her waist as he jerked off his shirt.

"Hmm," she said, running her hands up his thighs. Ever since she'd washed his beautiful body in her shower when he'd been injured the first time, she couldn't get his chiseled features out of her mind.

He rose on his knees and begin sliding his jeans down, then unable to get them off all the way, he moved off her to sit and pull them off.

He had them down to his ankles when she moved on top of him again, and he smiled at her, a wicked look that said he was going to pay her back. She rubbed her silk-covered mons against his briefs' covered erection, her hands sliding up his torso, palming his nipples, enjoying the feel of them tightening against her skin.

She leaned down again and licked his smiling mouth. He was trying to kick off his jeans still caught at his ankles.

She nipped his mouth, one of her hands planted on his chest, the other reaching down to rub his erection. He stilled for a second, all but his cock that jumped under her strokes. He growled, tried more vigorously to kick off his pants, but when he couldn't, he moved her onto her back, taking charge again.

She loved it, loved him, as he quickly yanked off his jeans. Before he realized what she was going to do, she tugged his briefs down, his fully engorged cock springing free. He growled and hurried to dispense with those before she took advantage and pinned him down again.

Then he was kissing her, stroking her tongue with his, and then pulling her to sit so he could unfasten her bra, and tossed it aside. Like a man with an important mission, he quickly dispensed with her panties. Then he covered her body with his, pressing his erection against her, showing her just how much he craved having her, how much she turned him on.

His scent and taste and touch and the sound of his soft growls filled her senses to overload as she ran her hands over his thighs and he began to stroke her naked nub.

She groaned in a happy and sexy way, loving the manner

in which he drew her to the top of the world with his sweet and powerful strokes whether they were in a car wrecked to pieces in the middle of nowhere, a hastily-made lean-to under the wide-open night skies, in a sleeping bag built for two, or on her soft mattress—now...their bed.

She felt the climb all the way to the top as if she was running as cougar, leaping toward the sun. Then it hit all at once, the sunburst of joy, and she clung to him as she cried out in relief and bliss. He was entering her then, pushing his broad head between her folds, claiming her for his own.

Leyton meant it when he said Kate had made him the happiest cougar in the world. He had no doubt of that as he pushed slowly into her before he began to thrust, thinking of all the other times, but because they'd declared their commitment to each other now, that made this time all the more special. His blood was sizzling as he pumped into her, loving the way she moved against him, trying to draw him out, holding him tight in her wet grasp. She spread her legs further, her knees higher, allowing him deeper. Settling into the core of her, then pulling out again, he began to kiss her, their tongues touching and stroking and teasing, their breaths ragged.

He savored the taste of her warm mouth, sweet and wine flavored, the smell of their heated sex, the feel of her soft skin against his, and the sound of their accelerated heartbeats. Their senses were attuned to all things and the whole while they were making love, he'd been processing every one of them, all tantalizing him and making him savor the minutes.

He felt the climax coming, stilled himself, shaking, trying

to hold onto the moment, then diving in, driving hard and fast and furious. He growled right before he released, and continued to thrust until he had fully come. He pulled out and began to stroke her again, feeling the tension in her body and seeing it in her face, before she groaned with release again.

He collapsed on his back and pulled her on top of him, and just lay there, wanting nothing more than to hold her close the whole night through.

"Shower, next time," he said. "After you applied your doctoring skills in there when you were washing me, I've never been able to get it out of my mind."

She laughed. "I'll have you know, I don't normally give my patients baths."

He smiled. "Well, for a novice, Doc, you sure have magical hands." Then he sighed, not wanting to leave Kate for anything, but he worried about Travis being on his own. "I've got to call Travis and let him know I'm coming home. I hate to leave you, but..."

"Understandable. With his leg in a cast, if Butch or his men come around the place, Travis has a big disadvantage."

"I kind of doubt they'll be coming into town to take us out with so many knowing who he is, but better be safe than sorry."

"Agreed."

"They'll probably put me on the guard detail for Dottie, but wanted to wait another day for me to heal up a bit. Will you put in a good word for me with Dan?"

She groaned. "Leyton..."

"Come on. You know I can take the bastard down if he shows up at Dottie's place."

"What about the kids?"

Leyton shook his head. "I don't want to do it in front of the kids, naturally. Or Dottie either. Just as I imagine no one wants to. It's going to be a tough call. One minute, he was just a bad guy. Now he's a dad with a couple of kids, even if he never raised them, and he's as ruthless as they come? It just turns the once clear water a little murky. If I could have taken him down before, out in the wilderness, that would have been perfect. But now? The bastard has been nothing but trouble. And he did kill my informant."

"Oh, Leyton, you never told me that before."

"I was undercover before. Now the whole sheriff's office knows, including Dottie. He framed me, putting my fingerprints on the gun used to kill my informant. I still have to locate it." He let out his breath, caressing her arm, loving the silky feel of her, the softness of her body pressed against his. "I didn't think I'd ever love a woman the way that I love you."

She took a deep breath of him and let it out. "I'll say you can serve on guard duty, but only during the day. I want you either here, or with Travis at night. And you can only have short shifts. I don't want you overdoing it."

"But this is okay, right?" He leaned down to kiss her again.

She greedily accepted the kiss. "This is good for you. And for me."

Then he made the call to Travis. "Hey, dude, I'm on my way back."

"Don't worry. You can stay there. I'll be fine. Just getting ready to tuck myself in for the night."

"No way. I'll be over there in a few minutes." He ended the call, groaned, and said, "I'll be back before you begin your work day so we can have breakfast in the morning." And he didn't mean just omelets.

"What do you want to do about telling everyone we're tying the knot?" she asked, rubbing her hand over his bare chest.

He smiled. "Tell them it's a done deal. Quickie marriage, or the works. Your choice."

"We'll have the wedding here. The roses are in full bloom, and so are the rest of the flowers. We can rent a party tent and have it set up in the back parking lot, tables, cook the meals here. When do you want to do it?"

"Whenever you want, Kate. I'll leave it all up to you." Then he frowned a little. "Formal?"

"Absolutely. Only time I'll ever get married, and I want you to wear something nice."

"Okay, for you, I'll do anything." He got out of bed and got dressed, trying not to groan as his shoulder hurt all over again. He'd been so careful not to show how much it was paining him, but she was watching, and she most likely saw him wince.

She shook her head. "I'll tell Dan you have two hours to watch Dottie, no more than that. And when you're at home, I want you to get some rest."

He smiled. "And then I'll work off all that sleep over here."

She got out of bed like a slinky cat and gave him a hug and kiss. "Wait, before you leave, I've got a key for you." She fished a spare key out of her bedroom drawer. "See you in the morning. And sleep well."

"Thinking of you? I will."

Then he hurried back to his car. If he hadn't had so many groceries to carry, he would have just walked over from his place. Next time he would.

He headed back to his place, thinking it wouldn't really be "his" place, except as an office. They'd have to hire a couple of new agents too to help with workload in the area. Even though he was thinking about what he'd wear to the wedding, who he'd invite, the boss, Travis, he was still watching out for any signs of trouble, Butch or any of his men lurking about.

He saw nobody, thankfully, and entered the house a few minutes later, saying, "She's mine."

Travis groaned. "Hell, Leyton, you woke me up to tell me that? I could have told you that before you even decided it."

"I had decided it. I had to let the doc decide if she was ready."

"Congratulations. Long wait for the wedding?"

"I doubt it. She's making all the arrangements. We need to get us a couple of tuxes. And I need to call Chuck and tell him to drop everything and be ready for the wedding."

"I'm ready. What about this place? You won't be staying here then."

"The house is the field office, and it's yours otherwise. We need to sell our houses, move our stuff, so we still have our work cut out for us. How are you doing?"

"Been better. I was sleeping."

Leyton smiled. "Okay, off to bed."

"You really didn't need to come home and leave her

behind, you know."

"Yeah, I did. I'll be leaving early in the morning to have breakfast with Kate."

Travis smiled. "Sure wish Chuck would have sent me on the job instead."

***

Three weeks later, the wedding was all planned. Kate hadn't wanted to wait that long, and neither had Leyton, but he was being super patient, staying with Travis at night after Leyton and she had made love, so he could watch out for him in case Butch came back to kill his witnesses off. Butch had to know that Leyton and Travis would be back on his trail, together this time, as soon as both of them were completely healed. Travis was doing great, the walking cast off, and he was walking without a limp now. Leyton had a little shoulder stiffness, but their faster healing abilities had really helped in healing him up more quickly. They were going to begin searching for Butch again after the wedding and Leyton and her camping trip honeymoon, so that was a little dark cloud on the horizon that she tried not to think of too much.

Everyone had become so involved in the wedding preparations and were so enthusiastic, she felt she had become the queen of Yuma Town. But she loved them and was glad to have some joyful tidings, because everyone was still on edge with not knowing if Butch was going to return to see his kids and Dottie. The worry was that he might try to grab them and run. But he had to know they'd catch him then.

Tomorrow was the big day. And then she and Leyton were off to make that camping trip really memorable.

She had just finished rounds and was headed home, expecting Leyton to arrive about an hour later. He always gave her time to unwind, which she appreciated, before he came over for supper, making it or helping her to prepare it.

It was still light out when she made her way through the gardens, her ever blooming roses just as beautiful as earlier in the summer and they'd be just perfect for the wedding tomorrow. Leyton has said he wasn't going to make love to her tonight, because he wanted to give her the night to relax and prepare herself for the big town event of the year tomorrow. But she knew Leyton better. At least she thought she did as she unlocked the back door, walked inside, closed, and locked her door.

She headed for the kitchen to get a glass of orange juice. As she approached it, she saw a man reflected in the mirror hanging in the dining room. Jeffrey Brown, or Butch Sanders—there was no mistaking him even if he had changed his appearance since the last time she'd seen him.

Her heart was beating a hundred miles a second as she whipped around to return to the back door, unlock it, and run off screaming. She prayed he didn't realize she'd seen his reflection, but he was looking straight at the mirror and must have caught hers too. She was glad she left Sheba at the clinic for the big day tomorrow, afraid she'd get stepped on with all the traffic there would be in the house.

She ran for the door, but he was on her in a heartbeat. She screamed, and he took her to the floor, pinning her arm behind her back, his voice snarled. "I don't want to hurt you, Kate. But I need you to call Dottie for me and have her bring the kids over. You'll do it without alerting anyone I'm here, do you understand?"

She nodded, feeling the muscle strain in her arm and shoulder where he was pushing her arm up so severely.

"Okay. I've got a gun, and I don't want you making any false moves, warning anyone, or else your wedding day with that damn cougar Leyton will be your funeral he'll be attending instead."

She nodded, trying to think of what to do. She was afraid Butch would kill her too, if nothing more than to prove to Leyton he had no power to stop him. She was wracking her brain on what to say to Dottie that would clue her in to stay away. And then what? She'd have to wing it.

But then Leyton would be on his way over and Butch would kill him for sure. Why hadn't she smelled the bastard in her house already? Hunter's spray. Had to be.

Butch let her up, but as soon as she was standing, her phone rang. She glanced up at Butch's hard face, more gaunt now, his eyes brown, but she could see they were contacts, the roots of his hair blond while the rest was dyed brown.

"Get it, but put it on speaker." He glanced at the caller I.D. and snorted. "Lover boy. Maybe you should just tell him to come right on over."

She knew she couldn't. She had to warn him that she was in trouble. If Butch killed her, well, she was really trying hard not to think of worse-case scenarios, but she wanted to give Leyton a chance to take this bastard down.

She answered the phone, putting it on speaker. That might clue Leyton in that something was wrong. She never did that. In fact, the only time she did was the time that Leyton had made her do it when Dan had called her that one

251

day. But Dan had never realized she had been held hostage. She had to be careful, but not so much that Leyton couldn't figure it out.

"Hey, Leyton, listen, Dottie's coming over with her kids. We've got some final wedding plan stuff we wanted to discuss. Since you weren't going to stay the night anyway, why don't we just see each other for the big day, okay?"

Leyton hesitated to respond, and she was sweating out that he was going to ask her if something was wrong and then the gig would be up.

"Ah, hell, Kate. All right. The guys had asked if I wanted to do one last bachelor fun night out and I said I'd make it later after supper, but that'll work for me. I'll just give them a call and tell them there's been a change of plans. I'll just see you tomorrow at the wedding. I just want you to know— I love you. And I'll always be there for you no matter the difficulties."

"I—" She had to say something more. Leyton had rattled off too long. She couldn't believe he'd just plan to go out with the guys. Damn it. But Butch gave her the kill sign, hand slicing across his throat, telling her in no uncertain terms to end the call. She thought of not telling Leyton she loved him, in case that might clue him in. But then she decided she couldn't do it. Not when it might be the last time she could say it to him. "I love you, Leyton. Have fun."

And then she ended the call.

***

Leyton called Dan and said, "Listen, maybe nothing's up, but Kate canceled on supper with me."

"Don't tell me she's got cold feet," Dan said.

"No. I...just feel like something's wrong. She told me she loves me."

Dan didn't get it. "Well, hell, I hope so."

"In a way that said if something bad happened to her, like it was a farewell, just in case, she had to tell me. She didn't give me a chance to even tell her I love her again back. She just abruptly ended the call. If that wasn't warning me she was in trouble, I don't know what would."

"Are you headed over there?"

"Yeah, but no siren's blaring. No squad cars. Or parked somewhere not close by. She said Dottie was coming over with the kids for last minute wedding preparations. Can you check on that for me?"

"No one's said a word to me about it. Hal's over there, but I'll check. And damn it, Leyton, don't get yourself shot up this time."

"I just worry about Kate."

"I hear you. Put your phone on vibrate."

"No way in hell. If Butch's there, he'll hear it. I'm going in silent on this one."

"Wait for backup."

"Yeah, got to go," Leyton said. Butch was a dead man. He wasn't leaving here alive.

"What's up?" Travis said, as Leyton began tearing off his clothes.

"I think Butch's at Kate's place. I'm not for sure, but highly suspect it."

"Do you want me to go as cougar backup or bring the gun?"

"Bring a gun. I'll try to slip in through the cat door, but if you get a shot at the bastard, take it. Even if it means hitting me. I don't want Kate hurt, no matter the cost."

"Understand."

"Let me go first. It's still too light out to make this completely clandestine. You'll have to really work at it to keep out of sight."

"Agreed."

Leyton knew Travis was well aware of that. He just couldn't help telling him that. Then he shifted and headed out through the pet door, one of the first things they did to renovate the place to make it perfect for the cougars staying there.

He ran through his gardens and through the two lots behind him, the last one butting up to Kate's gardens. She had a white picket fence covered in red roses, and he leapt over it, careful not to run into anything and make a noise. His heart was thudding in his ears, and he wanted to quell the sound of the blood rushing through his veins as he attempted to listen for any conversation between Butch and Kate. He had to know if he was even there, for one thing. Then he moved close to the house, brushing his body alongside the white siding so that if anyone peered out the windows, he wouldn't see Leyton. When he reached the cat door, he paused to listen. That was the hardest part for him. Waiting until he knew it was as safe as possible for Kate for him to make his move.

If Butch *was* in there, Leyton had to know where everyone was. He couldn't bolt through the pet door if they were in the living room and could see him tear through there.

From the kitchen, Kate said, "You don't want to do this,

Jeffrey."

For a second, Leyton wondered who the hell Jeffrey was, then remembering Jeffrey Brown was the name he went by while living here, though he wondered if it had been an alias even then, Leyton waited. Though it was killing him, until he heard Butch's response. If he was in the kitchen...

"I mean, what do you intend to do with Dottie and the kids?"

"My kids," he growled.

"I know. But if you took them from here, all of Yuma Town would hunt you down. What could you hope for by doing that?"

Leyton poked his head through the cat door, hoping it wouldn't make any sound—especially as sensitive as their hearing was. Humans might not hear anything, but the cats could.

All of a sudden there was a huge crash in the kitchen, the sound of water splashing. "Damn it," Kate said. "You're making me nervous. Put the gun away, will you?"

But the noise she made was enough to cover Leyton's pushing the rest of the way through the door and running for the kitchen. He didn't know if she was aware he was coming for her, or not, but knowing they were in the kitchen and that the bastard had a gun on her helped.

He wasn't taking this slow now, glancing at the mirror in the dining room, seeing Butch standing straight, but his head was bent as if he was watching her, and she was making a racket as if she was mad, cleaning up the mess nearer the floor, so she wasn't visible in the mirror.

Taking a chance that if he came around the wall blocking

his view of the kitchen, he could take Butch down before he could shoot at Kate—or him—Leyton took a couple of leaps toward the kitchen on silent paws, his ears still tilted to hear every movement in the kitchen, the paper towels dripping water, and Kate throwing them in the trash. Then she tore off more paper towels and leaned down to mop up the remaining spill.

Butch never saw him coming as he focused on Kate. Leyton's teeth sank into Butch's juggler, his fish-hook claws digging into the bastard's front and back. Leyton wasn't sure what happened exactly, but he heard a heavy thud and a crack of bone above his head, and the clatter of the gun as it hit the floor.

Leyton severed Butch's spinal cord, only regretting that he'd done so in Kate's kitchen and not outside or better yet, farther away that she would never have to see the brutality of the scene. But he wouldn't have done anything differently with Kate's life on the line. Or Dottie's and her kids' either.

Butch collapsed on the floor, dead, having breathed his last breath holding a gun on Leyton's mate. Never again.

Leyton shifted and Kate dropped the heavy skillet she'd been holding. Hell, that was the sound he'd heard hitting Butch's skull, his mate swinging the heavy cast iron skillet. She threw her arms around Leyton and held on tight, sobbing against his naked chest.

He meant to alert everyone that Butch was dead. But Kate was kissing Leyton, and she needed this more, right now, no talking, nothing but their shared love and hugs and kisses.

When she finally came up for air and he looked down at

her teary eyes, he smiled. "Hell of a swing, Kate. I was sure glad the skillet didn't hit me."

She smiled a little. "Even after you had him by the neck, he wasn't dropping the gun. I was afraid he'd try to fire it. If he'd hit you, I figured no one would ever get to use that hospital bed but you. Besides, we have a wedding tomorrow." She sniffled, then hugged him again. "How did you know that he was here? Did you guess because I had the phone on speaker?"

"That, and I didn't believe Dottie and the kids were coming over. Dan didn't know anything about it, though I was coming over to check on you no matter what. But the biggest reason? You didn't want to have supper with me. We'd planned this all along. I really didn't believe you'd cancel on me. And you didn't let me tell you I loved you in return. Just hung up on me."

Kate's phone rang, and she pulled it out of her pocket, but she wasn't letting go of Leyton for anything. "Dan," she said, and put the phone on speaker. "Butch, Jeffrey is dead. Leyton killed him. We're both fine."

"We're all out here, coming in." Dan ended the call.

"I have to unlock the door," she said, but Leyton wouldn't let her go, and with his arm wrapped around her, they went together and unlocked it.

Then Dan, Travis, and the deputies—all but Hal who was still at Dottie's place keeping her and the kids safe until he had word that everything was okay—barged into the house. Leyton pulled an afghan off Kate's couch and wrapped it around his waist.

Dan stayed with them while everyone else hauled the

body out.

"Hell of a job, Leyton," Dan said, everyone else echoing his comment.

"Hell, if Kate hadn't hit him with the skillet, the outcome could still have been different," Leyton said, squeezing her tight, and she appreciated he'd given her credit for helping and was glad she was able to.

Even though that wasn't her kind of job, mates helped each other out in times of crises.

With gloved hands, Travis carefully took Butch's gun into evidence. "This could be the same gun Butch planned to frame you with. No serial number on it. Bet we don't discover who it belonged to. And how much do you want to bet your fingerprints are on it."

"Got a car a block down the street that has false plates. Figure it's Butch's," Stryker said. "Found a gun and a rifle in it. One of them might be the one used to shoot you twice, Leyton. And the other? Might still be the one he planned to plant as evidence. It would be more likely that he wouldn't be using it or worry that he would smudge your fingerprints on it."

"We'll have it investigated further," Dan said. "But we can't go reporting this to any regular authorities."

"Hey, it's not a blue Mustang, is it?" Travis asked.

"Yeah," Stryker said.

"Hot damn. Bet it's mine." Travis frowned. "The condition?"

"Looks as good as new."

Travis sighed with relief. "Got to check it out."

"Do you want to stay at my place tonight?" Leyton

asked, rubbing Kate's arm.

"No. Butch's not going to make me feel bad about staying in my own house."

"Do you mind if I stay here?"

"I want you to." She hugged him again. She didn't want to ever let go. If the bastard had shot Leyton in some place that wasn't vital, she could imagine him going to the wedding no matter what and camping with her too even if it nearly killed him. She didn't even want to think of what might have happened if he had been killed.

Dan was helping direct the cleanup in the kitchen, making it appear as though nothing bad had happened there, which she so appreciated. "Good," Dan said as if he was part of the conversation. "Otherwise someone else would have stayed with you, Kate."

"Did you want one of the ladies to stay with you instead?" Leyton asked, but he looked like the notion didn't appeal to him in the least.

"No. You can leave after breakfast. You just won't see me wearing my wedding dress. The ladies will be over at ten. You have to be out by then."

He nodded, took a deep breath, and hugged her tight again.

Even though she wanted to fix supper for them, she just couldn't. The cleanup was done, including the mess she'd made when she'd dropped the pot of water she was going to use to boil bell peppers.

"I was afraid when I used the cat door, Butch might have heard me. Is that why you dropped the pot of water?"

"Yeah. I was making supper, anything to keep busy while

Butch was holding the gun on me. But when I heard someone come in through my pet door, I quickly dropped the pot of water, hoping to disguise the noise, hoping someone was coming to the rescue."

Even so, when Leyton went flying through the air as a cougar so all of a sudden and latched himself onto Butch, she hadn't expected it. She'd been so scared that Butch would still get the best of Leyton that it took her a moment to realize she had the perfect weapon sitting on the burner, the skillet she was about to cook the hamburger in.

"You folks want dinner out, on me?" Stryker asked.

Leyton waited for Kate to say. "Yeah, I'd like that." She smiled at him.

And that was it. The next thing they knew, they were having a barbecue at Hal's ranch with everyone who lived at the ranch, Tracey, Ted, the ranch foreman, and the boys, Ricky and Kolby, Dottie and Dan, and her kids, Shannon and Chase and their kids, Stryker, and Travis. They stayed up too late, but everyone was cognizant of what had happened earlier this evening—how Leyton had saved Kate's life, and she could very well have saved his. How they had protected Dottie and her kids. And the threat to even Travis had been eliminated. But Kate was glad for it. She loved seeing the sunset, and sitting with Leyton together on one of the loveseats, enjoyed the talk of anything else but about what had happened at her home tonight. Until everyone with sound-asleep children began to say their goodnights. And then Leyton and she headed home.

Tonight on the drive back, they were quiet, contemplative. When they arrived at her home, Kate said,

"Because of all the people and excitement of the wedding and our trip, I was leaving Sheba at the clinic. But if you don't mind, I want to bring her home for the night." She really wanted to cuddle her one last time before she was gone for a couple of weeks, though Sheba loved everyone and seemed perfectly happy to visit with the patients at the clinic while she was gone.

"She's family. Let's go get her," Leyton said.

As soon as Kate and Leyton went to bed, Sheba jumped onto the mattress and was trying to pick a spot to curl up next to them.

"No, Sheba," Kate said. "Not with Leyton here." She should have realized Sheba might want to sleep with them. Sometimes she slept with Kate, but mostly in the winter months and not so much in the summer.

Leyton smiled and reached out and scratched Sheba between the ears. Sheba purred and snuggled up on the other side of him as if he was her best friend now. Leyton chuckled and pulled Kate into his arms to sleep.

"You are going to be a terrible influence on her, I can see," she said, serious. What would happen when they had kids? She could just imagine him spoiling them terribly. She smiled at the thought of him playing with the kids and she couldn't wait.

He just kissed Kate and held her tighter.

Before they knew it, it was morning and time to send Leyton on his way.

"Are you sure?" he groaned, trying to pull her into his arms and brushing his whiskery cheek against hers.

"Yes! I'll fix you a quick breakfast. The ladies will be here in just half an hour. We slept in too late."

Leyton smiled and pulled her down for a real kiss, deepening it, loving her. In truth, they had made love twice during the night and it was way too early for getting up. He should have said they'd have a wedding late in the evening. But she finally pulled away from him and practically leapt out of bed before he could grab her again. He smiled and folded his arms behind his head.

He had never seen her so anxious before, and he watched her hurry into the bathroom to shower, sighed, and got up, threw on some briefs and headed for the kitchen to make a quick breakfast for them. Then he finished dressing.

She looked frazzled, her hair wet, but once she ate a little of her breakfast, he pulled her close and kissed her. "See you in a little bit, honey. Love you."

"Love you too," she said, practically shoving him out the door.

He laughed and was glad he wasn't feeling anxious. The ladies smiled at him as they hurried to exit their cars and pile into Kate's house.

***

Kate was so excited. Her big wedding day. The biggest tower wedding cake she'd ever seen with two cougars sitting on top, nuzzling each other, the icing white but covered in bits of chocolate to commemorate the s'mores she and Leyton had shared during their camping experience was sitting in the kitchen, waiting to do its part. Melanie Whittington had created the cake at her home in Loveland, where she made all kinds of cakes for every occasion, since she was Tracey's mother. Tracey and her sister, Jessie, and their dad, Jack, were there also. Ricky and his brother, Kolby, were dressed up as much for the occasion, and she thought how fetching they were.

All the ladies had helped her pick out a princess wedding gown—Dottie, Tracey, her sister, Jessie, their photographer, Shannon, her nurses, Helen Kretchen and Elsie, and they'd had a ball. They'd had their nails done, though once they shifted, they'd lose the nail coloring, and had their hair all curled.

The babies and toddlers she'd delivered were just as cute all dressed up in their finery. And Leyton couldn't have been more dapper. She'd never seen such a handsome cougar in her life, but then she was totally biased.

The retired FBI agents, Rick and Yvonne Mueller were there to help her celebrate, and she'd just learned from them they had been investigating Leyton from the evidence left behind in her house when she decided to take him with her camping—the story that everyone was now sharing—and learned he was one of the good guys. But she already knew that.

April Hightower, her receptionist, and Becky Sorenson, her emergency on-call operator, were there too, smiling broadly.

And Hal's parents were there, Roger and Milly Haverton. Roger was the reporter and making several big announcements about the wedding beforehand and would be afterward, and Milly owned the newspaper and was making it headline news. Luckily, Leyton didn't seem to mind, despite loving being undercover.

Travis was so happy for his friend. Even Leyton and

Travis's boss, Chuck Warner, was there, just shaking his head and giving her a kiss.

Kate had been disappointed that she couldn't get hold of her parents to attend the celebration, but she hoped they'd come for Christmas and meet their new son-in-law then.

Everyone was beautiful, she thought, as they shared in the celebration of her and Leyton's wedding, then enjoyed a steak dinner, champagne, and cake.

But what was coming next was what Leyton had planned. The two-week vacation camping trip that Kate had missed out on. Only they weren't going to her original camping sites either. They drove on the dead-end road, found the pile of rocks that Leyton had set up to let everyone know that they'd had a wreck here, and then parked.

"I can't believe we're coming back here," she said, excited about camping with him here, only this time, on purpose.

They had climbing gear this time, and though they had all the gear they needed and enough food for two weeks, plenty of bear noise makers, and even champagne, they didn't bring fishing gear. They'd fish to their hearts' content as cougars.

But what neither of them had planned for when they looked down at where her car had been before it was removed was to see a trail of rose petals.

"Are you sure you didn't do this beforehand?" she asked, eager to begin hauling stuff down.

"Yeah, I'm sure. When could I have done it?"

"True."

"I'm going to take a look down there, make sure there are no surprises."

She began stripping off her clothes. He arched a brow.

"Me too, only I'm going to take the easy way down." She was too eager to wait and shifted, then leapt from one narrow ledge to another to make her way down to the bottom.

He quickly joined her as a cougar. And then shifted at the base. A tent had been erected and from the smells of all the people who had been there—Hal, Chase, Stryker, and Dan—they had left not long before Kate and Leyton arrived.

"That's why everyone kept asking when we were getting on the road," Leyton said, amazed. "They wanted to make sure they didn't run into us along the road."

Enough firewood had been stacked for them to use for the whole two weeks they were there so they could just cook, enjoy nature, and make love.

Leyton smiled. "I'm going to owe them big time when we return."

"That's what being part of a cougar family of Yuma Town is all about," Kate said, wrapping her arms around Leyton, loving him. And she loved being here again to turn her last "visit" here into a real camping retreat with one hot cougar.

"I'm ready to make love to you, Kate Ellen Parker Hill."

"But we'll need our sleeping bag."

They peered into the tent, just in case the guys thought of dressing up the tent a bit. Candles, a table, a duplicate cougar print double sleeping bag, a handmade quilt with cougar prints of all sizes, and lots more rose petals. A note on the quilt said, "With love from all of us in Cougar Town."

Initialed on each square she saw the ladies' names and Betty Kretchen's, and she knew she had to be the one who supervised the making of the quilt since she was the only one of the ladies who was into quilting. Shannon, Tracey, and Dottie's initials were on it too, and she loved them for doing something so special. She wondered when they'd taken the time to do it.

Leyton smiled and swept Kate up into his arms and carried her into the tent. "Looks like we don't have to wait."

"As if you can ever wait for anything."

"Not…for this."

"Wait, what about bear noisemakers, just in case?"

"Right over there. Paintball gun without the paint, air gun, we've got it made. No more stalling, Mrs. Hill."

"Me stall? No way!"

And that was it as they zipped up the tent and settled down for a hot cougar lovemaking fest as the water rolled over the stones in the nearby creek and the breeze ruffled the branches of the nearby spruce trees.

Camping would never be the same. It just got a *whole* lot better.

ABOUT THE AUTHOR

Bestselling and award-winning author **Terry Spear** has written over sixty paranormal romance novels and four medieval Highland historical romances. Her first werewolf romance, *Heart of the Wolf,* was named a 2008 *Publishers Weekly*'s Best Book of the Year, and her subsequent titles have garnered high praise and hit the *USA Today* bestseller list. A retired officer of the U.S. Army Reserves, Terry lives in Crawford, Texas, where she is working on her next werewolf romance, continuing her new series about shapeshifting jaguars, and cougars, having fun with her young adult novels, and playing with her two Havanese puppies, Max and Tanner. For more information, please visit www.terryspear.com, or follow her on Twitter, @TerrySpear. She is also on Facebook at http://www.facebook.com/terry.spear. And on Wordpress at:
Terry Spear's Shifters
http://terryspear.wordpress.com/

ALSO BY TERRY SPEAR:

Romantic Suspense: Deadly Fortunes, In the Dead of the Night, Relative Danger, Bound by Danger

The Highlanders Series: Winning the Highlander's Heart, The Accidental Highland Hero, Highland Rake, Taming the Wild Highlander, The Viking's Highland Lass

Other historical romances: Lady Caroline & the Egotistical Earl, A Ghost of a Chance at Love

Heart of the Wolf Series: Heart of the Wolf, Destiny of the Wolf, To Tempt the Wolf, Legend of the White Wolf, Seduced by the Wolf, Wolf Fever, Heart of the Highland Wolf, Dreaming of the Wolf, A SEAL in Wolf's Clothing, A Howl for a Highlander, A Highland Werewolf Wedding, A SEAL Wolf Christmas, Silence of the Wolf, Hero of a Highland Wolf, A Highland Wolf Christmas, SEAL Wolf Hunting; A Silver Wolf Christmas, SEAL Wolf in Too Deep, Alpha Wolf Need Not Apply, Billionaire in Wolf's Clothing (Jun 2016)

SEAL Wolves: To Tempt the Wolf, A SEAL in Wolf's Clothing, A SEAL Wolf Christmas; SEAL Wolf Hunting, SEAL Wolf in Too Deep (Feb 2016)

Silver Bros Wolves: Destiny of the Wolf, Wolf Fever, Dreaming of the Wolf, Silence of the Wolf; A Silver Wolf Christmas, Alpha Wolf Need Not Apply (May

2016)
Highland Wolves: Heart of the Highland Wolf, A Howl for a Highlander, A Highland Werewolf Wedding, Hero of a Highland Wolf, A Highland Wolf Christmas
Heart of the Jaguar Series: Savage Hunger, Jaguar Fever, Jaguar Hunt, Jaguar Pride, Jaguar Christmas (Oct 2016)
Vampire romances: Killing the Bloodlust, Deadly Liaisons, Huntress for Hire, Forbidden Love
Heart of the Cougar Series: Cougar's Mate, Call of the Cougar, Taming the Wild Cougar, Covert Cougar Christmas, a novella (Dec 2015)

.

Made in the USA
Lexington, KY
10 November 2015